Sashie was decorative enough in his outraging-of-the-conventions way. Both his legs were artificial, the result of his service in the Air Force during the 1939–45 war, so that he walked in a mincing, unnatural fashion – but Sashie regarded his disability as his own private affair, and he concealed it by exaggerating it. He had adopted and dramatised, almost to the point of caricature, all the mannerisms accepted by conventional minds as peculiar to the homosexual . . . his clothes made him stand out among the more drably dressed men on the island like a parakeet among a flock of crows. He was small and slight, with something bird-like about his movements. Sashie had some Russian blood, which gave his eyes a Mongolian slant. About him there was always a quivering air of imminent movement . . .

D1612971

Also by Jane Duncan

MY FRIENDS THE MISSES KINDNESS
MY FRIEND THE SWALLOW
MY FRIEND THE HUNGRY GENERATION
MY FRIEND ANNIE

and published by Corgi Books

Jane Duncan

My Friend
Sashie

CORGI BOOKS
A DIVISION OF TRANSWORLD PUBLISHERS LTD

MY FRIEND SASHIE

A CORGI BOOK 0 552 10194 X

Originally published in Great Britain by
Macmillan London Ltd

PRINTING HISTORY
Macmillan edition published 1972
Corgi edition published 1976

Corgi Books are published by
Transworld Publishers Ltd.,
Century House, 61–63 Uxbridge Road,
Ealing, London W5 5SA
Made and printed in Great Britain by
Cox & Wyman Ltd, London, Reading and Fakenham

To Freddie

PART ONE

AFTER death has passed by, the trappings of life that remain are not tragic, not even sad. They have only the nuisance value of total irrelevance.

I stood in the study with the slide-rule between my hands, remembering, hearing again the impatient voice that called: 'Clorinda! Have you been tidying up in here again? Where is my slide-rule?' and feeling about me an echo like a ghostly wind of the flurry and bustle that used to fill the house until the slide-rule had been found. Then the memory, the voice, the bustle died away and I was standing there with the meaningless little mechanism between my hands as it and I along with it lapsed into irrelevance.

'Caleb,' I said, laying the thing on the drawing-table, 'everything connected with engineering and the factory, all the Chief's papers, pencils, drawing instruments, everything, put them here for Chief Mackie to take away.'

'Yes, ma'am. I will do it. You go and sit down. I will fetch you a drink.'

It was about three weeks since my husband had died and this day should have been his forty-eighth birthday but, like everything else now, the day had no significance. It was merely another day in a meaningless progression. I sat down in what had once been my drawing-room but was now an oblong box which contained a few crates packed with household possessions and a few pieces of furniture that had no longer any context or character but were merely waiting to be taken away into storage, to lie forgotten in the dark. I felt an envy for these chattels. I wished that, like them, I could be relegated, withdrawn from the stream of life where there were no contexts, no memories and no thoughts and as I drank the strong whisky and water that Caleb had brought to me, the outlines in my mind began to blur as if, indeed, I

7

were drifting out of the stream of life and into a backwater where nothing more could happen. In this drugged state of mind it was possible to ignore the present and the future and to see the past through a haze that made of the last ten years a golden dream.

It was not quite nine years since my husband and I had come to live in this house, Guinea Corner, in this West Indian island of St. Jago but these years had been so full that they constituted a lifetime, a lifetime that had now come to an end. His name had been Alexander Alexander which had led to his nickname of 'Twice', but the nickname, accidentally, had been curiously descriptive of his character. He had brought to living a vibrant energy, a sharp force of interest that gave the impression that everything he did was done twice over but death had destroyed in my memory even this mainspring of his character, for a man can die only once. Man has conceived the idea that he can be born again, but into eternal life. He has accepted the fact that, for death, once is enough. Sitting amid the meaningless disintegration of this room, the years of the past looked to me like a monstrous chain of accident, like a shapeless ink-blot on the white page of time, through circumstances and pressures not of our own making. Twice and I had come together, had arrived in St. Jago, had come to this sugar estate called Paradise where Twice, without seeking it, had achieved the position of manager. Then came his final illness and this was where I laid aside my empty glass and did some more packing until Caleb arrived at my side again with his: 'I will do it, ma'am. You sit down and I will bring you a drink.'

Caleb and I were friends of long standing. He had come to me, to help in the garden, as a skinny little boy but he was now over twenty, over six feet tall and ebony black, a true specimen of his Negro race with no taint of white blood in his veins. The bond between him and me was the deep one of our common peasant blood, for I am a peasant born out of the hard rock of Highland Scotland while Caleb was a child of the hot fertile St. Jagoan jungle and when we were together as we were now, we spoke as peasants do, of immediate practical things, such as the work in hand, the heat

8

of the day and the approach of evening when work would be over.

'Could maybe just pack the veranda books before you go back to the Great House, ma'am?' he suggested now.

'All right, Caleb. Let's do that,' I agreed and moved out to the veranda.

'You sit down, ma'am. I will fetch you a drink.'

Caleb's observation of white people in the tropics had shown him that they had drinks in every situation. They entertained their friends to drinks, arranged their business matters over drinks, had drinks at celebrations and funerals and his fetching of drinks for me was his means of trying to comfort me, to make things normal for me. I knew that I was drinking far too much but the alcohol served to blunt the edges, to make me less aware of the black guilt that had invaded my mind during the last days of Twice's life.

'It is good for you to be at the Great House, ma'am,' Caleb said as he began to take books from the case on the veranda and lay them in the crate on the floor.

'Yes,' I agreed with him. 'Madame and Sir Ian have been very kind to me.'

'Yes and you did ought to be with folks, ma'am.'

I agreed with him again but I was not sure of my own sincerity, for I was conscious of not being 'with' anyone in any real sense. I was aware of nothing but total isolation, alienation from the world of people and I did not wish to be otherwise. Hitherto, I had always lived in close involvement with people, had been acutely dependent first, as a child, upon my family and later upon a circle which I loosely termed my 'friends'. Indeed, I had often felt that I had no existence except in my relationships with other people and that if my family and friends were suddenly withdrawn from me, my personal identity would disappear like a bubble bursting in the air. At this time, after the death of Twice, my family and friends had not withdrawn themselves. They had done their utmost to draw me close to them but, in the grip of the terrible isolation that had come upon me, I was the one to withdraw, building a wall between myself and the people around me.

Paradise Estate was owned by the Dulac family which

consisted of three members, Madame Dulac who was about ninety years old and blind, her son Sir Ian and Sir Ian's son, Edward, who normally lived in London but who had come out to St. Jago shortly before Twice died. The Dulacs had been very kind to us from the first moment we had met them and it was regarded as natural and fitting that I, widowed, should live at the Great House as personal companion to Madame Dulac. Indeed, I had acted as part-time companion to her ever since she became blind, reading to her, writing her letters and trying to keep her au fait with the gossip of the island which was her main interest. Adrift as I was now on the stream of life with no will or desires of my own, I fell in with the arrangement because it called for no effort. Madame dealt in the conventions in the main and having told me with approval that my behaviour was very brave and dignified, she dismissed for good the reason for the so-called bravery and dignity and addressed herself and me along with her to the events of day to day, notably the Births, Marriages and Deaths column of the *Island Sun,* as the local newspaper was called. This suited me very well, as if I had been given official permission to live in a vacuum of non-thought, non-feeling, non-emotion and it was only when I spent a short time at my former home, Guinea Corner, so that Caleb and I could pack the insignificant relics of a former life, that my mind came alive and aware, between drinks of whisky, of the black arid desert that I carried inside me.

One of the most difficult aspects of these afternoons spent at Guinea Corner was my dog, Dram, a dark golden mastiff that Twice had presented to me on a birthday long ago. I had not taken him to the Great House with me because Madame Dulac did not like dogs and the animal had never been mentioned. Dram had been content to remain at Guinea Corner with Caleb and Charlie the cat with whom he had always spent most of his time. But now, when I went round to my former home, Dram would get up from the shady spot where he was lying with Charlie, come to me and put his large solemn-eyed head in my lap and while I packed he stayed close to me, pushing his head under my hands if they fell idle for a moment. The sight of him, the feel of his velvet hide under my hands, harrowed me so unspeakably with the memories they could evoke that I found myself wishing that he could be taken from my sight, that he might die, even, and disappear for ever.

Charlie the cat lived the independent life that she had always lived – in spite of her name, she was a female. She had always preferred to beg for her food or steal it from the other staff houses around the park than to feed at home and now she ignored me as she had always done. But Dram did not ignore me and would not be ignored. He was dignified and obedient as he had always been and made no fuss when I left to return to the Great House. As I got into the car, he would sit down on the veranda as I had told him to do and watch me out of sight with his large, dark solemn eyes. Those eyes worried me. At times they seemed to accuse me, at other times they seemed to question me, just as accusation of myself alternated with that question in my mind that I was afraid to face. Was I partly responsible for the death of Twice? If I had behaved differently would he still be alive? I would turn away from the accusing questions in my mind by busying myself with something or by drinking whisky but the dark eyes of the dog were there, like a physical manifestation of the questions in the mind.

In retrospect, I can see that I was living an extraordinary double life at this time, one side of it being the practical life of day-to-day, filled with trivial matters that required my attention, the other side being a perpetual flight from myself and life, a flight often aided by the means that came most readily to hand, which was alcohol.

My early training at my home in the Highlands of Scotland had made me efficient in a practical way, so that I could discharge day-to-day duties without effort and this outer shell of efficiency and normality deceived the Dulac household, and those who came to visit it, as to my condition, for people, in the main, are more interested in their own conditions than in that of the people around them. Also, in the midst of social living, death is an embarrassment, almost an indecency and society tends to ignore the aftermath of death in the form of widowhood, as it would ignore any other minor social lapse that threatened to interrupt the smooth

11

flow of trivial intercourse. It was simple, therefore, for me to pursue my empty way unnoticed.

Caleb drove the last nail into the lid of the crate of books, straightened his back and looked through the veranda screen. 'A Peak car is turning in at the gate, ma'am,' he said. 'Must be Mars Sashie. I will make some tea.'

'No tea, Caleb,' I told him. 'I am going back to the Great House.'

He went away to the kitchen and I looked sullenly out at Sashie de Marnay getting out of his car.

Sashie was another of the many people who had been kind to me. He had been in the house with me on the evening that Twice died, he had stood between me and the world, he had dealt quietly and efficiently with everything and I was deeply grateful to him. And at this moment, I hated the very sight of him, as I had hated him every time I had seen him since Twice died, which had been at least once in every forty-eight hours.

Sashie was not like the Dulacs or any of the other people of my acquaintance or any of the people who came to the Great House. Sashie had no conventional attitudes to death, to widowhood or to anything and he aired his views with the nerve racking persistence of a gadfly. Although, as yet, he had not said in so many words that he disapproved of my move to the Great House, I was aware of his disapproval and equally aware that the moment would come when he would put it into words, sharp-edged and clear.

'Packing your books, darling?' he greeted me. 'Good.'

'Caleb and I have just finished for today,' I told him, 'and I have to be back at the Great House in time for tea.'

'No, you don't. I have just been there and I told Madame that you and I would have tea here. Winston,' he said to the driver of his car, 'go round to the kitchen and ask Caleb to make some tea, please.'

I waited till the man was out of earshot, then rose to my feet and said: 'Sashie, you are an overbearing bore and a nuisance. You had no right to call at the Great House and make arrangements about me.'

'Somebody has to arrange about you, heaven knows,' he said, sitting down and arranging his sharply-creased trousers

12

in the finicky way that irritated me, while he contrived to convey that he well knew that it irritated me. 'You make a monstrous mess of arranging about yourself,' he added.

I could not be bothered to argue with him and sat silently, wishing that he would go away but Sashie did not go away.

Caleb brought the tea, Sashie poured it out and handed me a cup. 'I suppose you would prefer whisky,' he said, 'but I consider it too early in the day for that. One must abide by the conventions to some extent and four-thirty in the afternoon is tea time.'

In this way, he contrived to tell me that I was drinking too much, that I was living a life of hollow convention and that he disapproved of these things and I wished that I had the mental energy or even the will to send him packing but I had not that energy or will. I was merely bored and sat looking at him as if he were not a person but an object, for this was how I saw people now. As an object, he was decorative enough in his outraging-of-the-conventions way. Both his legs were artificial, the result of his service in the Air Force during the 1939–45 war, so that he could walk only in a mincing unnatural fashion but Sashie regarded his disability as his own private affair and he concealed it by exaggerating it. He had adopted and dramatized all the mannerisms accepted by the conventional minds as peculiar to the homosexual to the point, almost, of caricature and he wore silk shirts and linen trousers of brilliant colours which, in the year 1958, made him stand out among the more conventionally and drably dressed men of the island like a parakeet among a flock of crows. His resemblance to the little jade-green and vermilion parakeets of the island was stressed by his small slight stature, for he was not more than five feet six inches tall, some three inches shorter than myself, indeed. And there was something bird-like in the quick movement of his small dark head and the keen glance of his brilliant jet-black eyes. He had some Russian blood and the eyes had a Mongolian slant under the thin dark brows that flew outwards towards the temples. Even when he was still, as he was now in the chair opposite to my own, there was about Sashie a quivering air of imminent

13

movement, so that one would have felt little astonishment if he had suddenly spread wings and taken to flight.

'I entirely disapprove of this arrangement,' he said now.

'What arrangement?' I knew perfectly well that he was referring to my move to the Great House.

'You are well aware of what I mean. I refer to this move of yours from one deathbed to another.'

Most people might prefer to ignore the anti-social fact of death but Sashie did not belong to this majority. He did not belong to any group and as a rule took little interest in humanity except to comment cynically on its foibles, but for some reason that I did not understand, he had always taken a considerable and helpful interest in myself. In the past, he had been helpful in many ways but in this grey present his penetrating interest was the last thing I wanted, for it threatened to pierce the dull grey wall that stood between me and reality, the wall that protected me from pain.

'I wish you would stop talking ugly nonsense and go away,' I told him, trying to sound merely bored and not to show that I was afraid of him.

'I am not talking nonsense. You have just watched over one deathbed and now you are taking up duty beside another. You know as well as I do that it is not in the nature of things that Madame can live much longer. She is being pushed on to you to save Sir Ian and Edward any trouble and discomfort.'

I knew that he was being deliberately crude and outrageous in an effort to break through to me, to bring me into communication and although I wished to remain in isolation, my sense of loyalty and gratitude to the Dulacs came momentarily awake so that I could not let pass what he had said.

'Sashie, that is a very nasty thing you have said,' I protested feebly.

'Nasty!' he repeated on a mimicking whining note. 'Nasty! Janet, for God's sake be your*self*! Dear heaven, how odd that the cliché so often can be the only way of saying what one really means! Be your*self*!'

And suddenly, piercingly, I knew that this was the last thing I wanted to be. The sense of guilt that had come over

14

me at Twice's death seemed to burst into life in my mind like a scarlet flame, showing in its lurid light that this self I had been, this woman Janet, had somehow, in some way that I did not understand, that I was afraid of understanding, helped to destroy Twice. But for you, said an inner voice with sharp conviction, Twice would still be alive.

'No!' I said aloud and sharply, contradicting that inner voice. 'No! Stop it! Go away!'

'I will stop it and go away just when I choose,' said the voice of Sashie, bringing me, thankfully, out of the menacing inner darkness to the grey dreariness of the veranda, the crate of books, the tea tray and his presence. 'This thing of taking you into their service at the Great House is the worst sort of opportunism on the part of these Dulacs, for that is what they are by the habit of centuries – opportunists, exploiters of situations.'

'You are speaking about my friends, Sashie and I am not going to listen to you.'

'How very hoity-toity as your friend Madame would say. Friends, forsooth! What about your own life, your future?'

'All that is my affair, surely?'

'Then *make* it your affair. Get *affairée* with it. Don't sit around prating of your *friends*,' he said. 'What about your writing?'

'What writing? What do you mean?'

'Oh, very well.' He made an impatient gesture. 'If it is your secret, keep it secret but *keep* it, be active about it. *Do* something, *anything* but do it!' His voice changed, became less sharp and urgent, more gentle. 'Janet, you have to go on living. You are the living sort and you have to go on doing it. You ought to go back to Scotland. You have served your term on this island.'

'No,' I said. 'Not Scotland. I have no place there now.'

He sighed suddenly and rose to his feet, a curiously sad little figure in his gay lemon-coloured shirt and orange linen slacks. 'Scotland is the only place on earth where you belong,' he said. 'So you intend to carry on with this farce at the Great House?'

'I intend to stay with Madame for as long as she wants me,' I said, glad that he was going away.

15

'We have not quarrelled, Janet,' he said now and gently before his manner changed as he draped about him like a spangled cloak the affectation with which he usually faced the world. 'I shall wait upon you at the Great House from time to time, my sweet, suitably dressed and upon my best behaviour and if at any time I can be of service, you know where to find me. Good-bye but only for the moment, darling. I am gone.'

Thankfully, I watched him dance down the steps and get into his car, while I decided that another tête-à-tête with him was something to be avoided. I did not notice at the time that this was the first decision I had taken on my own behalf since Twice died, for such a small negative thing like avoiding private meetings with Sashie did not seem like a decision at all.

One more afternoon at Guinea Corner would be enough time for Caleb and me to pack the contents of the linen cupboard and after that this dreary stowing away of relics would be complete. After that, Sashie would not see me except in the protective cocoon of the Great House, in the presence of Madame, Sir Ian or Edward, where he could be kept at a safe distance.

In the early tropical twilight, I left the corpse of my former home and Caleb drove me across the park, past the sugar factory which hummed out its productive music to the Great House. I had known this parkland, dotted with clumps of palms, criss-crossed with roads that led to the staff bungalows, for years but nowadays it looked different and unfamiliar, as if the growing things and the buildings had withdrawn into another dimension. As we passed the factory and the distillery complex inside their high barrier of steel mesh, I felt a surge of hatred for them. It was largely the work of the brain and hands of Twice and it seemed to be obscene that it should still stand there, out-living its creator, but the feeble surge of feeling died away and was lost in my grey hopelessness, as the car swung through the gates and up the drive to the library entrance to the Great House.

The library, although large, was one of the smaller public rooms of the house and during the last few years, since she

16

became blind, Madame used it as a living-room. She and Sir Ian were there when I went in, the tea tray still between them on its low table.

'I'm sorry I did not come back in time for tea—' I began but Sir Ian broke in with: 'Sashie called on you, my dear? That's right. I sent him round. Well, Mother, now that Missis Janet is here, I'll take a stroll over to the factory.'

'You have had tea dear?' Madame asked. 'Then ring and have the tray taken away. I am glad that you have had a chat with Mr. Sashie. You must get into the way of going about a little now and seeing something of your friends. And, of course, as you know, you must invite people here just as you please. Did Mr. Sashie bring any news from St. Jago Bay?'

'No, Madame. He came up from Silver Beach. I think he spends most of his time there now.'

'Ah, of course. I am inclined to forget that he has given over the management of the hotel to Mr. Candlesham. There have been so many changes. I remember when the Peak Hotel, as they call it now, used to be a private house – the Poynters' place – a most uncomfortable house, where the northers used to blow the sand from the beach into one's soup. Mrs. Poynter, dear Maud's grandmother, she was, was a most unpleasant woman—'

Madame was now launched for the evening on the waters of her long past in the island, to which she had come from Edinburgh some seventy years before as a young bride. While she talked, I worked at a piece of embroidery, interjected a few phrases such as 'Really, Madame?' but heard little of what she had said and thought of nothing except that, very soon, the evening tray of drinks would arrive, then there would be dinner, then retirement to my rooms, to the bottle of whisky that was there and on into oblivion.

The days passed on a routine of luxury. The Great House of Paradise, like its mistress, was a survival from the past, where the servants went quietly about their duties which were all designed for the maximum comfort of Madame, Sir Ian and myself and there was no doubt, I tried to tell myself, that I was the most fortunate of widows, but in the grey twilight of the mind in which I lived, I did not hear even my own voice, did not believe even my own thoughts. I had

17

plenty of time to think, time which I spent in the avoidance of thought. Madame did not get up until noon, at which time I and her maid Letty helped her to dress. Then we had lunch, followed by a little walk round the garden before she went to her bedroom for her nap. After that, we wrote her letters or I read to her, then came tea, then drinks, then dinner and a little conversation before Madame went to bed at nine-thirty. When she had gone to sleep, I made myself drunk and usually fell into a stupor that lasted from about two in the morning until about six, when I would awake unwillingly to face another day. When I look back to this time, I can see that my robust health was one of my enemies.

I was forty-eight years old, had never had an illness in my life except one that was the result of an accident and I contrived to give an appearance of normal health to the people around me while eating little food, sleeping normally not at all and consuming an excessive amount of alcohol. In a mechanical way, I did everything that was required of me although I was dimly aware of turning into a split personality. The mechanical side carried out the duties that Madame required of me, wrote banal letters home to my family and packed my possessions at Guinea Corner, but this practical efficiency was no more than a veneer that hid from the people around me and sometimes from myself the dark chaos that had invaded my mind. This was something that I was afraid to examine, because I felt that a monster lived there, something that, if it were allowed to take form as a concrete thought, would destroy me utterly.

Nevertheless, the most extraordinary feature of life is its persistence, the force that, as long as a spark of sanity remains, sends one forward in time through minute after minute, day after day. Although I could not see any future, had no desire for a future, I went on, illogically, packing up the remains of my past life, books, china, cutlery, things that I no longer wanted and felt I would never use again, doing these things because they were what the people around me expected me to do. Guinea Corner had to be cleared of my possessions so that it would be ready for the new office manager who was to live there with his family.

18

There came the afternoon when Caleb and I tackled the last apartment in the house, which was the linen cupboard. This was a small room, shelved from floor to ceiling and it contained not only linen but all sorts of odds and ends that had accumulated there during our stay in the house.

'I think you should carry the linen down to the crate in the hall, Caleb,' I said, 'and after it is packed we'll tackle the other rubbish.'

It did not take long to stow the linen into the crate and then Caleb began to bring down all the other contents of the cupboard while I sat on the bottom step of the stairs with a glass of whisky and water beside me. There were battered old suitcases, shoes of mine that were unworn misfits, a large, hideous green metal vase with a dent in its side and the words: 'Home, Sweet Home' painted on it in gilt.

'The dustbin, Caleb,' I said.

'Missy Rosie would like it, ma'am.'

Miss Rosie was either his grandmother or his great-grandmother; I had never been sure which. 'All right. Keep it for her and keep anything else you would like, Caleb.'

On his next journey, he came down with a long, black metal trunk, like a coffin, with the words: 'Major A. Alexander, R.E.M.E.' in white paint on its lid, the trunk that Twice had had during his war service in India. No. Not Twice, but Major A. Alexander, a man I had never known. Caleb put the trunk on the floor beside the wall.

'Throw that out, Caleb,' I said.

'It would be good for all them papers, ma'am or do you want the carpenters to make another crate for them?'

'What papers?'

'All the papers in the linen cupboard and some in the back bedroom too.'

I remembered that these were the manuscripts of the novels I had been trying to write, brown paper parcels full of sheets of written words, valueless irrelevant lumber. 'We'll burn all that,' I said.

Caleb's big dark eyes regarded me gravely. 'Missy Rosie says not ever to burn papers, ma'am. Our Joseph went and burned his birth paper once. Miss Rosie says papers are always to be kept safe.'

19

'And Missy Rosie is quite right,' said the clipped voice of Sashie from the doorway. 'Bring the papers down and let us pack them, Caleb.'

'Are you back here again?' I said. 'I wish you would mind your own business.' But it was a feeble protest for I was tired and sick of all this debris that lay cluttered around me.

'I am doing precisely that,' Sashie said in a determined way, stowing the first lot of brown paper parcels into the trunk.

I said no more but sat on the step watching them pack the heaps and bundles of paper.

'That is the lot, Caleb?' Sashie asked eventually.

'Yes, Mars Sashie, every last piece.'

'Good.' Sashie dropped the lid of the trunk and while Caleb fastened the clasps he turned to me. 'Where are the keys of this trunk?'

'I don't know. They were lost long ago.'

He went to the door and called his chauffeur. 'Winston, you and Caleb take that trunk out to my car, please.'

I reached for the stair rail and hauled myself to my feet.

'Listen, Sashie, those papers are mine.'

'I am aware of that.' His face and voice were flint-hard. 'That is why I am taking them into safekeeping.'

'Sashie de Marnay, if you go poking about among that stuff, looking at it—'

'Don't be obscene, Janet,' he said and turned away from me.

I felt remorse but vaguely only, in the way that I felt everything now, when I felt anything at all and I sat down on the step again, looking at Sashie while Winston and Caleb carried the heavy trunk out of the house to the car.

'You are in a destructive mood,' Sashie said, 'and there is nothing more brutal than a constructive person bent on destruction.'

'Oh, rubbish.'

'I remember that once before you had a private holocaust in the backyard. I was too late to stop you that time.'

Dimly, as if I saw the memory through a cloud of smoke, I remembered how, after the death of my father, I had burned all my manuscripts in the backyard and how Sashie had arrived to find me among the black smouldering ashes. Out of the remembered heap of ash, a small white flame seemed to rise, a flicker of light in that darkness of my mind. Sashie had helped me that time and perhaps he could help me again now but help me with what? There was nothing left in me that was worthy of help, nothing that was of importance to myself or to anybody any more. I could feel Sashie's dark eyes looking down at me and again I wished that he would go away. Caleb, having put the trunk in the car, came back into the house and went towards the stairs.

'Is this packing business nearly finished, Caleb?' Sashie asked impatiently.

'Yes, sir, finished to the last little thing except for the two heads in the linen cupboard.'

'Heads?' I repeated.

'Yes, ma'am. Men's heads. I will fetch them.'

It was late afternoon. The sun had gone over towards the rim of Paradise valley and the light in the mahogany-panelled hall was dim. From my seat on the step I looked upwards at Caleb as he came down the stairs with a 'head' under each arm and wondered, morbidly but without much interest, if I had been responsible for the death of not only Twice but of other men as well. Had I, for years, been a mad woman who killed people and concealed their heads in my linen cupboard, as I had concealed the manuscripts of the novels I wrote against all the wishes of Twice?

Sashie reached for the switch and flooded the hall with light. Under one arm, Caleb was carrying the metal helmet of a bogus suit of armour, a thing that had once belonged to my friend Muriel and, before that, to a woman called Mrs. Whitely-Rollin. I could see the hall in her home in Kent now, with the suit of armour standing by the door to the drawing-room, like a tiny picture at the end of a long dark tunnel. Caleb set his 'heads' down on the stairs. The second one was a dirty grey plaster cast that had once been white, a cast of a man's head. The nose was chipped and the neck rose from a plinth on which was lettered the word 'Beethoven' and now the picture at the end of the tunnel changed to show an unfurnished room in a house called Crookmill in south-west Scotland. The room was, outwardly, like the

21

rooms around us at Guinea Corner at that moment, for it was full of packages, trunks, crates but in its inward nature the room at Crookmill was different. The packages that it contained were wedding presents, waiting to be opened, that their contents might be incorporated in the new life that lay before Twice and me, while the packages that littered the floors of Guinea Corner contained the meaningless relics of a life that had come to an end.

'The dustbin, Caleb,' I said.

'Missy Rosie, ma'am?' he asked.

'May I have the helmet, Janet?' Sashie asked in the same moment.

'What for?' I asked but before he could answer I had lost interest in why he wanted this bogus freak of a thing. 'Of course. Take it,' I said.

He took the thing from Caleb, raised the visor and peered into the cavity of the head before letting the visor fall again with a hollow clonk.

'Thank you, my sweet. I shall treasure it,' he said. 'It reminds me of so many people I know.'

I rose to my feet. 'I am going back to the Great House. Caleb, lock this place up and give the keys to Chief Mackie. Tell him the crates can go into storage as soon as he likes to have them picked up.'

'I shall come back to the Great House with you,' Sashie said.

'What for?'

He raised the visor of the helmet and let it clonk back into place again. 'You are ungracious,' he said, 'and parsimonious as well. It is sundown and I want a drink. It is mean to keep all your whisky to yourself.'

'Which door, ma'am?' the driver asked me as the station wagon with the long black trunk in the back came round the drive towards the Great House.'

'The library entrance, please,' I said.

'No, Winston, the east veranda,' Sashie countermanded and when we left the car we climbed the flights of outer stairs to my rooms on the top floor of the house.

These rooms were the old nurseries, the rooms where Sir Ian and his brothers had been brought up in the days when children were not heard and seen by their parents as seldom as possible. Like all the other rooms of the Great House, these rooms had dark mahogany floors and were panelled from floor to ceiling in more mahogany and beyond the dormer windows that protruded from the cedar shingles of the roof, the tops of the garden trees came between the windows and the sky so that the light was always a dim brownish green. Madame had always been acquisitive and down the years she had collected at auction sales, when the great houses of the island were being pulled down or turned into hotels, a vast amount of valuable furniture which was stored in the cellars four floors below. It would have been more reasonable to furnish these upper rooms from the cellars, rather than let valuable pieces lie neglected in the dark but Madame's convention was that the nurseries were furnished with throwouts from the more public and import- ant parts of the house, so that this top floor was an amalgam of rickety tables, curtains that were too long and chairs with broken springs that were upholstered in dark brown, dark red or dark green plush.

I had brief moments of feeling oppressed by these sur- roundings but for much of the time I was not aware of them. Yet now, when Sashie and I came into my sitting- room, I felt vaguely ashamed that I spent my days in such a place.

The Great House ran on oiled wheels of long habit and custom, however, and every room used as a sitting-room was provided with a large tray that held a decanter of rum, one of whisky, a siphon of soda water, a jug of water, glasses and a thermos bucket that was filled with ice morning and evening.

'I resent this place,' Sashie said, standing in mid-floor and looking about him, 'with its poor-relation atmosphere.'

I ignored this. 'There are the drinks,' I said. 'Help your- self.'

'You are being very ungracious, Janet. Your family would be ashamed of you.'

This was true. I felt hunted and desperate. 'Sashie, please leave me alone. I don't want to talk about – things.'

'But I do.' He poured whisky and water for both of us.

23

'Or rather, I want to talk about people, one person in particular.'

I could feel my eyeballs dilating, as if they would burst from their sockets. If he dared to speak the name of Twice—'

'Caleb, I want to talk about,' he said and sat down. 'What is to happen to him?'

'I don't know.' And I did not care which made me feel guilty. I was capable of only one attitude, it seemed, to all the realities of life when they were forced upon me and this was a feeling of guilt. I was behaving badly about Caleb who was my friend, by having ceased to take any interest in him. The three women servants I had paid off had been different. There had been no particular bond between them and me but Caleb – I had been the main influence in his life and now I had withdrawn that influence in my creeping away inside myself but I was tired and had no influence left to exert.

'I am going to give him some money,' I said. 'He will get another job and he has his guitar-playing down at the hotel.'

'I intend to ask him to come to Silver Beach as my headman,' Sashie said, 'but on the understanding that you may have him back when you have decided what you are going to do.'

'I am not going to do anything. I won't want to have Caleb back.'

Sashie looked round the room which seemed to echo the silence of the multitude of empty rooms below. 'You intend to spend the rest of your days in this cavern of nothingness?'

It was a good description of my view of the future. 'I am glad you are taking Caleb,' I said. 'He will enjoy cultivating Silver Beach. Thank you, Sashie. I must go down to Madame now.'

He put his glass aside and stood up. 'I shall come down with you and pay my respects.'

In the library, Madame was alone, sitting in her upright throne-like chair. 'Ian is in the office at the Instrument,' she said, using her own word for the telephone. 'The drinks are on the table, Janet. Mr. Sashie, what will you have?'

'Nothing thank you, Madame,' he said. 'Janet and I have

24

just completed the packing at Guinea Corner and I must go home.'

'Just as you please. I am very glad that it is all finished and done with. Janet, now that everything is over you must arrange to go out and about a little and you must call upon us as often as you can, Mr. Sashie. After all, now that you are less active in the management of the hotel, you must have more spare time.'

'That is true, Madame.'

'Very well. You must spend some of it with us and bring us the news as often as you can.'

'With pleasure, Madame,' he said, looking at me with what I felt to be a threat in his dark eyes, as if he were telling me that now he had Madame's official permission to come frequently to the Great House, I would never escape his vigilance.

Sashie must have gone back to Guinea Corner that evening for, the following forenoon, my maid told me that Caleb was asking to see me. When he was shown upstairs, he looked round my sitting-room and said: 'This is nice, ma'am. You are happy here?'

'Yes, thank you, Caleb, very happy.'

'I came to see you now that we are finished away with Guinea Corner, ma'am.'

'Finished away.' The dialect phrase was fitting and final.

'Aston from Engineer's House is going to cut the grass and the hedges until the new office gentleman comes to Guinea Corner, ma'am. Chief Mackie arranged it.'

'That is good, Caleb. We don't want the garden to run wild.' Caleb and I had made the big garden out of an area of jungle which had grown round the old house during long neglected years and we had both loved it but now, for me, it was only one more encumbrance from the past. I did not care whether it ran wild or not but was yet ashamed that Mackie the Engineer and Caleb had been left to arrange its future.

'Mars Sashie spoke to you about me, ma'am?' Caleb now asked.

'Yes. He wants you as headman at Silver Beach. Do you want to go, Caleb?'

His dark eyes shone. 'Yes, ma'am, I want to go. Silver Beach is a sweet property, ma'am. I can make money for Mars Sashie in that place.'

'I am sure you can, Caleb.'

'There is one more thing, ma'am.'

I sighed. There was always one more thing. Down all the years of living, 'things' had gathered around me like barnacles on the hull of a ship and I felt weighed down, as if I would never be disencumbered of them all.

'Yes, Caleb?'

'I am asking you kindly, ma'am, if I could take Dram to Silver Beach with me to be with Mars Sashie and me.'

I had forgotten about the dog, was ashamed of this and at the same time relieved that he would be provided for. 'But would Mars Sashie want him at Silver Beach, Caleb?' I had to ask.

'Yes, ma'am. I asked and Mars Sashie would like it. Dram is a good watch, ma'am, and them trash down on the coast won't steal the Silver Beach coconuts with Dram there, ma'am.'

'Very well, Caleb. Take Dram with you but he is yours, not Mars Sashie's.'

'Mine?'

'Yes, Caleb.'

'Ma'am, I thank you. I will look after him good.'

'I know you will. When do you go, Caleb?'

'One more week here, ma'am. Mars Sashie is fixing that little old house by the gully at Silver Beach for me. You will come to see it one day, ma'am?'

'Yes, Caleb. I will come to see your house,' I said.

When he had gone away down the veranda stairs, I felt that at long last I was finished with Guinea Corner, with all of life as I had known it, with all of life as I ever wanted to know it but there was still one more 'thing'.

The day before Caleb and Dram were to leave for Silver Beach, I sent Madame's chauffeur round to Guinea Corner with a small cheque as a parting gift to Caleb. The man came rushing back, sprang out of the car and into the library.

'Caleb says to come quick, ma'am. Dram is sick. The vet is round there.'

When we reached Guinea Corner, Dram was lying in the shade of the bougainvillea hedge with Caleb and the government vet kneeling beside him. Round his black muzzle on the green grass there was a great pool of foam-flecked blood and when I put my hand on his golden head, his large dark eyes looked into my face with what seemed to be an infinite pity before they became dull and expressionless in death.

'He had been running in the sun?' the vet asked after a moment.

'Chasin' mongoose in the cane, sah,' Caleb said. 'Him was everlastin' chasin' mongoose.'

Caleb's voice shook as he spoke in the island dialect which he seldom used nowadays and I looked at his big black hand which smoothed the golden coat of the dog while his tears dropped on to the grass.

'I am sorry, Mrs. Alexander,' the vet said. 'A haemorrhage of some sort – there was nothing I could do. Life is being more than hard for you.'

'It can't be helped,' I said senselessly, getting to my feet. I felt guilt wreathing about me like trails of black mist for, during these last weeks, had I not wished sometimes, that the dog was not there to trouble me with his big questioning eyes? 'He must be buried,' I said next, out of my knowledge that the flesh and blood and bones that life has left behind must be quickly and darkly hidden from the bright, corrupting tropical sun.

'I will do this,' Caleb said, standing upright. 'You come in the house, ma'am and I fetch you a drink. Then I will make a grave for Dram under the avocado tree.'

The vet went away, I sent Madame's chauffeur back to the house with instructions to return for me at the end of an hour and then I sat on the veranda with the drink and the cigarettes that Caleb had brought to me. The sun was at its midday zenith when he came to conduct me round to the back garden.

Under the avocado tree, there was the mound of earth, safely covered with large stones and on the stones lay a great spray of scarlet bougainvillea.

'Thank you, Caleb,' I said.

There was no more to say. The car came for me and Caleb asked for a lift as far as the Great House, having suddenly decided that he was going to his home at Missy Rosie's.

I do not know if he ever went back to Guinea Corner. I suppose he must have done, to fetch his belongings from his quarters there, but I did not ever go back to the house again. This time, my life there had ended for good.

It was with thankfulness that I dropped into my little slot at the Great House, shut away from all calls from the world outside. I now began to exist inside a glass case of social form, with an obscuring film drawn over my deeper consciousness, saying nothing and doing nothing, except in a surface mechanical way, trying not to think at all. For me, it was a farcical way of life and I ought to have known this. Perhaps, even, I did know it and chose to ignore my knowledge but however that may be, it was a way of life radically opposed to the way that had formerly been mine.

In my childhood at Reachfar, my family home in the north of Scotland, there had been little social form except for the hierarchy of the family and in the hierarchy I had my secure appointed place, so that my mind was free to pursue a life of curious intensity. On my dancing way along my Strip of Herbage, as I called the row of boulders that separated two fields, I would suddenly stop at a primrose that had come into bloom on a spring morning and, bending down until my eyes were within inches of its golden centre, I would stare into the flower and come to a consciousness of a whole living world contained among those pale stamens. Or I would sit high in the forked branch of my Waving Tree while the wind chased the clouds across the sky so that their shadows made the far hills seem to move like the waves of the sea and it would be as if I were part of the whole rhythmic symphony of the universe. And when something new happened, something that had never happened in my life before, I would retire to my Thinking Place among the tall fir trees above the well and there, in the dim brownish-green stillness that was like the dim shadowed depths of my own mind, I would sit 'thinking' as I called it but it was really a waiting, I see now, a waiting for the gleam of understanding to come, seeming to arrive for no reason from nowhere just as, sometimes, a sunbeam would find its way through the thicket of the Thinking Place, threading through the jungle of branches and fir needles to touch a brown tree trunk to a shimmer of pure gold.

This childhood of mine had caused me to grow up with a dislike of forms, conventions, habits, routines and all the modes of life that encouraged the mind to slip out of gear and idle like a de-geared engine, while the body lived through its days and nights automatically. During my young life in the south of England and London in the decade of the nineteen-thirties, my mind was always fully engaged in exploration of some kind and if a time came when nothing seemed to be 'happening', by which I meant that I had come to a point of little mental interest, I would, without conscious planning, break through the dullness by some means, frequently getting into mischief or creating some uncomfortable social situation among my acquaintances by way of shaking them and myself up into a renewed consciousness.

Now, however, I wanted to live and did live in a way directly opposed to this. I lived entirely within the forms and conventions and avoided all deeper awareness of any kind. This was easy to do by day in the company of Madame and Sir Ian who were hidebound and imprisoned in the web of habit and convention which had been spun round the Great House and its people down the long generations. They lived, if this mode of existence can be called living, mostly in the past. They made no new acceptances and still thought, basically, in the same way as they had thought at the age of twenty. This meant, roughly, that Madame's views were characteristic of a woman of her bourgeois class in 1890 and that Sir Ian's were those of a wealthy subaltern at Poona in 1913.

It was true that they had made an outward appearance of adjustment which caused Madame to invite the Negro apprentice engineers to the Great House about once a year but now that I was living in daily contact with her and Sir Ian, I came to know that it was an adjustment only in surface form. It was an expedient demanded by what Sashie had called their opportunism. Engineers were essential to keep the wheels of Paradise turning and these times enforced that engineers be Negroes. Very well. In an outward sense, they must be fitted into the social structure of Paradise but this did not mean that Madame or Sir Ian had changed their attitude to the Negro race. To them, Negroes, and, indeed, Frenchmen, Germans and all 'foreigners' had always been inferior breeds and always would be. It was typical of their mode of thought that the original Dulac of Paradise had been a Frenchman but he had lived long enough ago for them to bear his name with pride while pressing the man himself and his origins more and more deeply into the forgotten grave of the past.

While I lived within the routine of the Great House, I would become momentarily conscious that it was like some great lumbering barouche creaking along among all the modern traffic on the vast motorway of life but I would suppress the thought at once, as I suppressed every kind of thought. I would tell myself that these thoughts were disloyal and ungrateful to Madame and Sir Ian and in a masochistic way be ashamed of having thought them.

Human lives are linked together in strange and devious ways, so that whatever happens to one member of a network of relationships affects in some way all the other members. In an ironic way, the death of Twice, which had been tragedy for me, was beneficent to Madame and Sir Ian. It had broken through their lethargic routine and Madame, with me to look after, as she saw it, was restored to much of her former energy. Although she did not get up until noon, she had breakfast in bed at eight and when her breakfast had been taken in, the house took on an air of being about its business. Her bedroom opened off the central hall on the second floor and from eight onwards, this door was left open and enthroned against a heap of pillows on the bed, she would talk tirelessly, laying down the law in her imperious way about everything. The highlight of the forenoon was the coming of her mail at about eleven o'clock and when reading this to her, it was easier than ever to escape from the present. All the letters came from women nearly as old as

30

herself, most of them widows like herself and since I had come to live at the Great House, she had, with my help, revived old acquaintanceships and correspondences that had lapsed during the first years of her blindness.

Madame had always regarded me as something of a secretary for, in former days, when Marion Maclean was alive and she and I and all the staff wives were in the capacity of ladies-in-waiting to the near-royal Madame, I happened to be the only one of the retinue who could use a typewriter. Madame regarded me, too, as something of a 'new woman', a blue-stocking, a type of which she did not entirely approve but, since it existed, there was no harm in using it for her convenience, so I had been called upon to type all her charity lists and circulars.

When I came to live at the Great House, the first thing that Madame asked me to fetch from Guinea Corner was my typewriter and I realized that she intended to make me 'forget things', as she put it, by keeping me busy. During those first few weeks, I had written a great number of letters dictated by Madame, most of which began with the words: 'It is a long time since I wrote but better late than never' for Madame had never been one to despise the cliché. After we had completed each letter, she would say 'Poor Minnie—' or 'Poor Ella, I suppose she is dead years ago but it will be nice to know', behind which I could sense the triumphant thought: 'And won't they all be astonished to know that *I* am still alive!'

As it happened, an unlikely number of the Minnies and Ellas were also still alive, although one or two had gratifyingly died, so that we had to write letters of condolence to their relations which Madame found very enjoyable. Splendidly unconscious of her own ambivalence, she would sigh deeply while her blind old eyes filled with tears and say: 'Poor Mary, she was a dear old soul. Her niece must miss her sadly. We must write to the poor thing regularly.' I do not think that Madame had forgotten that, on the day that we first wrote to poor Mary, she had said: 'I suppose she is dead and it will be a blessing if she is really because she has been so selfish with that poor niece who looked after her.' No. I do not think that Madame had forgotten saying this

31

but it was her convention that you might say such things when you thought people were alive or while merely supposing that they were dead but you did not say them after you knew positively that they were dead. 'Death,' as her Cousin Emmie, who was one of our correspondents, would have said, 'made all the difference.'

The letters from Cousin Emmie did Madame more good than any of the others by setting her old blood boiling with rage.

Cousin Emmie had never lived within the forms and conventions. In Edwardian days, when Madame was in her heyday at Paradise as the queen of St. Jagoan society Cousin Emmie had been a militant suffragette in London and in recent times, after living as a spinster to the age of seventy, had topped off what Madame called 'her ridiculous career' by marrying a retired vicar. Even as I wrote, at Madame's dictation, the first cliché-ridden letter to cousin Emmie, I was estimating the reply to it, if Cousin Emmie bothered to reply at all and, sure enough, when the reply came, it opened with: 'Dear Lottie. I don't know why you've suddenly started to write to me after all these years but I suppose you can't bear to see Mrs. Alexander's typewriter lying idle.' By the same mail, though, I too had a letter from Cousin Emmie, couched in very different terms and it brought me more comfort than any of the hundreds of others I had received, for this old woman and I had met some years before when she spent a few months in the island. But Cousin Emmie did not like her Cousin Lottie and, unlike Madame, she did not see any reason to be other than open in that dislike.

And so Madame dictated an angry letter back to her and in due course Cousin Emmie replied with a letter even more outspoken than the first and so our days went past while Sir Ian woofed cheerfully round the house and estate and the hum of the machinery and smells of molasses and distillery effluent were borne on the breeze from the factory complex as they always were in Crop time.

While I was spending my empty days and oblivious nights inside the separate world of the Great House and its garden whose gate I never went through, the other world beyond those gates was going on its way. Edward Dulac, now that the crisis brought about by the death of Twice was over, when he had been replaced on the staff by two men less experienced, went back to London for he had never pretended to like the life of St. Jago or Paradise. Edward belonged to the cosmopolitan sets of the capitals like London, Paris and Rome and did not conceal his dislike for the cultural desert that he found St. Jago to be.

'So the eternal adolescent has gone?' said Sashie. 'What a blessing, darling.'

I had now put the past behind and could contrive to forget it for most of the time but I had learned that Sashie was one feature of it that was not to be put behind or forgotten. He arrived at the Great House, welcomed by Madame and Sir Ian, almost every other day and had become adept at arriving at times when I was not 'on duty' as I thought of it, when he would come quietly up the veranda stairs and into my sitting-room. If he arrived in the forenoon, he would go away when I went to Madame's bedroom to read her mail; if he came in the afternoon, during her nap, he would be invited to stay to tea and perhaps longer. I did not understand why he came and did not care and most of the conversations between us were mere squabbles, as we began to squabble about Edward now, for I had discovered that to get through his visits by squabbling about other people was the best means of preventing him from breaking through to myself and destroying my inner lassitude.

'Edward is all right,' I said surlily. In truth, I had always found Edward something of a bore, because he was so socially correct in manner, dress and attitudes as to be almost featureless.

'There is nothing in his mind but a few adolescent pimples,' said Sashie.

'His knowledge of pictures isn't a pimple,' I said, for Edward had amassed a considerable and distinguished collection of modern paintings.

'He has no knowledge or appreciation of *painting*, darling,' Sashie argued. 'What he has knowledge of is how to make money out other men's paintings.'

33

I rose, turned my back on Sashie and began to move books from one place to another on a shelf.

'You should have married him while he was here and you had the chance,' said the voice from behind me.

'Don't be so disgusting,' I said, turning about.

Sashie shrugged his shoulders. 'Somebody is going to do it one of these days and it might as well be you if all you want to do is sit around on your behind doing nothing. Inert people like Edward always get things done to them. People either have to do things or have things done to them. Why don't *you* do something although, for preference, *not* marrying Edward?'

'What, for instance?' I asked, pouring myself some whisky. 'Do you want a drink?'

'No. Do anything, as long as it is positive. That—' he indicated the glass in my hand '—is negative. You will never be a successful alcoholic. You simply are not the type. In my years in the bordello down at the Peak, I have come to recognize the types who can achieve real alcoholism. You are not one of them.'

'You talk a great deal of nonsense, Sashie.'

'I know and I irritate you to death too. Why don't you quarrel with me, darling?'

'I simply can't be bothered. You will have to go now, Sashie. I have to go down to Madame.'

His manner changed as he stood up and looked at me solemnly with his strange dark eyes. 'Janet, does it matter to you that I am worried about you?'

'Worried? Why? Why should *you* worry about me?'

'So it does not matter,' he said and his eyelids blinked rapidly for a second or two before he assumed his normal air of affectation and said: 'Yes, indeed, why should it matter? Good-bye, my sweet.'

I watched him leave the room, listened to his jerky hopping down the veranda stairs while, deep in my mind, there was a movement, as if feeling were coming awake. But if feeling did awake in me, I knew that it could only be painful, shameful or guilty for these were the only feelings of which I was now capable. There would be the pain of having hurt Sashie, the shame at having hurt him and these would be

34

followed by the guilt that I could cause nothing but pain and destruction. Hastily, I swallowed some more whisky, then brushed my teeth and went down to Madame's bedroom.

Three days went past and Sashie did not appear at the Great House and on the third evening I was forced into awareness of a sick uneasiness from which I took my customary means of escape. Physically, at this stage, I suffered frequently from nausea and giddiness which were, I knew, the result of my drinking too much and eating too little and the thought of Sashie induced in me a similar squeamish unsteadiness of mind. Although giddy and nauseated, I went on drinking whisky and although Sashie's penetrating presence frightened me, his absence induced in me a sickening sense of loss. Yet, when he arrived on the fourth evening, I felt a panic desire to run away and hide from him when I heard his hopping feet on the veranda stairs but I stood my ground although I could utter no word of greeting.

He was dressed in a jade-green silk shirt and grey trousers and struck a pose in the doorway while he declaimed the words of Ariel in *The Tempest*:

> 'Hail! I come
> To answer thy best pleasure; be't to fly,
> To swim, to dive into the fire, to ride
> On the curl'd clouds, – to thy strong bidding task
> Ariel and all his quality.'

He lowered his arms and came forward into the room. 'And how are you this evening, my sweet?'

'I am all right.'

Now that he was here, I wished that he would simply go away again. 'Why the dramatic entrance?' I asked.

He sat down, arranged his trousers, looked down at his small green suède shoes which, I was sure, had been bought in a women's shop. 'I had to say something when I arrived,' he said, 'only I couldn't think what and then these lines came to me and they were exactly what I wanted to say so I said them.' He studied his shoes for a few seconds and then: 'When I left you last time, I decided that you had been very nasty to me and had hurt my feelings but today I decided

35

that, as Twice used to say, you can hurt my feelings any time so that is why I am here.'

Nobody ever spoke to me about Twice but when Sashie spoke of him now and used the turn of phrase that had been his, I felt that something of him lived on. 'I am sorry if I hurt your—' I began but Sashie broke in on me. 'You are nothing of the sort,' he said. 'You don't care a damn but it doesn't matter.'

'I don't mean to be as horrible as I am, Sashie,' I said next. 'It's just that – oh, I don't know.'

'I know that you are not well, Janet.'

This irritated me. If, physically, I was unwell, I knew that I had nobody other than myself to blame and I knew too that my physical condition was not the reason for my behaviour and did not want it to be used as an excuse. 'Rubbish. I am as strong as an ox as you well know and it takes more than a death in the family to upset someone like me.' I said brutally.

A small wincing shudder passed over Sashie's face before it set into an expressionless mask. I wished I could talk to him, tell him of the blackness in my mind, a blackness like primeval slime that could bring to birth hideous monsters, but I was afraid that, if I told of the blackness and of my fear in words, the monsters would suddenly come to life, rush upon me and destroy me.

After a dark sightless moment, my eyes looked outwards again and saw that Sashie was holding out to me two small keys on a steel ring. 'I have had these keys cut for that trunk,' he said.

'Trunk?'

'The steel trunk that holds your papers. It is locked now and these are the keys.'

I took them from his hand. 'Oh, yes. Thank you, Sashie.'

I looked back as if from a great distance on these papers of mine. Like everything else from the past, they had no reality and even when it impinged on the present, that past had no reality. Only the day before, a contract for the publication of my first novel had come, the manuscript of which I had sent to London before Twice died. I had signed the contract, asking Madame's chauffeur to witness my signature, covered it with an efficient impersonal letter and sent it back to the literary agents. This duality of personality was in itself frightening, for it meant that although I could see no future and had no hope for the future, I went on doing things that bound me to the future. The signing of the contract was like the macabre twitching of the legs of a fowl after the creature is dead.

'I hope the trunk is not a nuisance to you, Sashie,' I said formally, absurdly.

'Nothing connected with you is ever a nuisance to me, darling,' he said in his light affected voice.

I looked at him dully. I wished again that he was not here, that he would go away and I continued to have this ambivalent attitude to him. If three days passed without his calling on me, I began to wish for his presence, yet when I saw him approaching, I felt fear and when he had been with me for a short time, I would begin to wish that he would go away. I did not have this morbid attitude to other people. I was merely bored by their presence but I could behave in it and speak to them in a manner that was superficially normal. It was Sashie alone who could break the barrier and induce the vague longing, then the murky fear, then the bitter desire for the alienated loneliness into which I crawled as into a cave when he had left me.

I turned away from him and looked out at the black tree-tops against the silver-grey of the moonlit sky before I went to the table that held the drinks. I paused with my hand stretched towards the whisky decanter, waiting sullenly for him to tell me once again that I was drinking too much. Neither Madame nor Sir Ian nor anybody else seemed to notice how much I drank, nor did they seem to notice my physical deterioration and my irritation at Sashie who seemed to notice everything rose hot inside me as angry words came ready to my tongue. But he did not say anything. He merely came across the room, poured whisky and water into glasses for himself and me before sitting down again and arranging himself neatly in his chair.

'Caleb sends you his regards,' he said, 'and, by the way, he is walking out – walking-out-serious – he calls it, with Trixie, one of the chambermaids at the Peak.'

37

Grateful to Sashie now for not talking about my terrifying self, I did my best to be interested. 'Really? I am glad. It is time that Caleb settled down.'

'Darling, you sound exactly like Madame. I had hoped that you would prove impervious to the influence of the Great House.'

I felt that I was impervious to influence of any kind, for even this news of my friend Caleb made no impact on me, but Caleb was a safe subject.

'Is Caleb still playing his guitar at the Peak?' I asked.

'Only on Saturday nights since the hot weather began. He is really rather bored with professional guitar-playing and only does it to oblige and for the money, of course.'

I was not thinking of Caleb. I did not think actively about anyone. I was half-dreaming, half-remembering a guitar playing in the garden of Guinea Corner in accompaniment to Twice singing in his study.

'Aren't you pleased that Caleb hasn't turned into what you once called a lick-spittling cabaret singer after all?' Sashie asked.

'I misjudged him when I said that.' I had misjudged everything and everybody in the past which was why I did not try to exercise judgment any more.

'On the contrary, you were right about what was good for Caleb and he has recognized it for himself now. He is very happy among his cabbages and carrots at Silver Beach. He even makes those beastly coconuts look more controlled and less frightening. Will you come down one day soon, darling, and inspect his cultivation? It is all really rather beautiful.'

'I am sure it is.'

'He permits me to assist him now and then but not to do anything on my own. Do you remember that rubbly place that the builders left when they dug the foundation for the new kitchen? I thought a patch of yellow would be attractive there and sowed a packet of seeds that the shop said would grow in rubble. They came up in no time and burst forth into the most grotesque flowers that were just like yellow rubber sponges, darling. Caleb was horrible about them and rooted them all out.'

'He had no right to do that, Sashie.'

'I didn't mind because he said—' Sashie suddenly seemed even to look like a large Negro as he broke into the island dialect of an angry Caleb '—Dem yellah t'ings was called mar'golds, Mars Sashie an' if de Missis come dahn hyah, her not gonna like 'em.' Sashie turned into his mischievous self again. 'I shouldn't wish us to have anything at Silver Beach that you wouldn't like, my sweet, so will you come down one day and assure us that you like everything?'

'One day, Sashie,' I said, wishing desperately now that he would go away.

Mechanically, I had noted from the sounds rising from below that Madame and Sir Ian were preparing to come upstairs. Very soon now I would see Madame to bed and one more long day could go down into the blackness of the night. Sashie stood up and laid aside his glass. 'I shall go home now,' he said. 'What did you do with those keys I gave you?'

'What keys? Oh those?' I looked round the room. 'There they are on that table.' I stared at the keys. They seemed to grow before my eyes into huge bars of metal attached to a gigantic ring, a great heap of steel that might crash to the floor and through it so that the walls of the house would cave in and crush Madame, Sir Ian, Sashie and me to death. I waited for it to happen but then my sight cleared and the keys on their ring turned into one more irritating possession, one more thing to be put away carefully, like the books and the china and the linen in the crates that were now in the cellars down below. I did not want the keys. I did not want to be bothered with them. 'I wish you would take them and keep them along with the trunk, Sashie,' I said.

'All right, darling.' He picked them up and dropped them into the pocket of his trousers. 'And when shall I see you again?'

He was always trying to make me decide things, I thought resentfully. 'I'm always here,' I said. 'Sashie—'

'Yes?'

'Oh nothing.' If I had been going to say anything, I could not remember what it was and it could have had no importance anyhow, for nothing had any importance.

'If at any time there should be something,' he said, 'do let me know. Good night, Janet.'

Thereafter, he began to call again every other day and always there was the longing for him to appear, the fear when he came and the closing in of monotony when he went away but there was no real communication between us. I could make no more than a few forced banal remarks and often achieved no more in his presence than a sullen silence. Yet, when he was with me, I was more truly alive than when his presence was withdrawn.

The hot weather began early. Before April was out, it was as hot as midsummer and it was an unusually enervating summer, even for St. Jago – a hurricane summer, as the Negroes said, for, although no hurricane struck the island, a number formed out at sea and spread their heavy humid atmosphere over us. But the routine of the Great House went on its well-oiled groove and everybody said that Madame had taken on a new lease of life – everybody except Sashie, that is. Sashie always had his own view of everything and when someone said this of Madame in his presence, he exploded to me in private afterwards: 'New lease of life, forsooth, the old cannibal! She lives on the people around her, especially you, Janet.'

'Oh, stop it, Sashie,' I said. His energy wearied me.

'I am sorry, darling.' He seemed to be genuinely contrite. 'I must try to mind my own business,' he added.

It was true that Madame seemed to have more energy than any of us other than Sashie, to feel less than any of us the pressure of the atmosphere, and she awoke each morning looking forward to the routine of her day. The mail was the highlight and on the infrequent days when a letter arrived from Edward, this day became the highlight of the month.

In her way, Madame was fonder of Edward than she was of anyone. I say 'in her way' because Madame, I think, had no great capacity for love or affection. Her relationships were more in the nature of attitudes and she had the Victorian attitude to the family and its continuity so that Edward, the sole representative of the most recent generation of the family had more importance in her eyes than any other person. She did not see him primarily as a person, an individual with a particular character but saw him in an uninterested, uninquiring uncritical light as her grandson, in whom the future of the family was vested. Her sole criticism of him was that he was now over thirty and was not married but this, with Madame, was a common criticism of both men and woman, whether they were related to her or not. Madame liked people to be married and settled down, as she called it, as if the marriage ceremony were a sort of cement that set people in their places in life for good and all.

On a day at the beginning of May, an overseas mail came in that contained a letter from Edward. In the terrible diversity of life, everything had a different significance for everybody and for me this rectangular envelope, postmarked in Rome, meant that I would have more time that day to be upstairs by myself, for Madame would spend hours mulling over its contents with Sir Ian.

'The mail, Madame,' I said, going into her bedroom, 'and there is a letter from Edward.'

'Splendid, dear. Read it to me.'

Propped on her pillows, she smiled expectantly as I slit the envelope. 'He is in Rome, Madame, and it is a fine long letter,' I said and began to read: 'My dear Granny, I write very good news and I am sure you will be pleased—'

My eyes were already running ahead to the next sentence and as the sense of it came to me, I paused and looked at the blind old eyes in the fat little face above the buttoned collar of the silk nightgown, at the plump little hands with their load of rings already in place for the day folded serenely on the white sheet.

'Yes, dear? Go on.'

'It is very exciting news indeed, Madame,' I warned and returned to the letter. 'Your grandson is now a married man which is something you have always wanted,' I read out.

'Good gracious! I didn't know he was even engaged, Janet! He must have forgotten to tell us. How very peculiar and extraordinary!' She was frowning with annoyance.

'Lots of people don't bother about engagements and announcements and things nowadays, Madame.'

41

'How very odd. Very well. Read on, dear.'

'Anna and I were married on the twenty-second of April at the Caxton Hall Register Office—'

'*Where*, dear?'

She had heard me quite clearly but I repeated the words and added: 'That is quite usual nowadays too, Madame.'

She sighed. 'I see. Please read on, Janet.'

The bride was French, her maiden name being Anna Delatour, was twenty-five years old – considerably younger than Edward, as Madame remarked in a pleased way for this, unlike other aspects of the marriage, was exactly within her convention with regard to husbands and wives – and the only child of Anton Delatour, a dealer in the fine arts who had business interests in London, Paris and the other capitals. Anna was, of course, more beautiful than any dream and Edward was in the ultimate heaven of happiness, as he told his grandmother in every other sentence. He and Anna were now nearing the end of their short honeymoon in Rome and they intended to fly from there to St. Jago in the middle of May. Factually, there was little more in the letter but Edward was sure that Madame would love Anna as he did and he asked her to tell Sir Ian his news because he had no time to write a second letter. As I folded the sheets and put them into Madame's hand, I was aware of irritation that the entire letter struck me as adolescent, the word that Sashie had used of Edward.

'Shall I call the factory and ask Sir Ian to come over, Madame?' I asked.

'In a moment, dear. Janet—' the blind old face wore a puzzled frown '—do you suppose that my new granddaughter is by any chance a – a divorcée?'

'Good gracious, no, Madame! Because of the Register Office, you mean?'

'I just wondered a little.'

'Madame, she is only twenty-five. It is very unlikely.' I knew of a married couple who had parted at the age of twenty-one but I saw no point in making life difficult for Madame.

She smiled a little. 'That is true, dear. You are so sensible.'

'She is evidently a very much-travelled young lady, Madame, and so is Edward and we can't expect them to do things in the old-fashioned way that we would do them.'

'You are quite right, dear, and I am being very foolish and old-fashioned as you say. Go to the Instrument and ask Ian to come over. Really, this is the most wonderful news!'

As I sat at the telephone, waiting for Sir Ian to be found in the maze of the factory complex and brought to the office to speak to me, I wondered at the hypocritical malleability of my own character. I had spoken the words 'in the old-fashioned way that we would do them' to Madame quite glibly and even in honesty although the fact was that Twice and I had done what was known as 'going away together' without even calling at a Register Office on the way, for Twice was already married and could not obtain a divorce. It took some time for Sir Ian to be found, enough time for me to conclude that I had turned into a mere reflection of Madame, seeing everything from her point of view, in my desire to make her long days as happy and peaceful as possible, the only desire that I had and even it was mild and fleeting in nature. As I sat there, I found myself hoping that this development would mean real happiness for her but hoped in a haunted distrustful way, for I had lost somewhere in the empty darkness all belief that I had ever had in happiness.

'Yes, me dear, what is it?' Sir Ian barked into my ear.

'Madame asks you to come over to the house, Sir Ian. She has some good news from Edward that she wants to tell you at once.'

'By Jove,' he said when I had read the letter a second time, 'this is something like! And a French girl too!'

Hitherto, he had invariably referred to all Frenchwomen in a near-bawdy Gay-Nineties way as 'Fifis' but by convention a bride of Paradise could not be so described, of course. 'Anna,' he went on, 'nice-soundin' name, not *too* French. An' I bet she is a beauty. Edward won't have fallen for any plain Jane after messin' about with all these Venuses all these years.' This was a reference to his son's interest in painting, an interest which Sir Ian did not share. 'Fine arts dealer?' he continued in his ruminating way. 'Edward would have met her at some o' these galleries, Mother. I bet Delatour is rollin' in money. All these chaps that deal in things are stinkin' rich.'

I thought of Jock Skinner the dealer in our village near Reachfar when I was a child. Jock 'dealt' in anything from coal to rabbit-skins and although I do not think that Jock himself became wealthy, he fathered an illegitimate son who grew up to be one of the 'spivs' of the aftermath of the 1939–45 war and this man had undoubtedly been 'stinkin' rich' by our village standards.

In my hazy unsteady mind, I was always drifting about among cloudy pictures of the past, pictures conjured up by words, as the word 'dealer' had conjured up the memory of Jock Skinner. Words had always held a fascination for me but now this facet of my mind, like the other facets, had taken on a morbid character so that I heard the words Sir Ian spoke as if from a distance, as if his voice, as he spoke to Madame, were passing through a web of associations conjured up by the name 'Anna'. There was Anna May Wong, a Chinese actress of the thirties in a tight black satin dress; Anna and the King of Siam, in a book read shortly after the war; Anna Karenina and her husband who cracked his knuckles all the time and Greta Garbo playing the part of Anna Karenina in a film. With an effort, I dragged my mind free of these encumbrances that made Edward's Anna so unreal and tried to focus my attention on Madame and Sir Ian.

'Pity we couldn't have the weddin' here like you say, Mother,' Sir Ian was saying, 'But young people these days don't like these sort o' fusses any more.'

Nevertheless, I could see that he was as disappointed as Madame at how the marriage had taken place and that, like myself, he was choosing every word he spoke for its comfort and compensation to the old lady.

'Very well, Ian,' she said at last. 'Go back to your office. Janet and I are going to write to Edward – to Edward and Anna – before lunch.'

'Better send it to his London flat. He'll be sure of getting it there,' said Sir Ian, ultimately revealing his distrust of all things foreign, even addresses, as he went away back to the factory.

In the end, the letter was addressed to Anna in London, but we had difficulty in writing it. To write to someone completely unknown who was suddenly in a relation of such intimacy was of great difficulty to Madame while I in my dullness and weariness of mind could give little assistance. My main feeling was that Edward, always a bore, had now reached a sort of nadir of boredom and with relief I sealed the envelope at last and dismissed all thought of Edward and Anna, as I dismissed everything that happened.

But an event of such magnitude as the marriage of the heir to Paradise and its millions was not to be ignored, even by somebody as withdrawn from life as I was. There was now no other subject of conversation at the Great House and all Paradise looked forward to the arrival of the bride and bridegroom, while I felt that I was suspended in mid-air, looking on hopelessly at the birth of an avalanche.

Madame, as a young bride, had come to Paradise and had taken the reins of the Great House into her firm little hands and she was confident that this pattern was to be repeated now. She was convinced that Edward and his bride would arrive, 'settle down' and take their place at the head of island society as she herself had done and she seemed to forget that Edward had never spent any length of time at Paradise except at periods of crisis, that he had never shown any interest in the estate or its people and had never had any inclination towards island society. Indeed, island society as Madame had known it in her early days no longer existed but she seemed to have forgotten this too, as she planned for the arrival of the bridal couple.

'Janet,' she said, 'I am the dowager now and I intend to move up to the old nursery floor beside you. Anna must have my suite, as is proper for the mistress of the house.'

Sir Ian and I protested at this because of the stairs to be climbed and the isolation of the top of the house but she would not be dissuaded and Sir Ian yielded unwillingly, while I yielded out of a weary lack of interest. While the house was cleaned from top floor to cellars and I supervised the making of new curtains and soft furnishings for the

45

great first-floor drawing-room and the bride's suite, I dragged myself about in the torrid heat while my mind was trapped in a hopeless foreboding. And Sashie was always there, like an angry little wasp.

'Janet, you are exhausted and this is your chance. Leave this madhouse *now* and let the bride take care of that old woman.'

'No, Sashie, I can't.'

'Why not?'

'I don't know but I can't.'

'*Why* can't you?'

'Oh God, will you go away and leave me alone? Go *away*, I tell you!'

'All right. I shall go but I shall come back.'

And he did come back, every other day, sometimes every day. While Madame made plans, dreamed of the future and asked little questions such as: 'I wonder if Anna is dark or fair? So stupid of Edward not to say,' I was growing more and more uneasy and distrustful of the situation but, at the same time, I recognized my own morbidity of mind that cast a distorting shade over every situation, so that I lived between a certainty of coming disaster and scorn for my own mental instability.

Anna did not reply to Madame's letter and this small incivility took on in my mind a disproportionate import-ance, so that every time the bride was mentioned, the im-polite omission would awaken the uneasiness I felt. And then there was the bustle and gaiety about the Great House, the air of everything being for the best in the best possible of worlds, which reminded me of the previous summer at Guinea Corner when Twice's and my way ahead had seemed to be set so fair. I looked with bleak distrust upon the gaiety and the bustle, my muddled mind haunted by a couplet from Shakespeare:

> For never-resting time leads summer on
> To hideous winter and confounds him there.

It was in vain that I told myself that I was no longer capable of sound judgment, alcoholic as I was, my mind distorted by

46

morbidity. The unease persisted and there was a constant strain in trying to ignore it, to suppress it, to be part of the confident gaiety that was all around me.

As the time of the arrival drew nearer, Madame began to think in terms of a series of 'entertainments' for the bridal pair, by which she meant lavish dinner parties for thirty to fifty guests, of the kind that she had been wont to give in former days. Here, however, she came hard against the social reality, for most of the people she used to entertain were already dead.

'Yes, Janet, I have been foolish,' she confessed. 'I do not know any of the young society but when Edward and Anna come, the younger people will call and they will make their own friends and arrange their own entertainments.'

I did not point out that, in the sense that she meant, there was no longer any young society in the island. Paradise was the last great house to be lived in in the grand manner. Mount Melody was now a hotel, Craigellachie Heights had been pulled down and the Great House of Hope had been sold by its owner, Mrs. Miller, to an American syndicate which had turned its green pastures into a golf course with the Georgian mansion as its club house.

At last, the great day that I half-dreaded, half-welcomed came. Sir Ian, immaculate in white drill and pith helmet, anachronistic but dignified in the planter's uniform of sixty years ago, stepped into the Rolls and was driven off to the airport. About three in the afternoon, I brought Madame down to the drawing-room into which, although it was on the first floor, the main entrance to the house opened, at the top of a flight of broad stone steps whose pillared balustrade was decorated with stone urns from which the growing orchids fell in cascades of bloom.

'The drawing-room is as it should be, Janet?'

'The room is beautiful, Madame. In the Coalport bowl on the bamboo table, I have pink roses and in the pedestal vase—' To beguile this last waiting time for her, I went round all the details of the room, trying to make her see it and from the room I went on to the orchids in the urns and the flowers in bloom in the garden.

And now the moment came. The car stopped at the

47

bottom of the steps and I helped Madame to her feet and led her to the spot where she always stood, just inside the wide door, to receive guests. I then went back to stand about two yards behind her. As the three people came up the steps, my glance was drawn to Sir Ian's face. It wore a puzzled frown and from under his bushy down-drawn brows his eyes stared anxiously at Madame's face. I then looked at Edward's bride. She was as beautiful as a dream, as beautiful as the visions which, I have read, are induced by opium but she was, to all appearances, a full-blooded Chinese.

At the top of the steps, Edward suddenly picked her up and set her down inside the room in front of Madame. There came from her an angry little spatter of French of which I caught only the last word 'fou' and then, standing on her tiny feet in their white spike-heeled shoes, she straightened in an irritated way the narrow skirt of her white silk suit.

'And this is my grand-daughter?' Madame was saying, her voice trembling with pleasure, her arms held out to embrace the girl but Anna was not looking at Madame or at any of us. Her brilliant black eyes swept round the big richly-furnished room with an appraising glance – a dealer's glance, came the phrase in my mind as I was reminded of the crafty eyes of Jock Skinner – before she very coolly took Madame's right hand in her gloved fingers and said formally: 'Madame Dulac,' and I noticed that, as she bowed her head slightly, the black eyes rested on the four heavily-jewelled rings on Madame's plump little fingers.

'Janet,' Madame said, groping with the hand that the girl had released.

I went forward and took her arm. She was trembling but I felt her stiffen her muscles as she said: 'Anna, dear, this is our friend Janet – Mrs. Alexander – who lives with us.'

The black eyes turned to my face, the appraising estimating glance swept over me, the gloved hand came forward: 'Mrs. Alexander?' The hand was withdrawn, the black eyes continued to look into my face and suddenly I saw a quick flicker as her tongue passed from left to right along the channel between her lower front teeth and the inside of her lip. It was an extraordinarily repulsive little mannerism and so incredibly rapid in execution that it at once brought to mind the flickering tongue of a snake.

Tea was now brought in and while I poured out and Sir Ian handed plates, Madame began to ask about their journey.

Anna spoke fluent English, with an accent so slight as to be no more than an attractive intonation, in a high-pitched but musical voice. But the conversation was not that of a bride meeting her new family for the first time and was not at all, I knew, what Madame had expected. The old lady's hands shook a little as she held her cup and saucer and her face wore an uncomprehending look as if she could not understand what had gone wrong. As I sat beside her, I was reminded of the night when I was very small when, for the first time in my life, the clock struck six and my father had not come home for supper. He had only been delayed at the farm where he worked but, for me, this was something that had never happened before, something that *could* not happen without my world disintegrating. I felt that Madame was suffering this same sense of disintegration. She had built up in her mind a picture of this girl whom her blind eyes would never see; she had imagined this home-coming so often that she could not comprehend its being other than as she had dreamed it and now, temporarily, her world had fallen apart.

Anna was more the mistress of the situation than any of us. Supremely poised, scrupulously elegant, confident in her beauty, she led the conversation with a vivacity and wit and with a metropolitan air tinged with patronage that made me feel as if I were Caliban at the court of the first Queen Elizabeth. Before she sat down, she went to a Chippendale mirror on the wall and took off her small white hat carefully, not disturbing a strand of her shining, straight jet-black hair and she now sat in her white silk suit, her beautiful legs crossed, her tea cup held in slim fingers with long, delicate filbert-shaped nails that were lacquered a pale rose pink. Her face was broad between the temples, coming to a point at the chin but its dominating feature, of course, was the wide-set and slanting black eyes under thin black brows. Her skin was like yellowed ivory in colour and texture and there was a faint flush of tawny rose on the high cheek bones.

While she talked, Edward sat looking at her in a way that I can only describe as besotted, in a way that brought to mind phrases like 'absolutely wrapped up in her' or 'unable to see anybody but her'. In a little spurt of rebellion against her patronage and Edward's besottedness, I spoke in my mind the words that my old friend Martha would have used: 'Edward looks at her as if the sun were shining out of her backside', but fortunately nobody was interested in the words that might be in my mind. Edward seemed to have no consciousness of Madame's puzzlement or of Sir Ian's heavy-handed attempts to conceal his shock. Edward had no consciousness of himself or of any of us. He was aware of nobody and nothing but Anna. He was utterly enslaved. This, to me, was a shock in itself. The Edward I had thought I knew fairly well had been a very cool-headed rather distant individual who was highly sensitive to every little nuance in social intercourse but it seemed that Anna had cast a spell over him that blinded and deafened him to everything except herself so that he could sit in the silken web of that spell and adore with all his senses the creature that had cast it about him.

Occasionally, she would turn towards him and throw out some little remark in French, as if she were throwing a sweet to a pampered poodle and the first time she did this, with such complete confidence that neither Madame, Sir Ian nor I could understand her, I expected him to reply in English, if not actually to rebuke her in a gentle way. It reminded me of my friend Rose who liked to tell dirty stories at the dinner parties that she gave and who would say: 'Talking of that, I heard a good story the other night but later. Pas devant les domestiques, you know!' I think this phrase was Rose's sole knowledge of the French language, if knowledge it can be called, but although French was Anna's native tongue, the effect of these interpolations to Edward was just as vulgar as Rose's four words used to be. But Edward did not hear the words as I heard them. When they were spoken, he would smile beatifically and reply in French with humble gratitude that Anna had singled him out. He made me think of a fawning dog.

And here, as in every pathetic, sad or even tragic situation, an element of the comic entered, for how were Edward and Anna to know that I understood French? By her attitude, Anna made it clear that in this pocket of provincialism she did not expect to find even such a minor accomplishment. In spite of many years spent in England and the West Indies, too, I still spoke English with a Highland intonation, especially on the vowels and I have never attempted to speak French unless I am very hard-pressed because I know that my larynx, designed to speak broad Gaelic vowels, is not suited to the delicacy of French and that my lips do not produce truly its front-of-the-mouth sounds and labials. But I can read the language nearly as easily as I can read English and no words that Anna and Edward spoke went un-understood. The remarks were either exchanged endearments or queries on her part as to where and how the various items of furniture and decoration of the room had been acquired and at one point she estimated in dollars the value of one of the carpets on the mahogany floor.

I had just poured second cups of tea for everybody and had sat down when Madame's hand that held her cup gave a convulsive jerk so that the cup flew from the saucer and landed plumb in the middle of Anna's white silk lap. She sprang to her feet, the old Coalport cup crashing to the floor in fragments, the black eyes glaring at Madame as she said in French: 'Old fool!'

I had observed such uncontrollable spasms of the muscles in Madame before, knew that they frightened her and I went to her and laid my hand on her shoulder. 'It is quite all right, Madame. The tea was not hot enough to do any damage,' I said while, over the old lady's head, I looked at the infuriated Anna, with Edward kneeling humbly at her feet, dabbing ineffectively with his handkerchief at the stained silk. In the greenish light of the room, which was shaded from the glaring heat out-of-doors, there was something macabre in the scene, something that was out of keeping with everything I had ever known, some total breakdown or distortion of all human feeling. There was what seemed to be a cold hatred that emanated from Anna, there was the grovelling subservience of Edward, there was the astonished misery of Sir Ian and the trembling fear of Madame. The muddle of feeling was out of all proportion to the little incident that had taken place. It was as if Anna, like some corrosive acid, had scarred and changed the characters of these three people I had known.

As if breaking out of a trance, Sir Ian rang the bell and a servant arrived to clear away the tea and fragments of china from the floor.

'Edward,' Anna said, 'take me to my room.'

They went away and Sir Ian said: 'I think you should go up and have a rest until dinner, Mother.'

'Yes. Come, Madame,' I said.

'Yes, Janet. Thank you.'

When I had helped her to undress and get into bed, I went to my own rooms across the hall where, suddenly, I felt violently sick and hung over the wash-basin, vomiting, while cold sweat broke on my forehead and down my spine. When the attack was over and I was able to walk, I lay down on my bed and stared out at the heavy orange-coloured sky.

During the preparations for the coming of Edward and Anna, I had told Madame that I would prefer to have dinner upstairs by myself in the evenings, so that she, Sir Ian, Edward and Anna might dine *en famille* and after some polite protest, she had agreed to this but, now, as I lay on the bed, I was torn between relief that I need not see Anna again that evening and guilt that I was withholding my support from Madame at a time when she might need it. When I had made the arrangement, I had not foreseen the Anna who had arrived.

I spent a restless unsettled evening and was relieved when I heard Sir Ian conducting Madame upstairs at an hour that was earlier than usual. I went across the hall to her bed-room.

'Do you wish to go to bed now, Madame, or shall Letty and I come to you later?' I asked.

'I shall go to bed now, dear. This has been a tiring day. Good night Ian.'

Sir Ian went quietly away and old Letty helped Madame to undress and wash while I put her clothes away. Madame was seldom silent. She had the Victorian attitude that when-ever even two people are gathered together, conversation must be maintained and in addition to this there was her propensity for laying down the law. There were always views on every subject that she had the need to express but, tonight, she seemed to have no views on anything or none that she wished to express to me. When Letty had gone and she was seated in bed against her mound of pillows, I placed her glass of hot rum and milk on the bedside table while she took off the six heavily jewelled rings that she always wore and arranged them in the familiar pattern beside the lamp. She now spoke for the first time, to say: 'Thank you, Janet. Good night dear.'

Uneasy, I left her and went back across the hall to my own rooms. Drinking whisky, the uneasiness continued while the thick hot darkness pressed down on the house. I tried to tell myself that the hurricane weather was the cause of this tension in the atmosphere but I did not convince myself and the following day, although Edward and Anna had breakfast in their rooms and then went out, leaving a message that they would not be back until time for dinner in the evening, the tension in the house persisted, as if invisible, tightly-drawn steel wires criss-crossed the air. Sir Ian kept out of sight, except for appearing silently at lunch and tea and Madame and I went through the routine of our day but she was withdrawn and showed none of her customary interest in the newspaper or her letters. For the most part, Madame and Sir Ian 'chatted' as they called it, within clearly defined conventional limits and now it seemed that what had happened was outside those limits and there were no words. I had the feeling that they were semi-stunned so that they could not even think rationally about Edward and his Anna. The silence in the huge house under the hot lowering sky, the sense of terrible separateness of the entities that were Madame, Sir Ian and myself, built up into a tension that made my head feel hollow, made me sick with exhaustion and yet I could not stop moving, prowling about the house, along passages and up and down the numerous flights of stairs.

When I took Madame up to her bedroom for her nap, she spoke to me in the sense of communication with me for the first time that day. 'I think you should join us for dinner this evening, Janet. It is not right that you should be up here alone.'

'But I shall not be alone, Madame,' I lied quickly. 'I have asked Sashie to come up.'

'Oh, that is different,' she said, but I knew that she was disappointed, that she wanted my support and I felt guilty.

'I could put him off,' I said, almost against my own will.

'Certainly not, dear. I am sure that you and he have business to discuss.'

Sashie was too different and exotic for Madame to understand to account for my friendship with him, which was also beyond her understanding, she had simply decided, in order to rationalize Sashie and the friendship, that Sashie handled my 'business' for me now that Twice was no longer present to do it.

'But perhaps you and he would join us for coffee?' she suggested as she got into bed.

'Very well. Thank you, Madame.'

I went straight from her bedroom to the house office on the ground floor and telephoned Sashie.

'Sashie, I am sorry to be a pest but could you come up here for dinner tonight?'

'Darling, this is so sudden,' came the mischievous voice. 'Are *you* inviting me or is it Madame?'

'It is only me I am afraid. And it is dinner upstairs in my place, then coffee down below.'

'So you have been relegated since the bride arrived?' The voice was different now.

I sighed into the telephone. Things were so tediously unlike what they seemed on the surface to be. 'It isn't like that at all. Don't be a bore, Sashie. And anyhow, what do *you* know about the bride?'

'Darling, don't be stupid. The whole island is buzzing. *You* may have got you to a nunnery but beyond the walls, life goes on, you know. Janet, is what I hear even remotely like the truth?'

'None of that now,' I said. 'Tonight.'

'What time?'

'Around seven.'

'And a black tie for the coffee, I suppose?'

'Lord, yes, I suppose so.'

'Darling, we shall be poor relations together, like Brontë governesses. I look forward to it. Thank you, my sweet.'

When I changed that evening, before going to help Madame to dress, I thought wryly that I did indeed look like a poor relation. When Madame, Sir Ian and I had been alone, we had dined at a table in a corner of the library and had not dressed formally. The colours that suited me best were white, black and a certain deep blue but although I had some white day clothes, I no longer wore white in the evening and standing before the mirror in the ankle-length long-sleeved black dress which I had not worn for many months, I saw looking back at me a pale-hollow-eyed haggard ghost. I sat before a glass twice a day to brush my hair but I had not seen my reflection until this moment and I was appalled at what I saw, but after a startled second or two, it ceased to matter. I swallowed a stiff drink, then brushed my teeth and went to Madame's bedroom.

She was silent while we helped her to dress, spoke only once, to say: 'Yes, dear,' when I took the long triple row of pearls from the case and held it over her breast from behind. I then snapped the diamond clasp at the back of her neck and she rose and took my arm to go downstairs.

Sir Ian was alone in the drawing-room when we went in and, seeing my long dress, he said heartily: 'So you are comin' down to dinner tonight, me dear? Good,' and seemed disappointed when I told him that I was not. I had a bleak sense of failing these people who had been so kind to me and guilt dragged at me like a heavy weight.

'Mr. Sashie is dining with Janet, Ian,' Madame said. 'They are kindly joining us for coffee afterwards.'

The conventional speeches in the midst of the tension were like a shrill vibration on the air.

'Good. Let's have a tot. Rum, Mother? Whisky, Missis Janet?'

'No, thank you, Sir Ian. Sashie will be here at any moment. I must go back upstairs.'

Once out of the drawing-room, I fled as if before some savage beast, yet felt guilty and ashamed even as I fled and

55

by the time I hurtled into my sitting-room up above, I was giddy and breathless.

'For pity's sake, Janet,' Sashie said, holding me by the upper arms as I stood panting with my back against the closed door, 'What in heaven's name is the matter?'

'Everything, Sashie, everything. It is all awful and I don't know what to do.'

I staggered away from him, poured myself a drink and sat down.

'Must you drink that?' he asked. 'It is of no use to you. You simply are not the type, darling, as I keep telling you.'

'It helps.'

'Helps with what?'

'Everything.'

'Let us make a little sense,' he said.

'There isn't any.'

'Darling, I know that. That is why one has to make it.'

'Anna,' I burst forth, 'is pure Chinese. I suppose her father is French but you wouldn't know it. Of all women, why did Edward have to bring a Chinese here for the whole island to talk about? For Madame and Sir Ian it is so bloody cruel, Sashie. Oh, you can say they are prejudiced and what does it matter what the island says, but they are old and it matters to them and they are what life has made of them and it is too much to expect them to change now.'

After the months of silence, after the new silence since Anna arrived, the words poured out in a torrent. 'And she is horrible, horrible. She is cold, cruel, pitiless. She – oh, what is the use?'

'What indeed?' Sashie asked. 'She is no concern of yours.'

'But I feel—' I began and paused.

'Yes, dear? You feel?'

'It is poor old Madame. I feel terribly for Madame.'

'You feel terribly, darling?' he asked quietly, yet with peculiar emphasis.

But my little burst of energy had exhausted itself and I fell into inertia. 'What is the use?' I repeated. 'There is nothing I can do.'

'You will do all you can, as you always do,' Sashie said, 'provided you don't become too ill to do anything.'

'I am all right.'

'You don't look all right.'

'Anna's looks will compensate for my lack,' I said, already feeling steadied by his presence.

Grateful for the steadiness, I sat down opposite him and looked at him carefully while he remained impassive. In his dinner clothes he was a study of black and white, every line clearly defined and I discovered that although he was so small in stature as to be almost a miniature of a man, the impression he gave was one of great size and strength. The huge oppressive house, now that Sashie was within it, seemed to be reduced, to have lost its power to dominate, to be no longer a crushing force but a mere artifact contrived by the hands of men. The tensions between the members of the Dulac family fell into insignificance, ceased to gnaw at me.

'I think,' I said, speaking to myself more than to Sashie, 'that the worst thing about it all is its smallness.'

'Smallness?' his voice repeated.

'Yes. What has happened here would be more bearable if it were tragic but it isn't. Anna isn't a monster of villainy. She is just a nasty little bitch. And Edward's bringing her here is not unfilial. It is merely inept. It is all so small, Sashie, so pitiably small.'

'Small people, small doings, darling, and they are not worthy of the size of reaction you bring to them. Madame and Sir Ian have to dree their Chinese weird in their own small way and nothing you can feel or do will make the slightest difference.'

When we went down to the drawing-room later on and Sashie was presented to Anna, she began to sparkle. It seemed that she was one of the large tribe of women who make no social effort except in the presence of males of a marriageable age and although she was a bride of only a few weeks' standing, Anna was true to her type in her response to Sashie. She launched upon a monologue which went from opera to the anti-novel, from ballet to the philosophy of Teilhard de Chardin, with a great confidence that she was giving a scintillating display of critical wit. While Sashie stared as if in solemn wonder at this erudition, Edward sat looking from his wife to the rest of us in his besotted way, Madame and Sir Ian sat in relieved silence that Anna seemed pleased and I sat wondering how Anna could be stupid enough to imagine that she was impressing Sasha de Marnay. In the cosmopolitan art circles in which she moved, she must meet people less complex than Sashie, I thought, if she was taken in by him as completely as she seemed to be. I had never seen Sashie look so naïve and innocent as he looked that evening. Gone were his airs of affectation, sophistication and exoticism. In his black dinner jacket and white shirt, while he had been up in my room, he had looked dramatically clear-cut but now he contrived to look like a colourless little man, overpowered into insignificance and fading into the background, so impressed was he to be invited to have coffee in this large drawing-room and more impressed still at being singled out in conversation by this brilliant young lady. It was an astonishing performance and although in my sick and sorry state I seldom, these days, felt like smiling, there was, deep inside me, the warmth of inner laughter.

After Anna had held forth for about three-quarters of an hour, I rose to my feet and found myself making a humble speech of gratitude for the coffee served to myself and my guest, whereupon Sashie and I withdrew upstairs. As soon as we had shut the sitting-room door behind us, Sashie sat down and and said: 'Darling, what a very secondhand young woman!'

'You were quite awful, Sashie,' I reproached him. 'You even had *me* doing it. Did you hear me almost thanking her for having us? What do you mean by secondhand? She is very beautiful in her way.'

'One either likes the oriental or one doesn't. I don't. I don't like those hideous horses and buffaloes or those tortured jade carvings and I don't see beauty in this young woman either. Secondhand? I meant her mind. That set piece about the anti-novel was straight out of the second-last number of the *Paris Review*. She is a cold, hard little monster as you indicated and a fool to boot. The adolescent art-dealer has bought himself a real fake this time, poor innocent.'

'Oh, Edward is all right,' I said. 'He is potty about her.'

'You know—' Sashie was thoughtful, '—I thought I had seen nearly everything but I have never before seen a man go from adolescence to senility in a single step.'

'Senility?'

'Edward looks like a rich old man who has taken on a young trollop that he is uncertain of managing. He almost drools in his anxiety to please her.' This was an apt description of Edward in the presence of Anna. 'When do they leave, darling?'

'Leave? I have been given the impression that is is their home, that they are here for good.'

'Then do not *take* the impression, my sweet. That young woman is spending an afternoon slumming and intends to be back in her hotel in New York, London, Paris or Rome in time for dinner. They won't stay here for very long.'

'You really think not?'

'I am sure of it.'

I sighed, relieved. 'I hope you are right. They go out all day but they usually come back for dinner and Madame and Sir Ian want me to dine downstairs with them now. When I rang you this afternoon, it was because I suddenly couldn't face them all and the tension and everything. Thank you for coming up, Sashie.'

'Then I shall come up every evening.'

'No. That would look odd.'

'Darling, I *always* look odd and you get odder-looking every day. Or I can send the car up to bring you to Silver Beach in the evenings.'

'No, Sashie. Madame might need me.'

It was a curious dilemma. I knew that as soon as Sashie had gone, the house would begin to depress and oppress me again so that I would long for escape and yet I knew that I would not be able to leave it even for an hour or two. I had a dark sense of waiting in this place although I did not know what I was waiting for.

'Then expect me tomorrow evening,' Sashie said. 'Even if we have to go down for coffee and listen to that one going on about bourré and plié when she knows no more about either than a hole in the wall, I shall be here.'

'Oh, please yourself, Sashie,' I said, weary now. 'I hear Madame coming up to bed. I must go to her.'

Thereafter, Sashie arrived between six and seven o'clock every evening but we did not again go down to the drawing-room for coffee.

'I think not, darling,' Sashie decided on the second evening. 'You know what a bitch I am. Sooner or later I would tell that little bitch what a bitch she is. You tell Madame nicely that we have business together and let us be up here on our own.'

I became less bored and irritable with Sashie now for, except for occasional remarks about how ill I looked and about my drinking too much, he avoided discussion of my personal affairs. He seemed to accept the obsessive sense of duty that tied me to the Great House and concentrated upon being amusing for which he had a talent, so that I began to look forward to his evening arrivals after the strained un-communicative days spent with Madame.

At the end of about a week, Edward and Anna stopped returning to the house even for dinner in the evenings and Madame and Sir Ian began to dine upstairs in Madame's sitting-room across the hall from my own where Sashie and I would sometimes join them. Edward and Anna were never mentioned on these occasions and Sashie, with selfless kind-ness and skill, kept the two old people entertained with reminiscences of the past life of the Great House, such as the time we had celebrated Christmas by acting a farcical melodrama entitled *Varlets in Paradise* which I had written. He took on for me the character of a slender lifeline between the dim half-life in the shaded mahogany-panelled rooms above the empty echoing house and the real world that went on its way beyond the walls.

Edward and Anna, in the course of a few days, became the leaders of what might be called the café society of the fashionable hotels of the Platinum Coast, as the north side of the island was known and it was strange to sit in the dim house at the centre of the Paradise Valley and read about them in the local newspaper. The gossip columnist was busy day after day with descriptions of Anna's remarkable clothes and jewellery but I did not read these paragraphs

aloud to Madame, nor did I tell her of the noontide cere-
monial when Edward and Anna were ready to go out and
the cases containing her wardrobe for the day were carried
out and loaded into the boot of the Rolls. I would watch the
ceremony going on in the driveway below while I read the
newspaper to Madame, watch the car slide away out of sight
among the trees, whereupon Madame, whose hearing was
keen, would say: 'I suppose Edward and Anna have gone
out for the day, Janet?' and I would reply: 'Yes, Madame'.
There was a dreary sterility in it. There would be no other
remark, so that the few words were like a padlock closing on
the silence.

Madame withdrew further and further into herself and no
longer wished to see the few old women with whom she had
something of the past in common and whom she used to
invite to tea fairly frequently. She stumped around the
shaded rooms as firmly as ever on her fat little feet, weaving
her blind way uncannily among the furniture, her lips tightly
pursed, two frowning, vertical little wrinkles above the
bridge of her nose. I did not know what her thoughts were
but sensed about her a spiteful anger.

And, relentlessly, the heat of the summer increased. May,
always a humid month, was more oppressive than ever this
year, with a sullen heat that bleached out and drained away
the last scrap of energy and even in these rooms, high at the
top of the house, neither dawn nor darkening brought the
relief of a slight breeze. The monstrous pile of emptiness
that was the Great House lay brooding sullenly, as Madame
seemed to brood, under the sullen orange sky by day and by
night the hot darkness pressed inwards through the open
windows. But very soon the silence of the nights began to be
broken when Edward and Anna returned from their day's
outing in the small hours of the morning, when Madame
was sound asleep.

The floors of the house decreased in area towards the top.
The ground and first floors were equal in area but the third
floor was smaller, the top nursery floor was smaller again
and this floor had no surrounding verandas, only a small
landing where the wooden staircase came up from the veranda below. My rooms were on the east side, Madame's on

the west and Sir Ian used the rooms on the north side of the first floor far below but Edward and Anna had east side rooms, immediately underneath mine.

As soon as Madame was asleep – she slept as if by an act of will as soon as she had drunk the glass of rum and hot milk that she took every night – I would sit by the open window, the decanter of whisky beside me, trying to drink myself into some state of insensibility before I fell into bed.

Edward and Anna had been at Paradise for only a little over two weeks when the first argument took place in the rooms down below at about two o'clock in the morning. Edward had never spent much time at Paradise and probably Anna had never visited such 'bush country' before. They were both accustomed to the life of the cities, to the privacy of rooms which are closed and shut off from the world, especially at night and they had never learned the technique of living in a house where the glazed windows are never closed except during hurricanes and where much of the outer walls consist of wire mosquito mesh. Every word they uttered came floating up and in at my window. Anna did most of the talking and always in French and the burden of her discourse was that she would be buried no longer in this savage island. She wished to make a tour of the United States, culminating in New York in the autumn for the opening of the season at the Metropolitan Opera House. Edward suggested in gentle tones that St. Jago was quite amusing and that, after all, it would probably not be very long that they would have to stay here. He and Sir Ian intended to sell Paradise after Madame died. Anna replied that 'la vieille', as she called Madame, looked as if she would live for ever. Edward now pointed out that Madame had her own life on the top floor of the house with Sir Ian and Mrs. Alexander. Anna replied that she found 'la veuve', her name for myself, I gathered, insupportable and, my God, of a dullness unbelievable.

Every night, after this opening overture, the arguments took place and with each night Anna's fluting voice, which had extraordinary carrying power, became more angry and more bitter. She had conceived a dislike for Madame and myself that seemed to be out of proportion to our minor impingement on her life and with every night that passed her barbs against la vieille and la veuve became more cruel and venomous.

Each forenoon, before they went out, Edward would come upstairs and spend a little time with his grandmother and this seemed to be the core of Anna's resentment. She did not come upstairs herself, did not know that I left Edward and Madame alone, chose to disbelieve this when Edward told her so and chose to think that Edward was paying clandestine visits to myself. I did not care what Anna chose to think or say of me but when Edward let pass without protest her cruelties about Madame, the inhuman ugliness of it all induced in me an unreasoning fear that sent me silently across the landing to the open door of Madame's room to listen to her breathing, to make sure that Anna's spite had not physically injured her in some way. But, at last, the voices from below would cease, the black silence of the night would take control and I would go to bed and lie somewhere between nightmare and waking, waiting for the morning to come.

There is always morning. Although, now, I was moving all the time, except when Sashie was with me, in a grey twilight, the coming of morning brought me things to do and in an automatic way I did them. Old Letty came up, assisted Madame in her bath, dressed her in a fresh nightdress and brushed her hair before helping her back into bed to have breakfast but, before having the meal, Madame would take the six rings she always wore from the table by the bed and put them on her fat little fingers. With the putting on of the rings, a subtle change came over her, transforming her from a blind old woman into the self-willed mistress of the Great House who issued her commands from her throne of white pillows. It was sitting thus enthroned that she received Edward each forenoon and on a day early in June, when he and Anna had been in the island for little more than a month, he stayed with Madame for an unusually long time which brought Anna, dressed to go out, up to the nursery landing.

'Where is Edouard?' she demanded, standing in the open doorway of my sitting-room. Her French accent was more pronounced on Edward's name than on any other word.

'With Madame,' I said, indicating the closed door of the bedroom across the hall.

Anna went to it, rattled a tattoo on the panels and called imperatively: 'Edouard!'

Almost guiltily, Edward appeared. 'Come and see Granny,' he said in a coaxing voice.

'We are already late,' said Anna. 'Good morning,' she threw from the doorway to Madame in the bed, turned about and went tapping down the wooden stairs.

'Well—' Edward was shame-faced, apologetic, shambling as if all will of his own had been taken away from him '—good-bye, Granny,' he said.

'Very well, Edward,' the old lady replied and as if she had been interrupted in reading, she picked up the newspaper from the table by the bed and held it upside down in front of her blind eyes, while I watched Edward creep almost furtively down the stairs.

When his footsteps could no longer be heard, Madame's voice came: 'Are you there, Janet?'

'Yes, Madame.' I went into the room and she let the newspaper fall on the sheet.

'Edward is leaving for Miami on Friday,' she said, 'and Anna too, of course.'

The words should have been: 'Anna is leaving for Miami on Friday and Edward too, of course,' for I had heard Anna declare this decision two nights before.

'They have a great many friends in the United States,' Madame added and then: 'Janet, there is something I wish to know, or, rather, have confirmed.'

I felt suddenly cold in the humid heat that hung over the room like a steaming blanket. 'Yes, Madame?'

'This woman Anna is of Chinese blood, is she not?'

'Yes, Madame and she is very beautiful.'

'I thought so. I could hear it in her voice.' She nodded her head in satisfaction that her blindness had not prevented her from recognizing this fact. 'Well, dear,' she said next, 'let us attend to the newspaper.'

I noticed, however, that she paid little attention to the newspaper, making no comment, even, when I read out the death notice of one of her former acquaintances and for the rest of the day she was more silent than usual.

'It is all so sad because it is all so futile,' I said to Sashie that evening while Sir Ian sat with his mother. 'She used to be so important in her own eyes and now it is as if she sees herself and all she stood for dwindling into nothingness. She is going to die, Sashie.'

'It is the only thing left for her to do,' he said. 'I am not being harsh, Janet. I am only speaking the truth as I see it. I have never been fond of her and I feel that there have been many sadder deaths.'

'Even if that is the truth, don't say it. It is this thing of Edward and Anna that is going to kill her.'

'Not entirely if at all. I believe that people, except those killed by war or accident, die of something in themselves.'

'Not always,' I argued. 'People can die because of other people.'

Dense and black, the guilt enwrapped my mind and I was glad when Sashie went away, leaving me to my dark thoughts and my whisky, but the next morning Madame seemed to be more like her practical self than she had been since the arrival of Edward and Anna as she got back into bed and prepared to have breakfast. However, she did not put her rings on as she usually did, but took them from the table and arranged them, glittering, round the rim of her bread and butter plate. She then picked out two of the six and returned them to the table, before fingering the four that remained.

'Janet,' she said, taking up one, 'this is the half-hoop of diamonds, isn't it?'

'Yes, Madame.'

'And this is the sapphire and diamond one and this the rubies and of course this is the memorial ring?' she asked, holding up a hideous hoop of black enamel with a tiny plait of hair under glass.

'That is right, Madame. You know every one of them,' I humoured her.

'And so I should,' she said with some asperity. 'I have worn them for long enough. They were my mother's and she died shortly after Ian was born. I wish you to pick them up

65

Janet. Put them on your fingers. Examine them carefully. The ruby one must not be confused with that other ruby one.' She indicated one of the rings she had set aside on the table. Feeling foolish, I put on the rings which were too loose for my long bony fingers, so that I had to hold my hand with the fingers stiffly upright that the jewels might not fall to the floor.

'I want you to have those rings when I go, Janet. My other jewellery belongs to the Dulac family and will go to Edward but I want you to have those. I shall tell Ian, of course, but gentlemen are so foolish and careless about such things.'

'But, Madame—' I began but she interrupted me. 'Now, dear has the newspaper come yet?' she asked, putting on the rings which I had clicked down on to the plate.

While I read the newspaper to her, the phrase 'I want you to have those rings when I go, when I go, when I go—' was repeating and repeating itself in my mind. Madame did not dwell on the subject of death, except to speak a few conventional phrases when it struck at some of her acquaintance.

After the death of Twice, she had touched me deeply by saying: 'You will never know how gladly I would have gone in his stead' and I believe that, in that moment of loss, she had meant what she had said, for she had been fonder of him than she was of most people. But as soon as the funeral was over and Sashie had brought me to her at the Great House, she had taken up the reins of life again in her firm little hands, directing the servants as they arranged my rooms, directing my life which I had no interest in directing for myself.

But the most uncharacteristic feature of what she had said was her arrangement for the disposal of her rings. To dispose of anything, especially many hundreds of pounds' worth of property, was utterly uncharacteristic of the Madame Dulac I had known. The entire Great House testified to this. The cellars were full of furniture that she had acquired down the years, her cupboards were full of furs that she had not worn since her last trip to Britain many years ago but they were all stored in linen bags inside cedar

66

chests and inspected regularly against the depredations of the island insects. Even on the nursery floor, stored in a cupboard, were the tattered Latin grammars and outdated textbooks on algebra which had been used in the education of her family but she would allow none of them to be thrown away. Madame was acquisitive, possessive, tenacious of property of every kind, or thus she had been. This was why the episode of the rings impressed me so deeply. With a hollow sense of foreboding, I remembered that Twice had undergone a change of character shortly before he died. His main characteristic, that paralleled Madame's tenacity of property, had been his vital interest in everything that life held. He loved, he hated, he held this opinion, he despised that but he was never indifferent and yet the time came when he lapsed into a morbid indifference that was lit by no spark of interest in anything.

But as the days passed and Edward and Anna had gone, rendering the huge house stiller and more silent than ever, I became more and more numb towards Madame, felt less and less pity for the bewildered prowlings of Sir Ian from room to room. I suppose that my physical condition was deteriorating even further, my mind becoming more clouded by alcohol, but I could still feel guilt, a further burden of guilt because I could no longer feel pity or compassion for Madame and Sir Ian. There was nothing but a dreary futility and the guilt that dragged at me like a physical weight.

Sashie continued to arrive every evening and would sit with me while, across the hall, Madame and Sir Ian sat together. Sashie was not dominated into subjection, as I was, by the dull weight of the house or the heaviness of the sullen air but, evening by evening, he became more silent. The great hollow house seemed to be waiting passively, as I was, for what was to come but Sashie was not only waiting, but watching and in my diseased mind he constituted a curious menace. When this waiting was over, I felt, he would spring into action as a cat, after patient waiting, pounces on its prey and the thought of action, in which I would surely become involved, terrified me. After all these weeks of non-life, the only form of existence that seemed possible to me, the idea of taking up any other form of life, of coming to full consciousness of myself and the guilt that I carried within me, was unbearable and I began to shrink away from Sashie as one shrinks from an instrument of potential pain. Yet I did not try to stop his visits, for this would have entailed effort and action and evening after evening, the gaily-dressed little figure would arrive to sit in almost total silence through the hot dark hours.

The processing of the sugar cane through the factory and rum distillery ended for the season during the last days of June and Sir Ian decided to entertain the senior staff to drinks one evening to celebrate Cropover, as the end of the processing period was called.

'And you will come down to the drawin'-room, Mother, won't you?' he asked. 'You will enjoy a chat with young Mackie an' them all.'

'Very well, Ian. Janet and I shall come down and, Janet, you must invite Mr. Sashie.'

The little gathering, between six and eight in the evening in the large drawing-room, had a nightmare quality. I had attended so many parties in this room down the years that the shadowed corners seemed to be filled with ghosts of the dead while the living people who stood around in groups seemed unreal. The atmosphere was tense and awkward, everybody obviously thinking of Edward's Chinese wife as they looked covertly at Madame in her high-backed chair, while Sir Ian tried vainly to be his bluff, hearty former self, but it was soon over and Madame, Sir Ian, Sashie and I came back to the top of the house for dinner. Then that too was over and Sashie and I retired to my sitting-room. One of the few feelings of which I was capable was a gratitude that one more thing, one more hour or two were 'over'.

'Well, that is one more Cropover,' I said.

'And I hope it will be your last,' Sashie said.

'Don't. Don't say things like that.'

'Somebody has to say them, Janet. I have been thinking of writing to your family about you.'

'Don't you dare! Do you think I am an idiot? I can look after myself.'

'I do *not* think you are an idiot but you *cannot* look after yourself. Janet, that old woman is simply not worth what you are doing to yourself.'

'Do you imagine that you are God, knowing what everybody is worth? Get the hell out of here! Go away!'

He went and I began to drink myself into insensibility, at which I was successful for I did not become conscious until about four in the morning, to discover myself sitting, fully clothed, in the chair where Sashie had left me. Guiltily, I started up. Madame might have needed me, might have been calling out and I had not heard her and I rose to cross the landing to her bedroom but I was overcome by giddiness and nausea and had to crawl to the bathroom to vomit.

Weak and sweating, I came back through my rooms and into the hall where I halted, my cold flesh crawling, as I became aware of furtive movement among the black shadows and shafts of moonlight in Madame's bedroom. When I reached the bedroom door, Madame was sitting on the edge of her bed but her name was arrested on my lips as her hand groped towards the bedside table and brought a brilliant greenish flash from her rings as she picked them up. With concentration, she examined them, before her hand moved to the table again and I realized that she was setting aside the two that belonged to the Dulac family. Then, carrying the other four, she went to her bathroom on the other side of the room. I heard her moving about in there for a little time before she came back to her bed and with a sigh of satisfaction lay down, pulling the sheet up to her chin. I remained there, watching and listening until she was obviously asleep, quietly and peacefully.

When I went in to her at eight o'clock in the morning, I looked first at the table beside the bed and there were the six rings, arranged in the familiar pattern around the lamp. I felt my stomach heave with nausea while I wondered if the episode that I thought I had seen during the night was some macabre dream, if at long last my brain was becoming unhinged. After that first sickening convulsion of the stomach, I did not care any more about my own state but because of Madame, I wanted to know if the macabre episode had really taken place. That evening, I kept Sashie with me much later than usual so that I would drink less heavily, pretending to take an interest in what he was telling me of the latest collection of folk-songs of the island that he and Caleb were making. Shortly before midnight, when he was about to go, Madame appeared across the landing in the doorway of her room, a stout, robust, solid unghostly figure in the long silk nightdress. She passed the four rings from one hand to the other, so that the light from our room was caught in flashes by the diamonds. I sat with one of Sashie's hands clutched between my own and we watched while Madame removed a Victorian novel from a bookcase, put the rings into the cavity and then replaced the novel. She then went back to bed, took a drink of water from a tumbler on the table and went back to sleep. Quietly, Sashie shut the door of the sitting-room, came close to me and whispered: 'My God, Janet, it's too ghastly! What was she hiding?' I was so relieved that the episode had actually happened that I could have laughed but, with that duality that characterized everything, I was so worried by this manifestation in Madame that I was afraid.

'I don't know,' I lied to Sashie.

'Janet, you cannot go on like this,' he protested. 'That old woman needs professional nurses. Her mind is going.'

'Don't, Sashie.'

'Darling, there is not one damn of use saying don't. You have to face facts. With your sort of nerves, you are simply not fit for this.'

'I am not in the least nervous. What is there to be afraid of in the eccentricities of an old woman?'

'I am going to speak to Sir Ian.'

'Don't you dare, Sashie de Marnay! Don't you dare to interfere. If I want your help, I shall ask for it.'

'Darling, is that a promise?'

'Oh, don't be so bloody intense. You must go, Sashie. Sir Ian has been in bed for hours.'

'If he isn't prowling round this damned mausoleum hidings things too,' Sashie said but he went away.

Thereafter, the hiding of the rings became a nightly commonplace but, at eight each morning, they were always back on the table by the bed. Sometimes I saw Madame replace them there and I was sometimes certain that she knew consciously what she was doing while at other times I thought that the actions were unconscious and carried out in her sleep. The effect of this manifestation of senile decay, however, was to render my own mind still more uncertain and unsteady. I did not mention this nightly activity to Sir Ian because there did not seem to be any point in worrying him with a thing that was beyond our control and led to no danger for Madame, blind as she was, was as safe, physically, moving around by night as she was by day.

But there came a morning when I went to her room and only two rings lay on the table beside the lamp. I knew that the others were in a vase on the landing but what worried me was the break in the routine. I stood looking down at the old lady, as the hands of the clock crept towards her waking hour of eight and as if aware of my glance, her eyes opened and she said: 'Good morning, Letty. Has the Master rung for his coffee yet?'

The Master. She did not ever refer to Sir Ian as 'The Master'.

'No, Madame,' I said quietly.

'How very annoying. He should have been up and about hours ago. Have his coffee taken in at once.'

With an impatient jerk, she tried to sit up and I noticed that the left arm, which she was trying to push against the mattress in her effort to raise herself, was as limp and powerless as a wilted branch. Yet, grotesquely twisted as her body was, half-sitting, half-lying, her mind and voice were still imperative. 'He knows that we have the Governor's Garden Party this afternoon and must be away by ten. Have him called at once, Letty.'

She then slumped back on her pillows, her eyes closed and she seemed to sleep. Old Letty came into the room and I sent her for Sir Ian.

When the doctor came, he told us the obvious, that Madame had suffered a stroke, that there was some paralysis of the left side and that her memory had gone.

'Not much we can do, sir,' he told Sir Ian. 'But Mrs. Alexander will need help. I shall engage nurses?'

71

'One will do,' I said, 'for night duty. Letty and I can manage the days. Is Nurse Delgado free?'

Nurse Delgado had been one of the nurses in charge of Twice during his last illness and I liked her. She was young, coffee-coloured, pretty, very capable and did not talk too much. She was free and arrived for duty that afternoon in her white nylon dress and cap, making the shaded rooms at the top of the house more ordinary and less macabre. Madame, physically robust, ate and slept as if nothing had happened but her mind roamed up and down the long years of her time illogically and unpredictably. And there were intervals when she was perfectly lucid, apparently securely anchored in the hour and the day.

That day, before Nurse Delgado arrived, I had taken the four rings out of the vase on the landing and had replaced them on the table by the bedside. The nurse arrived at mid-afternoon and when I took her to the bedroom and said: 'Madame, this is nurse who has come to—' Madame interrupted me to say: 'Ah, Nurse Porter. And how is your clinic this week?' Madame had decided that her visitor was the redoubtable Nurse Porter who managed the estate clinic but Delgado and Porter were friends and Delgado at once took over the part that had been assigned to her.

'Less busy than usual, Madame,' she said. 'There was not a single accident in the factory this week.'

Desperately, I tried to cling to the realities of the present and its personalities.

Madame tried to sit up and we helped her, propping her with pillows. 'I'm not very well,' she told the nurse now, 'a touch of malaria but I shall be up again tomorrow' and what she said had a certain truth. Her left arm was limp, which she seemed to accept, but the rest of her body was unaffected and she was so certain that she was not ill that she came near to making my uncertain mind believe that I and not she was mentally unsound.

That first night, I sat with Nurse Delgado in Madame's sitting-room after Sashie had gone home and, it already being evident that the old lady could get out of bed and walk, although her left leg dragged, I told the nurse about the rings.

72

'It is a sort of obsession, I suppose,' I said apologetically for I found something shameful in Madame's preoccupation with these baubles. 'She has been hiding them for some time. I have just let her do it.'

'Much the best thing,' Nurse Delgado said, 'but you must not worry about it, you know.' A little surprised, I discovered that I had indeed been worrying about this hiding of the rings, had been wishing that I could make Madame stop doing it, had been shamed by the triviality of it. 'I am glad that you have warned me about it,' the nurse continued, 'but don't think about it any more. It doesn't mean anything. And now you must go to bed, Mrs. Alexander. You are very tired and there is nothing to worry about. You can trust me, you know.'

'I know that,' I said and went to my rooms. There was nothing to worry about because nothing meant anything, as the nurse had said.

The days settled into a routine again. Nurse Delgado came off duty at eight in the morning and on again at eight at night and under her efficient management I had nothing to do all day except to see that Madame had her meals and listen to her ramblings up and down the years that she had lived.

I was drinking less now but the giddiness and nausea were always with me and frequently I felt as if my feet had no contact with the ground or my body with the chair in which I sat, as if I were floating in space. And all the time I was aware of Sashie each evening, watching, waiting, keen-eyed, silent.

I think this was the worst time of all. Madame seemed to sleep soundly at nights, no longer getting up to hide the rings so that I wondered if Nurse Delgado was thinking that I had fabricated this story but during the day her mind was very active as it rambled about in the past.

When, after the death of Twice, I had first come to the Great House, I had thought that all I wanted was oblivion, to forget everything I had known, that memory should be utterly destroyed, but as I sat with Madame day after day, I came to know that I no longer wanted this. Madame, with her mind out of control, all reticence gone, exposed herself in a shocking way. Everything in herself that had been concealed under convention and Victorian decorum came to light and most of it was very ugly. It was as if, day by day, we relived her life together and her favourite period was the last decade of the nineteenth century and the first decade of the twentieth, that late Victorian and Edwardian heyday of hers. Through her babblings, she emerged like a ghost from the past, indeed more solid than a ghost, more like a figure on a lighted stage in the corner of the shaded room. The apparition that stood there and at whom I looked over Madame's shoulder was a vain hard woman, power-conscious and tyrannical, revelling in her position as the social queen of the island, a woman capable of the utmost social cruelty. It struck me like a blow that this early Madame who was being re-incarnated was not unlike Anna. There was a disorienting confusing fusion of past and present as my mind veered between the Madame of the past, Anna and the Madame of the present.

Sitting across a small table from her, I was sometimes in the role of her husband, Letty or one of her sons but there were uncanny times when I became, it seemed, the very self of Madame, the self that we talk when we talk to ourselves and it was at these times that the most horrid revelations took place. 'Another child! How I *hate* Edward! And I wanted to spend the summer in London. Beast! Pig!' or 'The Buckleys must be mad, entertaining these Millers of Hope. Miller is *coloured*. They certainly shan't come here. Someone must keep such trash in their places,' and in her voice was the gloating confidence that she was in a position to blackball the Millers in island society.

Staring at the wall of the room while I tried not to listen, yet listened in spite of myself, I could see, standing on that stage in the corner, the arrogant young woman, see the colour of her dress, hear the swish of her petticoats because for a short time every morning, I was in the part of Letty, while she told me what she would wear that day and when the strutting figure became too real, I would try to steel myself to look at the figure that sat opposite me. This was hard to do because, unattractive in many ways as was the

Edwardian lady in pink taffetas and diamonds, she was more alive than the blind old woman in the chair who was in a state of decay that lacked the dignity which is the redeeming feature of death. At last, I would turn my head and look at the reality of the drooling, babbling old woman and 'No' I would think, 'I must not let my mind go. I must never come to this' and bending towards her, I would shudder as I wiped away the spittle that had gathered like venom at the sides of her mouth.

It was better to go as Twice had gone, taking all his secret thoughts with him than to have to submit in the end to this indecent exposure of one's inmost self.

Although I was drinking less now, I was still drinking more than I should. The need for alcohol was now, I suppose, a physical one, an appetite that grew by what it fed on and which was encouraged by Sir Ian's favourite phrase: 'Well, let's have a tot.'

When the fits of giddiness overtook me or when I felt that hollow floating sensation, I always seemed to be slipping down a slope whose summit was the time that Twice died and which was going further and further into the distance. Like Madame, I was no longer rooted in the present and although I did not think that I spoke aloud as she did, my mind wandered in time very much like hers, but less freely. In my mind, there was a dark monolith, a pillar of guilt and regret that stood between me and all the days before Twice died, so that I could see beyond it an expanse of time that had been happy but which was now like a garden from which I was excluded for ever. My mind began to have periods of obscurity, like the moon in a windy, cloudy Highland sky, going away into darkness and then lighting up again to show grotesque shadows, then darkening again and the people around me, Sir Ian, the nurse and even Sashie became more and more remote and less and less real.

As for Sir Ian, he seldom came upstairs now for he was shamed and embarrassed by the babblings of Madame. He made the excuse that the estate took all his time while my own sense of time was only that it was very long, that it went on for ever and ever, like the eternity or the hell of the Old

Testament. And yet, I know now that, factually, in time as we measure it in life, Madame lived for only three weeks after her stroke.

There came an evening when I was almost beyond consciousness of her babblings until she said suddenly, loudly and spitefully: 'No, she shan't have them! She shan't! A Chinese! She shall never have them!' and she began to struggle out of her chair.

Since her stroke, Madame's hands and feet had become grossly swollen, so that she could no longer wear her rings and even her wedding ring had had to be cut from her finger. But still the obsession with the jewels remained and they lay beside the lamp, where she could touch them during the night while, frequently during the day, she would ask me to bring them to her so that she might sit with them in her lap, turning them about between the fingers of her right hand. They seemed to my morbid mind to symbolize all that was left of Madame, her tenacious love for wealth and her hatred for Anna and it was sickening to watch the swollen hand fondling the jewels while the spiteful voice issued from the tight little mouth: 'She shall never have them! Never!'

I knew now that, in her struggle to stand up, she was trying to reach the rings in her bedroom next door and I pushed her back into the chair and set out to fetch the jewels but before I reached the door of the bedroom, she was on her feet, quivering with a galvanic energy, yet swaying uncontrollably. She came stumbling towards me, falling forward and as the fat, heavy short body thumped like a dead weight against my chest, I knew that I no longer had the physical strength to hold her. Sashie was already in my sitting-room across the hall and I yelled his name on a wild desperate note as Madame came stumbling on into the bedroom, pushing me in front of her. Before Sashie could reach us, she suddenly knocked me aside so that I staggered and hit the wall before she pitched forward on her knees, her one hand scrabbling after the rings on the table which tilted forward, sending the lamp, the bottle of tablets, the tumbler flying across the room as well as all six rings which flew through the air, making streaks of greenish-white and blood-red fire.

Sashie and I were trying to lift the body, which was now a motionless leaden weight, when Nurse Delgado came into the room, cool and professional, her white uniform normalizing the chaos of the shadowy room.

'If you will lift here and here, please, when I ask,' she said unmoved and under her expertise and instruction and with her help we raised the heavy body on to the bed.

'Never! Never!' Madame panted. 'I hate—' and here her voice failed before her body twitched and then lay still. 'Please take Mrs. Alexander to her room, Mr. de Marnay, and be good enough to ring for a servant for me,' Nurse Delgado said, her pretty musical Negro voice dropping into the shuddering air of the dim room like the notes of a silver bell.

Sashie led me to my bedroom, sat down on the bed and beside me and gripped my hand.

I pulled my hand away, clenched my fists and spoke the words I had to speak while trying not to let my voice rise into a scream. 'Those rings!' I said. 'Those ghastly awful rings!' and suddenly there were huge rings of fire spinning everywhere in the room, white fire, red fire and a great ring of black, fringed with black plumes of smoke that curled and swayed among the other fiery rings.

'She is grossly over-tired,' I heard a voice say, the voice of the estate doctor, Gurbat Singh.

I opened my eyes to see him, Nurse Delgado and Sashie standing in a row beside my bed.

'Madame—' I said and sat up, guilty, ashamed at having gone to sleep when I ought to be looking after Madame.

'Janet,' Sashie said. 'Madame is dead.'

He was looking at me intensely out of his black eyes and the nurse and the doctor were watching me too. They were all expecting me to say something for, where a few people are gathered together, there are always things to be said but it was not fitting to say what was in my mind which was: 'I am glad' and yet I could not speak the lie either and say: 'I am sorry'. I looked about the room, then to the dark rectangles of the windows where the night, moonless now, hung like a black velvet curtain between me and the outer world.

'How very dark it is,' I said socially. 'Such a long night and so very dark.'

I was aware of Sashie's presence in my rooms throughout the hours of the night and he and Nurse Delgado came to my bedside shortly after the sun came up at six in the morning. The nurse carried a tea tray and looked fresh and normal in her white uniform while Sashie was silent and urbane but I knew that they had come because things were not normal, to be with me while Madame's body was carried down all the flights of stairs to the ground floor of the house. The men tried to move quietly but they could not avoid slips of the feet, slight bumps and low-voiced instructions to one another amid the awkwardness of it all. The sharp angles of the wooden stairs were like the awkward corners of life, I thought, the awkward corners that make us all stumble, as the stairs were making the men stumble.

I did not attend the funeral that afternoon, but Sashie did, while Nurse Delgado and I sat in my sitting-room, Nurse working at a pink crochet tray-cloth that she was making and which looked very gay and brash among all the faded plush. About four in the afternoon, the butler and a maid came up, bringing tea and they were followed by Sir Ian and Sashie.

'Well, well, it's all over,' Sir Ian said. 'Nothing more to be done.'

I envied him. Everything seemed to be so simple for him. He got things finished, so that there was no more to be done.

I began to pour out tea, as was expected of me. I had always done the pouring out for Madame. There was no reason for me to be here now except to do the pouring out of tea.

'We have to think of the future,' Sir Ian said now. He spoke as if the future were a new and separate thing, quite unconnected with the past.

Nurse Delgado took her cup of tea from me, took a biscuit from the plate and said: 'Please excuse me. I must pack my things.' Nurse too had an air of finality, of having completed a phase and moving on to something new and different.

Sashie got up and left the room along with her.

'I am very grateful for all ye did for Mother, me dear,' Sir Ian said. 'You made her last days happy.'

But I had not. Madame's life had ended in bitter disappointment and feeble hatred that made of her long years a mere futility. Sir Ian had not seen that last terrible grasping at her rings, had not heard the bitterness of that recurring: 'Never! Never!' but I let his conventional words pass for there was no point in disputing them. Sir Ian was comfortable in his delusion. Let him stay that way. 'I am plannin' to go over to London in a day or two,' he said. 'Lot o' business to be attended to. Goin' to sell the place. Edward don't want it. Don't want it meself either. Too old to be bothered with all this any more. This ain't a white man's country now anyway.'

He spoke awkwardly and jerkily, with long pauses between each sentence and I knew that, like 'the place', these thousands of acres with the Great House, all the other houses and the huge factory complex, I was one more encumbrance of which Sir Ian wanted to be rid.

He was not a hard or unkind man, but the very reverse, but I knew that he had stayed at Paradise down the last few years because of Madame who refused to leave it and that he wanted to end his days in Scotland. Now that his release had come, he was itching to be away.

'Have you any plans, Missis Janet?' he brought out at last, for I was the most difficult of all his encumbrances to dispose of. 'Ye are welcome to stay in the house here for a bit. It has to be looked after until we find a buyer. That'll take six months anyway, maybe a goodish bit longer. And your salary will go on as long's you're here, ye know.'

'You are very kind, Sir Ian—' I began and saw Sashie in the doorway behind the old man's back. I knew that he had been listening to every word and as if to indicate that he knew that I knew this, he now raised his dark eyebrows and shrugged his shoulders before coming forward into the room.

'Ah, there ye are me boy,' Sir Ian said. 'Missis Janet and I are just makin' a few plans. What about a tot? Pour them out, will ye?'

'Janet,' Sashie said, busy with the whisky decanter, his back to us, 'I know you want to go back to Scotland soon but I wondered if you would stay here for a tiny bit longer.' He handed me a glass of whisky and water, standing between Sir Ian and myself. 'Our accountant at the Peak has got his work permit for the States and I wondered if you would take over down there until we find a new man.'

'By Jove,' said Sir Ian, 'the very thing, Missis Janet! It's very cheery down at the Peak. Just the thing after the dull time you've had here, me dear. Thank ye, me boy,' he ended, accepting his drink from Sashie but it sounded as if his thanks applied to a great deal more than the drink.

'Then that's all settled,' said Sashie, his eyes very hard and bright as he looked into my face. 'It *is* nice to have everything all settled and everybody all comfortable.'

Momentarily, I feared that Sir Ian would notice the venom in his voice and feeling that I could cope no longer with all the complications that surrounded me, I said, 'Thank you, Sashie. If it is convenient, you can drive me down to the Peak this evening. Then Sir Ian will be free to shut up the house and make all his arrangements.'

Sir Ian, as if released from bondage, could no longer even sit. He stood up, gulped down his drink and said: 'Well, well, me dear, I'll be off. See ye before ye go.' Then he went clumping down the wooden stairs while I dragged myself out of my chair.

'I had better go and pack,' I said.

'Sit down!' said Sashie angrily. 'Delgado is doing it. Are all your things in your bedroom?'

'Yes. I have only a few clothes. Tooth brushes in the bathroom.'

'What about your household things?'

'Down in the cellars here. Mackie knows about them.' I was bored by the thought of those crates in the cellars. I felt exhausted, lost. 'Sashie, I don't want to go to the Peak. It is years since I have done any accountancy.'

'You are not going to the Peak. I don't need an accountant. You are coming to Silver Beach.'

'Silver Beach?' I repeated. 'But—'

'Janet, will you cease to make a nuisance of yourself and do as you are told?'

Staring at the wall, I studied his words. There was no doubt that, now that Madame was dead, I was a mere nuisance here at Paradise and my grandmother had always said that I must always do as I was told. It seemed simple, after all the complications.

'All right, Sashie,' I said.

Looking very capable and confident, as if he knew all about everything and how to deal with every complication, he went away and I heard him talking to Nurse Delgado in the other rooms. It was a relief to be treated as a disposable piece of baggage and not as a person of will any more.

I have no recollection of leaving Paradise for the last time. Memory begins again with Caleb carrying my two suitcases, leading me into a room in the east wing of Sashie's house. I knew this house because I had seen it in all its stages of reconstruction and helped Sashie with its decoration and the arrangement of the furniture, but all that seemed to be very long ago although in actual time only about a year had elapsed.

I was so tired that I hardly spoke to Caleb and when he had gone away, I sat down in this familiar and yet unfamiliar place, but feeling frightened now. I had become so accustomed to those dim panelled rooms on the top floor of the Great House with the tree tops all around that all this open space was menacing. I had not been downstairs on ground level since Madame had had her stroke and here there was not only the cultivated earth and grass just over the low window-sill but a few yards away, there was the sea, rolling in long soft waves on to the silver sand of the beach. And everything was so bright, with a light that seemed to penetrate my skull and search through my brain. I remembered with hatred yet with longing the dark panelled rooms of the Great House, the dark mahogany floors, the dark insect-damaged curtains and the broken-springed chairs with their brown, green and dark red plush upholstery. Here the walls were white, the curtains white with pale green sprigs all over them, the floors of silver grey tiles that were cool to the eye and the feet but it was all too clean and bright for a creature of the darkness.

I got up to go through the short passage which I knew to lead to the bathroom of this little suite but in the archway I stopped dead. Lying by the wall of the passage was the long black steel trunk, with the little keys attached to one of its handles and the white-painted letters: 'Major A. Alexander. R.E.M.E.' on the lid. I stared at its blackness among all the white and silver-grey and turned back to the bedroom.

The first few days and nights at Silver Beach were a time of starting out of reverie or half-sleep into guilt that Madame might have called and I had not heard her and this would pass into the relief of realizing that she was dead and could not call to me any more and this in its turn would be replaced by guilt that I was glad that she was dead. If one of these sudden starts into awareness took place during the day time, I would go and find Sashie or Caleb and try to talk to them but at night I would lie still or sit at the window at the mercy of the guilt. During the days, while that clear searching light played about me, I longed for the dark of the night and when the night came, I waited, tense and frightened, for the dawn to break over the sea. I seemed to be caught in an endless present, as if in a bubble, that was surrounded by fear. I could not look back, to face the guilt that stood behind me and when I tried to look forward, I could see nothing in the future except more fear and I tried in a desperate way to interest myself in the day-to-day life around me while ignoring both past and future. But all the time I knew that past and future were there.

Silver Beach was a busy place, a happy place, where the cook sang in the kitchen and Trixie, Caleb's pretty girl-friend, sang as she dusted or pinned laundry on the line, while Caleb himself took another patch and yet another patch of derelict bush into cultivation. The restoration and development of this property was something that, once upon a time, would have interested and delighted me but it held no interest for me now and this inability to be interested in, concerned with or involved with anything or anybody was another feeding ground for the greedy guilt that consumed me. I was a monster, I told myself, a monster who had

82

helped to kill Twice, helped to kill Madame, a monster incapable of gratitude, fellow-feeling or any human attribute.

As the days and nights passed, I came to have less and less sense of time and place, for all normal laws fell into abeyance as I became further and further alienated from reality. I was aware of my alienation, tried to fight it, to free myself from its grip but when, momentarily, I had it in subjection, I was faced with the guilt that lay behind me and the future that I could not see, so that I shrank away again into the alien dimension where there was no reality but only grey blurs of half-thought, like dim objects vaguely outlined in the surrounding dark.

I walked about the property a great deal, through and around the plantation of coconuts, to and fro along the beach and although I felt in one sense permanently tired, in another sense my body seemed to be tireless, driven by some demon of energy that was beyond my control. When I was in the presence of Sashie or the servants, speaking to them, I seemed to be watching myself, listening to myself, as if from a distance and this sensation brought to birth the notion that my essential self had left my body which lived on as an automaton which could be observed from a distance by its departed spirit.

There next came a stage when the dull greyness in my mind was peopled by three obsessions. The first was the black rectangle of the steel trunk, the next the circles of green and red flashing fire among which revolved the black circle with its waving plumes and the third was the dark slanting eyes of Sashie. Every rectangle, be it the top of a silver cigarette box on a table-top, the table-top itself or the wall of a room was the black rectangle of the trunk. Every circular or oval shape – the plates on the dinner-table or the moon in the sky – turned into the circles of fire and smoky plumes that spun through the air and the eyes of Sashie were everywhere, looking out from the dark shaded depths of bushes, from between the soft dark waves of the night sea, even from between the folds of a black dress hanging in my bedroom cupboard. I was afraid of the rectangles and circles but I was even more afraid of the eyes so that I came to hate them and, because of them, to hate Sashie himself.

83

Or, rather, it was the thought of Sashie that I hated. When I was in his presence, I had that alienated feeling of seeing myself and him from a distance and physical features such as his eyes were of no account but when I was apart from him, those eyes would appear everywhere, watching, waiting, full of dreadful menace and I would be filled with helpless hatred. Yet, all the time, I lived a life that seemed outwardly to be normal.

No demands were made upon me. If I did not come out to the veranda for breakfast, a tray was brought to me and so with all the other meals. If I joined Sashie at any time, he would go on with whatever he was doing and talk to me about it or about Caleb's vegetables or of the latest news from the Peak Hotel. He did not talk of the past or the future or of intimate things but only of the trivia of every day, and he did not question any of my stayings in my room or my comings and goings along the beach or around the property.

But all the time tension was growing in me as if a steel spring were being compressed inside my head to the point where it must find release by splitting my skull apart and in the early hours of a morning when the moon hung low over the sea, I tiptoed across the hall to the drawing-room and carried back to my room the bottle of whisky from the tray. To fetch a tumbler from the bathroom, I had to pass the steel trunk in the passage way and it seemed, physically, to enter my mind in all its hard indestructible blackness. Sitting on my bed in the light of the waning moon, I stared at that coffin-like shape on the silver floor by the white wall, while I drank great gulps of neat whisky. The black trunk and the black guilt in my mind became merged into one, for the trunk contained the novels that I had written against the wishes of Twice. It was on the day when I had told him of the acceptance of one of these novels by a publisher that he had decided not to live any more. If I had never written that novel, Twice would still be alive, I reasoned with cold calm logic. I should have burned that manuscript instead of sending it to London. Still staring at the black rectangle in the passage, I struck a match to light a cigarette and the flame was pale yellow in the grey light, but the flame that flared inside my head was a vicious scarlet. I would open that trunk and turn its contents into consuming red fire like the fire that was burning away my brain.

I staggered towards the trunk, whisky bottle in one hand, matches in the other and knelt on the floor, fumbling as I disengaged the key-ring from the steel handle. Suddenly, Sashie was beside me and I sprang up, raising the whisky bottle like a club above my head. I was taller than Sashie and I knew that I might kill him if I brought that bottle down on his head but I did not care. But as I tensed my arm to strike the downward blow, Sashie reached up almost casually, took my upheld wrist in a grip like a vice and although I exerted all my strength, a frenzied strength, against him, he forced my arm down and down until the bottle was standing on the lid of the trunk, where he forced my fingers to relax their grip on its neck.

'And now that is all over, darling,' he said quietly, 'come back to your room and lie down.'

'Feel sick,' I said and threw myself headlong into the bathroom.

While the sour reeking whisky heaved and belched from my mouth, I felt a sharp pain in my abdomen which made my whole body clutch itself into a wincing huddle so that by the time the vomiting stopped, I could only sink exhausted to the floor, but when I opened my eyes again, an extra-ordinary thing happened, so that I felt my mind at gaze with the wonder of it. I was looking into those black eyes of Sashie's as he bent over me – I knew this as one recognizes any fact – but at the same time I was looking into the deep black water of the well at Reachfar where I could see a reflection of myself as a child, short pigtails sticking out on either side of my head. If I went on looking into those black eyes, I suddenly knew, I would free myself from that grey place where the rectangles and the circles made their ter-rifying gyrations, but I must go on looking and not draw back, as I had drawn back when I was a child from the strange reflection in the well.

'Janet, I am going to call Caleb,' Sashie said.

I clutched his arm in both hands, staring into his face.

'No!' I said and then the pain wrenched at me again, making me close my eyes.

'Darling, I must call him. I can't pick you up because of these damned tin legs of mine and we must get you to bed.'

I looked at him again, looked hard into the dark eyes. 'I can get up,' I said, clutching the edge of the bath, hauling myself to my feet, looking all the time into those eyes. At last I was on my bed. Sashie pulled the sheet over me and was about to turn away but I grasped his arm again and he stood beside the bed looking down at me.

'I must go and telephone Gurbat Singh,' he said.

'No!' There came another spasm of the pain and although I jerked my knees up almost to my chin and clutched his arm even more firmly, I did not shut my eyes.

'But Janet, you are ill!' he protested. 'I must get help.'

'Please don't go away,' I pleaded and everything in me was concentrated into that upward stare into his eyes.'

'But you are in pain, Janet.'

'It will go away. Get the doctor later. Please don't leave me, Sashie.'

His eyes changed, seemed to grow larger, as his thin eyebrows rose above them. He put his head on one side interrogatively as he sat down on the edge of the bed and released my tense fingers from his arm.

'All right,' he said. 'We shall call Gurbat Singh in the morning.'

Still looking up at him, I gave some slight consideration to those stabs of pain. I drew a tentative breath which brought no further spasm, so I tried a deep breath and again there was no pain, only a curious sense of release and I began to sink in delicious ease into some beautiful place where I belonged and yet the place was, at the same time, the soft darkness of Sashie's eyes. No. The place was my Thinking Place above the well at Reachfar, where the light was soft and dim but it seemed impolite and uncivil to drift away into comfort and peace like this after I had behaved so badly, getting drunk and waking Sashie in the middle of the night. I made an effort to come out of the soft warm darkness that was embracing me so that I might apologize.

'I am a nuisance, Sashie,' I said. 'And I am sorry. Why do you bother with me?'

I heard his voice answer me gently but from far away. 'You are well worth all the—' Sashie always hesitated before using a word that was not normal to his vocabulary and even from the distance of the warm dark, I now noticed this hesitation and his stress on the word: '—bother.'

INTERLUDE

'BOTHER.' I was six years old and deep inside my Thinking Place above the well at Reachfar. I conned over all the circumstances of my life as I always did at the beginning of a sojourn in the Thinking Place. Reachfar was my home, a croft on top of a hill in Ross-shire, where I lived with my family, which was made up of my grandmother, my grandfather, my mother, my father, my Aunt Kate and my friends George and Tom. George was really my uncle but he did not like the name uncle and neither did our friend Tom, who helped us around the place. The place, Reachfar, was a reasonable sensible place, that stayed there on top of its hill looking down on the Firth, day in, day out, winter and summer, but my family, although I would not have allowed anyone else to say a word against them, were, I admitted in my own mind, not always reasonable and sensible.

It was an autumn evening and warm, although growing dark, with a warmth that made the tall fir trees that hid my Thinking Place give out their resinous smell and the late-working bees were humming in the heather and I was in here on my own, thinking, because I had been a bother again. I was not worried about this, for I had long understood that it was inbuilt in me to be a bother, especially to my busy grandmother, because I was always ask-ask-asking. This was because there were so many things I did not know and my grandmother was very patient and told me many things but, frequently, the moment would come when she would say: 'Ach, be off with you, Janet, and stop bothering me with your ask-ask-asking!'

On this day the moment had come because of Miss Tulloch, the grocer in our local village of Achcraggan. That forenoon, George, Tom and I had gone off with the trap loaded with butter, eggs and honey, most of which we would

89

exchange for groceries from Miss Tulloch and just as we were turning out of the yard by the granary gable, my grandmother called after us: 'Oh and bring a puckle of tea as well as the things in the book!'

'Aye, aye,' George called back to her and said to me: 'You mind on that now, Janet, for Tom and I are not good minders. We'd better not come home without that tea. The Tea Man hasna been this year yet, Tom. I suppose it is the war.'

The year was 1916 and the war had started away back before I went to school when I was five. This war was a terrible thing, causing all sorts of upsets, like the Tea Man not coming. The Tea Man came from far away Edinburgh, wrote your order in his book and shortly afterwards George or Tom would have to take the trap to the station at Fortavoch and come back with the big cube-shaped wooden chest that was lined inside with silver and full of tea. You would think there was enough tea in it to last all your born days but, as Tom and George said, Granny drank tea everlasting and a new chest came to Reachfar every year. But this year, the chest was empty, the Tea Man had not come and so we had to buy some from Miss Tulloch.

Well, I remembered and we bought it. We had a bit of an argument about how much to buy, how much my grandmother meant by 'a puckle'. Miss Tulloch said a pound would be about right, she thought, but George said: 'Ach, the ould leddy drinks tea ever-lasting. A pound would go nowhere.'

'Better make it ten,' Tom said.

'I canna spare ten the-day with this war,' Miss Tulloch said and in the end she weighed out five pounds for us, put it in a big brown paper bag and wrote '5 lbs. tea' in our book.

We were very pleased with such a reasonable settlement until we arrived home for supper and my grandmother opened the account book.

'Five pounds o' tea you brought?' she asked us, in a scandalized voice. 'And the price of it! It's a penny a pound dearer than the Tea Man's tea!'

She was very angry. But I have to explain that when we went to Achcraggan, Tom and George always did some business at the Plough Inn while I visited my friend Bella Beagle in the fisher town and business at the Plough, my grandmother said, made all sense roll off them like water off a duck's back. And business at the Plough made my grandmother's anger roll off them too.

'You are buying it in bulk from the Tea Man, mistress,' Tom said, although he would not normally dare to speak back to my grandmother.

'And poor Miss Tulloch needs a penny or two for her bother,' said George.

This was what had led to the real trouble and to my being alone in my Thinking Place. I had not known before that bother was worth money and had begun to ask-ask-ask about this for I thought that my capacity for bother ought to make a milloinaire out of either my grandmother or myself, although I was not sure which and my grandmother, already annoyed about the five pounds of tea and the sense rolling off Tom and George like water off a duck's back, had sent me scudding out of the kitchen when supper was over and up to my Thinking Place on the moor.

And 'bother' was a funny word anyhow. Words were very interesting and the more you thought about them, the more interesting they became. Now then, as Tom would say, take this word bother. On the face of it, it ought to rhyme with 'mother' if you were writing a poem but it did not. To make it rhyme, it would have to be 'buhther' or mother would have to be 'moth-er' like a collector of moths. And it was nothing to do with my mother anyhow, for she never accused me of bothering her. She only told me sometimes to try not to be a bother to other people. Other rhymed with mother. Was there a rhyme for bother? Go through the alphabet. A was no use, B was in the word itself, cother, dother? On I went through the alphabet but there was no real rhyme, so bother was just a bother of a word, no good for anything and it was just because Tom and George had been to the Plough and the sense had rolled off them, I decided, that George had said you could get money for bother.

And now it occurred to me that I had been hiding in the Thinking Place for quite long enough. The only bad thing about having a think in the Thinking Place was that it made you forget all about the rest of the world and the people there and the things that had to be done there, like getting on with your work and going about your business and nothing annoyed my grandmother more than people who did not get on with their work or go about their business. If I was too late to shut up my brood of chickens for the night and the rats got at them in the dark, there would be more bother, even, than there had been about the tea.

I suddenly became aware that it was broad daylight, that the sun was shining white beyond the dark screen of the fir trees.

But I had come in here in the evening, when it was growing dark! Had I been in here all night? Had I slept in the Thinking Place? I began to struggle out among the heather and the low branches that clung to me, clutching at my clothes and my hair, impeding me. Impatiently, I thrust them aside and the daylight brightened still more. This was going to be what George and Tom called the very marrow of a bother ...

PART TWO

'It is all right, Janet,' the voice was saying from far away, 'you are not being a bother.'

'Raise her head a little,' another voice said and then I felt something cold on my lips. Milk. Cold milk. Very surprising. I swallowed, there was more milk and I swallowed again. This was all very queer, a proper to-do, my grandmother would call it. But this was not my Thinking Place. This was a bed and I had been asleep, dreaming and now I opened my eyes and looked up into the black eyes of Sashie.

'Good morning, Janet,' he said, took his hand away from under my head and stood erect. 'You remember Nurse Delgado?'

'Yes.' I looked at the nurse, then back to Sashie. He looked peculiar, as if he wanted to cry. I smiled. Imagine Sashie crying! The idea was too silly. He turned away without speaking any more and went out of the room.

'Am I sick?' I inquired of Nurse Delgado.

'You have been rather sick,' she said and I tried to remember but it was all too much trouble. I let my eyelids fall and went drifting away back to Reachfar.

When I look back from the standpoint of the present to this time, I see that, for me, the normal values of sleep and waking were reversed. When I was asleep, I was always back in my childhood home and acutely aware of the exact spot where I sat or stood in that place and equally aware of the time of year and the time of day. I can remember every detail of these lapses into sleep or subconsciousness or whatever the state may be called but I cannot remember in any detail the early spells when I was awake, when I was fed, bathed and attended to by Nurse Delgado. I remember only that these things happened and were always a great nuisance to me but at last the day came when I awoke normally, with the feeling of returning from sleep into time and place, instead of feeling that I was leaving time, place and coherence behind.

After this, the physical recovery seemed to me to be very slow although, in reality, it took only two weeks before I could walk from bed to chair unaided. During this time, life seemed to take the form of one long effort to move my limbs. It was a matter of deep concentration to sit up in bed, turn and swing my feet down to the floor but a day came when Nurse Delgado said: 'We must try to wash all that hair today'. The phrase 'all that hair' caught my fancy and I kept repeating it in my mind while I sat on the high kitchen stool, my head over the wash-basin, while the nurse rubbed and scrubbed among 'all that hair'. It was, in my opinion, very dull hair, a darkish brown now going grey and absolutely straight, but it had never been cut, was very thick and hung below my waist. When Nurse had scrubbed it to her satisfaction, she led me out to the veranda at the front of the house, where she began to brush the hair, spreading it out to dry in the warm wind from the sea.

'I am a person like this,' she said, 'I just love long hair.' I clutched at the arms of the wicker chair while my mind clutched at the words: 'I am a person like this', for I was suddenly beset by inexplicable terror. This was my first sortie beyond the white walls of the little suite of bedroom and bathroom and the world was suddenly and crushingly huge. Beyond the veranda rail, there was a strip of grass, then the sand of the beach and then the sea that stretched away to the far horizon to become one with the blue of the sky. I felt that I might disappear into nothingness among all that vaporous blue, that I was anchored to the earth and reality only by my grip on the chair, the nurse's hands among my hair and the words: 'I am a person like this, I am a person, a person—' The nurse arranged my hair down my back, took her hands away and went into the house. In stark terror, I gripped the arms of the chair, shuddering as I tried not to scream.

' 'Morning, ma'am,' said Caleb, coming up from the grass on to the veranda. 'I am happy to see you out here.'

Each day, since I had recovered consciousness, he had

94

paid calls on me forenoon and evening. I looked at him, could not speak and the broad smile faded from his face as he dropped his straw hat from his hand to the floor and came towards me. He held out his emormous black hand with the pink palm and I, calculating my risk of losing all contact with the world, as a trapeze artist high in the air calculates his risk as he times his spring from one swinging bar to another, released my grip on the chair arms and clutched at Caleb's hand.

'Is all right, ma'am,' he said, holding my hands tightly between his own as he called: 'You there, Mars Sashie, sah?'

Sashie came out of the house, put his arms round my shoulders and I began to cry with relief that the terror had gone, ashamed as I heard myself sobbing: 'I was all alone, all alone.'

'I should not have left her,' Nurse Delgado said, arriving beside us, 'but she seemed so normal.'

'She always seems too bloody normal,' said Sashie angrily. 'That is a large part of the trouble. Nobody is as normal as she is, especially she, if I make myself clear.'

'Sashie, don't be angry,' I said childishly. 'I *am* normal.'

'Of *course* you are normal!' he snapped at me. 'And if one more person utters the word normal, I shall go out there and drown myself.'

'Let me tie your hair back,' the nurse said, extending a length of blue silk between her hands. 'This is the belt of a dress but it will do.'

She tied the silk under the hair and into a bow on the top of my head while I sat very still, very ashamed of myself.

'I go now, ma'am?' Caleb ask. 'Come to see you again later?'

'Yes, Caleb. Thank you,' I said, too humiliated to look at him and he and the nurse went away.

'For God's sake, Janet,' Sashie said now, 'stop being ashamed of yourself, blaming yourself, harrowing yourself to pieces.'

'One can't help being ashamed,' I said. 'It is all too silly.'

'Silly or not, people are always afraid of coming out into the world after a serious illness. That is how people are.'

'Have I been seriously ill? Yes, when Nurse Delgado is

here and the doctor is always coming, I suppose I have been,' I said. 'I must have been an awful nuisance, Sashie. I am sorry. What has been the matter with me?'

'Physically, you had some sort of haemorrhage from your insides, all very feminine and Delgado will tell you about it but that was all over weeks ago.'

'Weeks?'

I looked about me, truly observing Silver Beach for the first time since I had come there and now the wide blue expanse of sea and sky held no terror. What Caleb called a gully, a watercourse that dried into a stony hollow in the hot weather, ran down to the sea a few yards from the end of the veranda and I saw a silvery dancing stream at its centre. Suddenly, I remembered the heavy humid heat in the dark panelled rooms at Paradise, a heat that would have been diminished if rain had come, but no rain had fallen.

'Sashie,' I asked, 'what is the date?'

'Thursday the fourth of September, 1958, darling.'

'But Madame died in the middle of July!' I protested. 'Have I been here ever since then?'

'We-ell—' Sashie drawled but his black eyes were very intent.

'If I have been in a loony bin, you might as well tell me. I promise you I won't create any more scenes.'

'You haven't been in a loony bin. Your body has been here,' he said carefully and then with an air of choosing his words he added: 'But there were eleven days when—' he hesitated and I broke in with: 'I was at Reachfar.'

'You remember about it, Janet?'

'Yes, as if it were a very clear dream or a series of dreams, all mingled and overlapping one another, yet all clear. Yet they weren't dreams. They were memories, memories from my childhood.'

'And what do you remember from before that dream and memory time?' Sashie asked quietly and carefully and I thought suddenly and with indignation: 'He and the nurse and the doctor and Caleb and everybody – they all think I have gone off my head, that I am a lunatic!'

'Everything, of course!' I said angrily. 'Do you think I have gone out of my mind?' but to assure myself that I could indeed remember, I made a deliberate effort to recall and a dreadful uncertainty came over me as memory, like a tangled web of guilt, sorrow, shame and horror, defied my reason to rationalize it, put it in order.

Sashie took my hand in his, looking at it as if he were examining my finger-nails, as he said: 'Do you remember the night that Twice died, darling?'

'He didn't die at night,' I said. 'He died in the forenoon, just after the mail came in.'

I felt Sashie's grip on my hand tighten but suddenly my reason had a grip on the tangled web of memory, as tight and sure as Sashie's grip on my hand.

'No,' I said. 'That is where I went wrong. Of *course* he died at night. It was a Saturday, late at night. You were there, Sashie. He died twelve days after that day the mail came in.'

Sashie put my hand gently in my lap with a curious air of satisfaction and I felt that I might have come out of a dark wood that was full of furtive distorted shadows into a sunlit space as high, broad and clear as that expanse of blue beyond the beach. I had no fear now, only a desire to disentangle the web, rationalize it and put it behind me.

'Would you let me tell you about how things went wrong, Sashie?'

'I shall feel very wronged if you don't, my sweet.'

At that moment, Trixie came on to the veranda carrying a tray that held a decanter of sherry, some glasses and bottles of rum and lime juice. At sight of the bottles, in my new clarity of mind, I felt a hot flush of shame rise over my chest and throat.

'Please take the rum and lime to Nurse's room, Trixie,' Sashie said and the girl went away while I remembered with a searing acuteness how often I had 'wronged' Sashie, culminating in that hideous scene in the passage beside the black metal trunk.

'And what are you ashamed of, blaming yourself for *now*?' he asked, handing me a glass of sherry.

'That awful night when I got drunk and tried to hit you over the head with a bottle,' I said. 'I can never apologize for that, Sashie.'

'Have done with apologies, my sweet,' he said and then with that air of care, of calculating the risk of his words, he added: 'As *Twice* used to say, you can try to hit me over the head with a bottle any time.'

To assure him that I remembered Twice whose name he had emphasized, to assure him that I liked, now, to remember Twice and the things he used to say, I smiled. I then put the fingers of my left hand round my right wrist and felt again that grip that had forced my arm down and the pain of the pressure across the back of my hand that had made my fingers release the neck of the bottle. 'I won't try again, Sashie,' I said. 'It hurt too much.'

'I am sorry, darling. I was a little rough, perhaps, but I did not want Caleb to come in in the morning and find *both* of us in a heap on the floor. Too utterly compromising.'

I now had a sudden awareness of the world, the people beyond the boundaries of Silver Beach, as if I had dropped back into a slot in the social scene after a long time spent in another distant dimension. Since the passing of that terror that had made me clutch Caleb's hand, my awareness was like a brightly lit stage on to which items of scenery were being pushed in from the wings and dropped from above and always suddenly. At one second, my awareness had been limited to Silver Beach, at the next the world beyond had moved in close to its boundaries.

'If I have been here since the middle of July,' I said, 'we are fairly well compromised by now I should think.'

'It is a little late to think about that,' Sashie said lightly. 'Indeed, I should think that as a topic on verandas we are already outdated.'

'There seems to be no end to the pest I can make of myself. I am terribly sorry I did all this to you, Sashie.'

'But you did *not* do it to me, darling. I took it upon myself in my officious way. From the moment Twice died – no, even before that – it was obvious to me that you had gone wrong somewhere, as you put it a moment ago.'

'Was I being queer all that time at Paradise? I mean did Sir Ian or any of them see—?'

'No. The Dulacs don't see very far beyond themselves at any time. Besides, I flatter myself that none of them knew you as well as I did. As Delgado would say, I know a little of what you are a person like.'

'I wish *I* knew what I am a person like,' I said.

'You are not fond enough of yourself to find out. You have to like a person to discover what he is a person like and you have been liking yourself even less than ever during the last few months. Why?'

'It is so difficult to know where everything started,' I said.

'For you, Janet, everything started at Reachfar.'

'I suppose it did. Yes, it did. Sashie, this sounds irrelevant but it isn't really. Ever since I was a youngster at Reachfar, I have wanted to write. I have never told you this in words before but you have always known this about me, haven't you?'

'I have known more than that. I have known for a long time that you *can* write, Janet.'

'Have you been poking about in that trunk?' I snapped suspiciously and was at once ashamed of myself. This desire to write had so long been held secret that secrecy about it had become a habit, even when I had broken through that secrecy to Sashie. 'I am sorry,' I apologized at once. 'Of course you haven't. But why do you say I can write?'

'Because of *Varlets in Paradise*.'

'Oh, that!'

Varlets in Paradise was the title of that melodrama I had written when I first came to the island. Originally, it had been intended to amuse Sir Ian and some of the Paradise staff who fancied themselves as amateur actors but had, in the end, been the centrepiece of one of Madame's 'little entertainments' of that time and had been performed in the garden of the Great House before an audience of hundreds, with Sashie bringing the house down in the role of the Jester.

'That was a lot of trash,' I said now.

'On the contrary, it was a very clever skit on Paradise, its life and times,' said Sashie and added with dignity: 'I *never* act in trash, darling.'

'I didn't know you acted at all.'

'But all the *time*, dear, *all* the time, except now.' He became grave. 'À nos moutons. Ever since you were a youngster, you wanted to write.'

'Yes, but it was not the sort of thing that was done in families like mine. You won't understand this, brought up as you were.'

'How was I brought up, darling?'

I was nonplussed, facing the fact that I did not know. Around Sashie in my mind there was a vague aura of cosmopolitanism, with his French father, his Russian mother, an atmosphere of the arts, with his ability to paint and his knowledge of music that had led to his making a collection of the folk songs of St. Jago.

'*You* know,' I said impatiently, 'in Paris and European capitals and all that – a bit like Anna.'

'*Never* have I been so insulted,' he said. 'That you should liken me to that – that – words fail me!'

'Cheers for something new under my sun,' I said and he laughed.

'Happy as I am to hear you sound so much like your real self,' he said, 'let us not quarrel. So writing was not done in your family?'

'No. If my grandmother had known that I tried to write poetry after I was grown up – writing rhymes as a child was all right – children will play, you know – she would have had me taken away in a plain van. But my father was – was different. I told him about it once and he seemed to sort of believe that I might be able to do it. Only I never did. I only dabbled at it and then my father died.'

'And that was the time that you burned all your papers in the backyard at Guinea Corner?' Sashie asked.

'Yes,' I paused, looking out at the sea. The next part was the most difficult to say for it was the basic cause of this illness or breakdown or whatever it was that I had suffered. I was only beginning to understand what a trial this illness had been to Sashie and that, but for him, I might be dead or in a lunatic asylum by now and I felt that I owed him an explanation of what had led to the trouble. 'Twice did not like the idea of my trying to write, Sashie,' I managed to say, as if I were betraying an important secret and yet it was a relief to have spoken the words aloud. 'He said that people like us didn't write, that in trying I was being a fool.'

'But you went on trying?'

'Yes. You knew that, didn't you? You even encouraged me, always presenting me with pens and paper and things.'

'Yes, I did,' he said firmly, refusing to recognize the blame that I was imputing to him.

'Well, last year when Twice and everybody were away watching cricket all the time, I typed up a manuscript I had in a cupboard and sent it off to an agent in London. I got the name of the agent out of that book you gave me,' I added, imputing blame to him again.

'Yes and I posted the package for you,' he said, 'and I refuse to repent of it so go on, darling.'

'Well, the agent placed it with Canterbury, Arden & Company—'

'Can—' Sashie began, then stopped his mouth and eyes wide open, disconcerted as I had never seen him disconcerted. 'You are telling me, Janet, that Canterbury, Arden have accepted a manuscript of yours?'

'Yes.'

'You have a contract?'

'Yes. They sent me a hundred pounds as well but that isn't the point.'

'Then what, pray, is the point?'

'The thing is – you remember that the Paradise Cricket Club wanted a lemonade barrow for the final against Retreat? You were at Guinea Corner when Twice was designing it.'

'Yes, I remember that. You and he had a bit of a spat about it and you settled your difference in the impressive way you always did. Go on about the barrow.'

'The junior engineers took the design and made a mess of building the barrow. Twice didn't find out about the mess until the last afternoon before the match. He started in from scratch and built another barrow, all by himself. That was what over-taxed his heart and made him ill – physically ill, I mean. He was all upset in his mind about Mackie and Percy already, the broken engagement and everything.' I suddenly felt tired of it all, all this that was now in the far past, as if on the other side of a dark hill. 'All this is very tedious,' I said.

'Not to me. Go on.' Sashie's voice was hard and imperative.

'Well, the afternoon that Twice came home after building the barrow, he was so ill and I was so frightened that I said a terrible thing. I said: 'Twice, that you should have done this for a lemonade barrow!' It hurt him. I was sorry as soon as I had said it but I had said it and you can't call things back. He simply got more and more ill and further and further away – but you remember that – and I forgot all about that manuscript I had sent to London. Then, one day, there was the mail. I was always trying to interest him in things, everyday things, like the mail. There was this letter from the agent, telling about Canterbury, Arden and I was so – so, well, flabbergasted that Twice felt it and I had to tell him what was in the letter. It was then that he seemed to decide to die, Sashie. All he said was: "Some people build lemonade barrows. Some people write books". Then he shut his eyes as if we did not need each other any more. It was twelve days after that that he died.' I paused, looking out at the limitless sky. 'All these months I was at Paradise, I felt that I had killed Twice, Sashie, but that was silly. I am not big enough or important enough to kill anybody.'

'Except yourself,' Sashie said quietly. 'You didn't quite bring it off, but you had a very good try.'

'But Sashie I wasn't trying to kill myself!' I protested. 'If I had wanted to do that, there are lots of cleaner, quicker, more efficient ways of doing it than by trying to assault your friends and vomiting whisky all over their bathrooms.'

'You are no mincer of words and a hard facer of facts but I do wish you would get the facts right before facing them. As you say, you did *not* kill Twice, darling, and as Twice said, some make lemonade barrows and some write books. We all have to do our own things, tell our own life stories and we all die our own deaths.'

'I am not sure of that. It is not that simple,' I said. 'There is a frightening paradox in human relationships. One cannot hurt anyone who does not love one and these are the people one least wants to hurt but one hurts them all the same. As I see it, I have to accept some responsibility for the death of Twice but accept it as an inbuilt part of the relationship between us, not as a thing for which I am totally and guiltily responsible. But even that is only a tiny part of the complexity.'

'I have always looked on death – death as opposed to untimely barbarous death in war or by other forms of murder such as traffic accidents – as a refusal to come to terms with life,' Sashie said. 'It is possible, to put it crudely, to become fed-up with life and I think that Twice was fed-up at becoming ill again, turning the house into a sickroom again – something he had always hated – not being able to do what he regarded as a simple little job without his body playing him false. From what I knew of him, darling, I think this was a factor.'

'I think you knew him well, Sashie,' I said, 'and I agree with you and with Madame, old as she was, there was a refusal to come to terms. Madame was all right until Anna came on the scene. Anna was the one thing in life that Madame could not take. And yet it was Edward that brought Anna upon Madame. If Edward ever felt even mild affection for anybody – God knows what he feels for Anna – it was for Madame and yet he introduced the unacceptable factor.' I remembered that evening in the dim panelled room and shuddered: 'Sashie, you remember that the last words Madame spoke were: I hate—?'

'I remember but I give the words no importance,' he said. 'Madame Dulac never said anything of any significance in all the time I knew her and it would be illogical to claim that the words that happened to be her last had any more meaning than all the others she uttered in her time.'

'You are hard on her, Sashie. She was kind to me in her way.'

'I can never understand,' he said, 'Why you should be so astonished when people are what you call *kind* to you, as if it were extraordinary for people to try to help one another. Isn't this largely what life is about?'

'Perhaps, but most people don't behave as if it were. You are a little different, Sashie.'

'But for my unusual nether limbs, I am perfectly ordinary,' he said, thrusting aside, as he always did, any discussion of himself.

'Just an ordinary person,' I said, began to laugh and then became aware of the puzzlement in Sashie's face. 'At one time,' I explained, 'I had a friend called Muriel who had one of those bogus suits of armour left to her by a woman who died.'

I became aware now that Sashie's face was a little too intent, as if he were suspecting me of being overcome by delirium. 'I am all right,' I assured him. 'This makes sense in what my nephew Gee calls the very very end.'

'Do go on, darling. I love things that make sense in the very very end.'

'Well, Muriel had this suit of armour lying on the floor and she unscrewed the head from the rest of it.'

'How very peculiar of her. Why?'

'She was moving house. She was packing the armour and she and I were having this row.'

'What about?'

'I had discovered that Muriel wasn't the sort of person that I had thought she was and I was annoyed about it.'

'I see. Go on.'

'And she just went on sitting there, fiddling about with that screwdriver among that suit of armour and in the end I kicked the helmet-head-part of it through a window into the garden. Twice was out there and he picked the head up and took it home with us. He didn't know what the row had been about and I said that I had always thought until that day that Muriel had been an ordinary person. Twice said that there was no such thing as an ordinary person because, to be ordinary, people would have to have nothing but emptiness inside their heads like the helmet. After that, we called it the Ordinary Person for a long time. I wonder what happened to it?'

'You gave it to me. I asked you for it. Don't you remember?'

'So I did,' I said, remembering with relief the day at Guinea Corner when Caleb brought the helmet downstairs, for I was still a little uncertain that my memory was functioning properly. 'Anyway, that was why I laughed when you said that you were ordinary. You have more inside your head than most people, so you must be less ordinary than most people.'

'Let's leave the contents of my head and attend to the contents of your stomach,' he said. 'You have had a long hard forenoon. Lunch and then bed for a bit. Come along.'

'But I feel so much better than I have felt for such a long time, Sashie.'

'I'm glad to hear it but come along,' he said briskly.

After lunch, when I went to my bedroom, I was glad to lie down because my wilting spine would no longer keep me upright, but this purely physical illusion of weight dragging me down was a relief after the mental weight that had dragged at me throughout the long months. It was difficult, now that rationality had established itself, to recall how real and pressing my sense of guilt had been. Indeed, it was difficult to believe that I had spent those dark nightmare months on the top floor of the Great House of Paradise or that the Great House itself really existed. But it does, I told myself, staring at the ceiling. I could go up there and visit it but I will not. I shall never go back there again. I knew this with a finality that I had never known in my life before. It was only now that I began to wonder where I *would* go and it was strange to realize that I could go wherever I pleased, that there was nobody to make a demand on me to go anywhere, to stay anywhere or to do anything.

'Sashie,' I said that evening, 'where do I go from here, do you think?'

'I have not the slightest idea, my sweet and it is too soon as yet to talk of your going anywhere. You will just stay here and bear me company for a bit and get properly well.'

'But I don't need Nurse any more,' I said.

'I agree and now that she has washed *all* that hair as she kept calling it, she will go quietly.'

I laughed and then: 'She has been so good. It is difficult to tell her to go. If I had died, she would have gone as a matter of course.'

'I prefer you alive, even if it meant an embarrassing interview with Delgado but it doesn't. She and I are hearty old chums. She has been coping with our hypochondriacs and alcoholics at the Peak for years. We are talking about you, Delgado,' he said as the girl came on to the veranda. 'We think we can manage on our own now and that you should hie you back to St. Jago Bay.'

'And I think so too, Mr. de Marnay,' she said.

'If I get into trouble with all that hair, I can send for you.'

'You do just that,' she told him and went away for her evening walk along the beach.

'Honestly, Sashie, what will that girl think?' I protested.

'Delgado is a person like this,' he said in Delgado's own phrase, 'she does not think. She has more sense than to get herself into trouble by thinking – tell me about this book you have written.'

'No. You can read it if it ever gets itself into print.'

'If the publishers have paid you a hundred pounds, it will get into print all right.' He put his head on one side and studied me as if I were a specimen under a microscope. 'You chose a firm of literary agents at random out of that Writers' Index I gave you?' he asked.

'I have never been sure what random is,' I told him. 'The dictionary says it comes from an Old French word meaning to gallop.'

'The things you know! If not at random, *how* did you choose those agents?'

'The Germans kept on dropping bombs at a place they called Random during the early days of the war.'

'Janet, about the agents.'

'Their name is Bush which sounded out-of-doors and they were established in 1910, the same year that I was and they said they were interested in the work of new writers. These things to me are reasons, not random.'

'Please don't keep on saying random. What interests me is the way your mind works. Did it never occur to you to send your manuscript to Roddy Maclean, an established author, to try it on his own publishers?'

'No. I never thought of that.'

'You have an inbuilt flair for doing everything the hard way.'

'It isn't that. I simply didn't want anybody except distant

people like agents, and publishers to know about the book at all.'

'Have you told your family about it?'

'No and that is another thing. I must stop this loafing about and write to my family. Not about the book but just in a general way. I think I wrote to my brother to tell him that Madame was dead but I'm not sure.'

'You did. At least you gave me a letter to post to him the day after we came down here. Do you think of going back to Scotland eventually?'

'I haven't thought of anything yet. I feel as if I have come back from the dead, as they say. I suppose I shall go back to Scotland in the end but I have nowhere to go there. I am not going to foist myself on my brother and his wife and I am certainly not going to my awful old stepma at Achcraggan. I think I shall find a room in a boarding house in the Bay for a bit.'

'If you do, I shall never forgive you for preferring some Bay flea-house to my desirable residence here. If you are worried about what people will say, I have already told you that it is rather late for that. Besides, you have to remember that you are a *writer* now, one of these peculiar people who behave so *oddly*, as Madame Dulac always said. What is the use of belonging to a suspect sect without accepting some of its fringe benefits? So let us consider that part of the matter settled.'

'You are very kind, Sashie, and I shall never understand why you have done all this for me.'

'That is easy to explain. I love you and I did not want to lose you. You look startled. It is so strange that if one says one loves a woman, everyone hears wedding bells and the patter of tiny feet or imagines darksome illicit intrigue and if one says one loves a man, they think of dire goings-on in seedy bedrooms. I have loved Twice and you, especially you, I now tell you for the first time, ever since I saw you at St. Jago airport. I have never loved any woman in a wedding bells and tiny feet way and I have never wanted to be dark-some and illicit either and contrary to all appearances—' he re-arranged the crease in his jade-green trousers '—I have never done dire things in a seedy bedroom with any man

107

either. And if all men and women would admit the truth, which they won't, I do not think that I am in any way unusual. Sex is fashionable in this age and to admit that it is not of supreme importance to one is as outmoded as wearing Louis heels. As for marriage, people do it for all sorts of undeclared reasons that have no connection with sex or the procreation of the race.'

'But not for love, to quote Roddy Maclean, not to say Shakespeare?' I asked.

'Precisely.'

'Actually, I agree with you,' I told him. 'They-fell-in-love-married-and-lived-happy-ever-after is the meaningless cliché of our times. I can see now that what brought Twice and me together was an amalgam of a million things held together by a sexual urge. This is how it was on my part anyhow. I think even that part of the amalgam was that I would get my living made for me and have some free time to try to write. That sounds dreadful when one says it in cold words but one might as well face it. I didn't know this about myself at the time but I know it now. Why do things have to be so complex?'

'Because the people who do the things are so complex. Tell me, do you feel that you are going to go on writing?'

'Oh, lord, yes. All the time at the Great House, all the time from when Twice died until the night of the bottle—'

Sashie laughed loudly and the sound rang out across the moonlit sea. 'I shall hereafter always treasure the Night of the Bottle as one of my historic moments,' he said.

'Well, all that time I thought that I would not write any more because it was a wrong thing to do, because – oh, I don't know what I thought but all the thinking was wrong and distorted anyway but now I know that of course I shall go on writing.'

'Then the sooner you go on the better. You have had one acceptance. Publishers do not like one-book authors. You should follow it up as quickly as you can.'

'You think so? Well, I have six more.'

'Six what?'

'Novels.'

'Where?'

'In that trunk.'

'But you said you burned all your manuscripts after your father died!'

'That was in December of 1955.'

'But this is only September of '58! People *don't* write six – no, seven – novels in less than three years, in two years, actually, for I am sure you were not writing while Twice was ill.'

'No, I wasn't,' I admitted, 'and maybe the things in the trunk are not novels but they all have about seventy-five thousand words in them. Besides, I only put them down on paper in the two years. As I told you, I have been writing on and off all my life.'

'And having periodic bonfires?'

'Yes. I had a fizzer in London before I joined the Air Force. It stuffed up the flue of the furnace in the basement and then I made the bottom fall out of a big dustbin as well with the weight of torn paper. But one remembers what one has written and what one wants to say so I said it all the more fluently when I started in on that lot through there in 1955.' I jerked my head in the direction of the passage where the trunk lay and Sashie laughed. 'What is so funny?' I asked.

'Darling, I adore you.'

'You are very civil. And you really think I should send these publishing people another one?'

'Yes, I really think so.'

'Mightn't they think I am being rather a nuisance? After all, it seems like trying to take advantage when they have been so kind about the first one.'

'Darling, I can hardly believe that you are so naïve about this and yet you honestly are. Listen, publishers are never *kind*. If they don't like the second one you send, it will come thumping back to you with a rejection slip or worse still, a polite letter taking twenty words to say they don't want it.'

'I shouldn't like that either,' I said. 'My novels are poor things but mine own. I think I shall wait a bit.'

'I never thought to see you faint of heart, darling. Nonsense! Tomorrow, we shall open that trunk, tie up a neat package and send it off.'

'We can't. All the scripts are in scribbly handwriting. Anything I send off, I have to type first. By the way, where is my typewriter? Still at Paradise?'

'No. You have not that excuse. It is in the cupboard in your bedroom.'

'The first thing I have to do, though, Sashie, is to write to my family. I wrote to them several times from Paradise but with the way I seem to have been going on. I may have written anything and I can't remember any of it.'

The next forenoon, I wrote the two letters, one to George and Tom, the other to my brother and sister-in-law, confessing that I had been ill but was now better and I also told my brother of the acceptance of my novel for publication. I did not tell George and Tom of this, however, for I felt that this news would bewilder them and I preferred to wait and tell them of it face to face. It was probably while writing that letter that I decided to return to Scotland but I was not aware of the decision at the time. I had even begun to toy with the idea of finding a little house somewhere in St. Jago, for the island had been my home for so long that I could not visualize any place for myself in the great world that lay beyond it.

The first response to my letters came from my niece Liz.

'Dear Aunt Janet, We were all sorry to hear that you have been sick and I thought I would write you a letter to cheer you up. We have just had Sandy-Tom's second birthday party and it was Mum and Dad and Granny and Aunt Sheila and Roddy and Fat Mary but not George and Tom because they are up north at Achcraggan. They were here when the cablegram came saying that Uncle Twice had died and then they went to Achcraggan and did not come back, not even through the whole summer holidays but Dad went up for a week-end to make sure they were all right and they are very well. Mum says to tell you that Sandy-Tom's hair is still bright red like you wanted it to stay and she will send you one of his birthday pictures that she took at the party. Roddy wrote another book and had his picture in the newspaper last Sunday and it said

110

Another Blast from an Angry Young Man so I am thinking about writing a book that will be a Blast from an Angry Young Woman. Dunk and Gee are all right but they play football all the time so this letter is just from Sandy-Tom and me. Love from Elizabeth and X Alexander-Thomas his mark. P.S. Please tell Mr. Sasha de Marnay which is a beautiful name to have that we thank him very much for looking after you.'

I handed the letter to Sashie. 'Better read it. There is a message for you,' I said.

When he looked up from his reading, his expressive eyes had lost much of their hard brilliance. 'How old is she?' he asked.

'Rising eleven and a very angry young woman indeed a lot of the time,' I said. 'She is a young-for-her-age child compared with those sophisticated little horrors who come to the Peak but she has plenty of character in her young-woman sort of way.'

'Just like her aunt indeed?'

'No, Sashie. I am not an angry young woman any more. In fact, I never was angry in the sense that Roddy is. And my novels are not angry either. Among all the blood, sex and social protest, my stuff is going to look pretty silly. That thing that Canterbury, Arden have got is going to fall as flat as a pancake.'

'Canterbury, Arden haven't stayed in a cut-throat business for over a hundred years by publishing pancakes,' Sashie said. 'Do let's open that trunk, darling.'

'No. Tomorrow maybe.'

Sashie did not insist and there was always tomorrow and every day as it came had its own interest. Silver Beach was a beautiful place and when my legs grew strong enough to carry me about, I spent a lot of time in the garden with Caleb.

'This is a wonderful piece of land, isn't it, Caleb?' I said one day, as I looked out over his vegetable beds by the stream to the acreage of bush coconuts, their dark green fronds shining in the sun as if each strand had been hand-polished.

111

'The best in St. Jago, ma'am,' he said with pride. 'You able to walk round to the house garden, ma'am?'

'Of course.'

The 'house garden' was a walled area that was almost part of the house itself. When Sashie had bought the property, this area had been a jungle of wild bush but this had been subdued by Caleb and much of the ground laid with flag-stones which turned it into a sort of patio that could be reached through french windows from the hall of the house or through a gate in the grey stone wall. At its centre, there was a cement-lined pool in which little jet-black fish which Caleb called 'mollies' swam about.

'Was up at Paradise yesterday, ma'am,' Caleb said and out of the shade by the wall he produced a battered bucket that was full of muddy wilted vegetation. 'Brought these back.'

I looked into the bucket and recognized water-lily plants from the Great House lake. I had imported them to the lake from a little village in the hills, a village called Siloam, where the lilies grew in profusion in a swamp by the River Pedro. It was so long ago and so much had happened since I had first seen the lilies of Siloam. 'Isn't stealing, me taking these from the lake, ma'am,' Caleb said, worried by my silence. 'In the beginning, the lilies at Paradise were yours and I only took three, one white, one red and one blue.'

'Of course it was all right to take them, Caleb,' I reassured him, 'there are hundreds in the lake now.'

'Only,' Caleb looked shame-faced. 'I forgot that this pool is a cement bottom and not a swamp. Will the lilies grow in the gully, ma'am?'

'I am afraid they would be washed away when the gully comes down in spate.'

Ruefully, Caleb looked down at the mess in the bucket and I sympathized with him and his shame that he had up-rooted plants only to let them die.

'Wait a minute,' I said, 'lilies *are* grown in artificial pools. You plant them in a bucket of earth and stone and sink them.'

'And what is that in that bucket, may one ask?' Sashie, arriving beside us, inquired. 'How very smelly.'

'We thought you might like some water lilies in your pool,' I told him.

'Lilies?' He looked sadly into the bucket. 'I *have* read somewhere that lilies when they fester smell worse than weeds. Do put them in at once if the pool will stop them festering.'

'Oh, you and your over-delicate nose!' I said impatiently. 'Let's go and find something to plant them in, Caleb. I wish we had some of my half-oildrums from Guinea Corner.'

'I got them, ma'am. I got Big Sammy and a truck from Chief Mackie and brought all our garden things down here to Silver Beach. Guinea Corner got no right to them things, I told Chief Mackie and he said the same.'

'Then let's get a half-drum and plant the lilies,' I said.

Caleb brought the drum to the side of the pool and filled it with earth and heavy compost while I held the lily roots in place. Sashie sat back in a deck-chair, immaculate in pale blue, watching while Caleb and I sloshed about among the mud. Then, having laid stones over the earth and roots, Caleb stepped into the pool and between us he and I lowered the drum into the water. Out of a cloud of mud, as the drum sank, the lily stems, having found their element, came swirling upwards until the broad pads were floating on the surface and at the centre of one group there was a half-open white bud, with golden stamens reaching for the sun. The little cloud of mud settled and the swirling stems stilled.

Sashie looked down at the green pads, the white bud. 'Thank you, good people,' he said. 'All I need now is a frog, that is really a fairytale prince, of course, to come and sit on those pads to wait for his princess to come and love him and turn him into a prince again. You two are great beautifiers of the earth, Janet,' he added as Caleb left to put away the tools we had used.

'Those lilies came originally from Siloam,' I told him. 'Remember Linda Lee? I never see a water lily without thinking of her.'

Caleb came back. 'And, ma'am, there is these coronations over here.'

'Coronation' was Caleb's name for the carnation which was difficult to grow in St. Jago but which, after much trial

113

and error, I had succeeded in growing from seed at Guinea Corner.

'They want doing to them what you used to do to them, ma'am but I ain't sure how to do it,' Caleb explained.

This was the 'stopping back' process by which the top of the slim seedling was pinched back at a joint to encourage more bushy growth.

'You want to take them just here, Caleb,' I said, pinching out the top of a seedling with my thumb and forefinger. 'And these are beautiful plants, far better than I ever had at Guinea Corner, Caleb.'

'You think so, ma'am. But everything grows good here. This is sweet land, ma'am.'

'Caleb is right,' I said to Sashie when we had gone in to lunch. 'This is sweet land everything grows good here. I find myself wondering now if that nightmare at the Great House really happened.'

'It happened,' Sashie said, 'but it was only a nightmare. What an instinctive grubber-about in the earth you are, Janet. To me, the transformation of that mess in the bucket into those beautiful plants in the pool was like a miracle.'

'I shall never be anything but a Highland crofter. As for the lilies, anything that is out of its own element looks a mess. A water plant needs water, that is all. Well,' I rose from the table, 'I think I shall go through and have a look through that rubbish in that trunk.'

Sashie stared at me before breaking into a broad smile. 'And an earth-grubber needs earth,' he said.

'What do you mean?'

'I have been stupid. I should have sent you out to grub about with Caleb long ago, my sweet. All right, be gone to your trunk. It won't disturb you if I tinkle my piano or play some records?'

'Of course not, especially if you play ballet music again.'

'You like Tchaikovsky?'

'Yes and all the other ballet music too.'

'So do I but then I am very light-minded and frivolous,' he said, 'and I like pretty miracles, such as princesses that turn into swans and frogs that turn into princes and messes that turn into water lilies.'

114

The steel trunk contained much more than the six brown paper parcels which held the manuscripts of my novels. Sashie and Caleb had packed into it all the paper material from the linen cupboard and back bedroom at Guinea Corner – old theatre programmes, old photographs, old diaries kept by both Twice and myself and all sorts of old rubbish. Among the photographs was a large coloured one of a painting, a painting that no longer existed, having been destroyed by fire many years ago. I laid this photograph on the floor beside the trunk, thinking that the story of it might amuse Sashie and began to undo the strings on the parcels of manuscript. After some time, I selected one sheaf of paper, decided to read it through, to consider putting it into typescript and then put the other papers back and locked the trunk.

When I went through to the veranda, I was amazed to discover that it was tea time and I remembered, as if rediscovering a lost pleasure, that I always went out of time into another dimension when I was engaged in my writing activities.

'Sorry,' I said to Sashie. 'I got involved in all that rubbish.' I propped the photograph on its stiff mount against the wall. 'I thought this might amuse you,' I said.

Sashie stared at the head and shoulders of the 'Peasant Girl' as the painting had been called.

'Janet, you were something of a beauty!' he said after a moment. 'How old were you when that was painted?'

'Why are you so sure it is a painting of me?'

'Of course it is you!' he said almost angrily.

'I was in my early twenties. The thing is that it was painted without my knowledge. I did not sit for it and when it was identified as a portrait of me it caused me more embarrassment than you could shake a stick at.'

'Is the original at your home?'

'Lord, no. That was destroyed in a fire in Chicago years ago but Monica's old Cousin Egbert had a photograph of the original painting and he had that copy made for Twice but I would never have it around. The whole thing was too embarrassing.' I felt embarrassment flood over me even now and wished that I had left the thing in the darkness of the trunk.

'How did it come to be painted?' Sashie asked.

'Oh, this young man, the artist, was staying with friends in Achcraggan and I – well—'

'I know,' he said. 'Before you knew it you were luring the unfortunate young man to his doom—' he looked at the photograph again – 'and quite a lure, I must say. And then the moment came when, as Twice used to say, you opened your great big eyes and said: Go away, you bloody fool!'

'No, I didn't. It was far worse than that. He got all intense one day and I didn't say a word. I was so taken aback that I just ran like a stag. Lord, what a fool I was when young, Sashie. I am sure you never were just as plain stupid as I was.'

'I didn't get as much time to be stupid as you did, my sweet. I went into the Air Force in 1939 when I was twenty-two.'

'And I was twenty-nine in 1939. I often forget that you are seven years younger than I am, Sashie. You often seem older.'

'That is most impolite of you,' he said and then: 'Actually, I used to be a lot older than you but the gap is closing. I was a hundred years older than you were when we first met at the airport in 1950. I shall never forget that day. I felt as if I had been stunned.'

'Stunned? I don't remember it like that. You didn't act like somebody stunned. You hopped about like a flea on a blanket.'

'Oh, that.' Sashie looked away towards the horizon. 'You were wearing a white dress. It had no sleeves and a wide skirt that was about calf-length—'

'What was known as the New Look, God save the mark.'

'—and white flat-heeled shoes, so very unusual in those days.'

'Because of Twice,' I explained. 'High heels made me look taller than he was because I was so skinny and he was so broad.'

'You came down out of the aircraft and walked a few steps along the tarmac and then did the most extraordinary

116

thing. You rose on to your points, raised your right arm and pointed away into the distance. You seemed to dominate the whole airport.'

'There was nothing so extraordinary, except to *me*. I remember what it was,' recalling the surprise and joy of that moment. 'It was these extraordinary St. Jagoan hills. I had never before seen hills – mountains – with trees growing right to their tops. It was as if I had landed in fairyland.'

'Where did you learn to rise like that?' Sashie asked.

'Rise?'

'On to the points of your toes. Did you go to ballet school as a child?'

'Ballet in Ross-shire in my childhood?' I laughed at him. 'I didn't know ballet existed until after I went to university. No. Betsy taught me to stand like that.'

'Betsy?'

'The plough mare at Reachfar.'

'A *horse*?'

'Yes. When one took Betsy into the dung midden to load her cart or, indeed, anytime one asked her to stand still, she would put her off fore up on the point of its shoe.' I rose from my chair and put one foot on its toe. 'I thought it looked pretty and I began to stand like that too. By the way, it was a trick that little Percy Soames had. She often stood with her right foot on its toe. But to go back – I was always being told that although Betsy was very clever, she was still only an animal and that people ought to be cleverer than animals, so I began putting my other foot on its toe which Betsy never did. Then I discovered that I could stand with both feet on their toes, which made me tall enough to reach things I had never been able to reach before, like the high shelf of the kitchen cupboard where Granny kept the jar of sweets.' I stood on both toes and reached up to the beam of the veranda roof. 'Here endeth the history of my training in ballet.'

'I had never imagined that the day would come when I would feel indebted to a horse,' Sashie said.

'Indebted? What do you mean?'

'Indebted for that stunning shining moment at the airport.'

He was still looking out towards the sea and spoke as if to himself. 'It was so long since I had—' He frowned, broke off abruptly, turned to face me and took a new direction. 'What is that bundle of papers in your lap, darling? Or shouldn't one ask?'

'A manuscript. I thought I would read it through and see what I think of it. Not that it will do any good for I shall never know what I think of it except that it is not as good as it ought to be but the best I can do. You know how the Negroes say: Every John Crow t'ink 'im pickney white? Well, I think all my children are perfect too. Obviously. I wouldn't have written them like that if I did not think it was the best way I could write them. But it means that I have no standard of criticism with regard to them. As I said, they are just poor things but mine own. That apart, I haven't got your critical sense about anything, anyway.'

'Am I critical?'

'Don't be ridiculous. You bend a very beady critical eye on everybody and everything.'

'Then let me bend it on that manuscript.'

'No. Mind your own business,' I said.

With the coming of September, the cooler weather had come too and at Silver Beach, of course there was always a breeze from the sea. And with the cooler weather, the rich tourists came to the island, filling the Peak Hotel to capacity. Although ostensibly retired from the management of the hotel, Sashie went along there once or twice in the week and Caleb went there three or four evenings a week to entertain the guests by singing the island folk songs to the accompaniment of his guitar. I did not go beyond the boundaries of Silver Beach but spent all my time in the garden or among my papers and was utterly content in a way that I have never known since I was less than ten years old.

'I suppose it is old age,' I said to Sashie.

'Or that, at last, you are doing what you really want to do. How is the script?'

'I wish I knew but I think I shall put it into type and have a go,' I said, and now I sat in my bedroom, rattling my typewriter all day while Sashie came and went and amused himself in his own many ways.

118

One day, he went off to the hotel after lunch and came back just as the six o'clock darkness was falling over the sea. We always spent the evenings on the veranda together and I finished the page I was typing, covered my machine for the night and came out to join him.

'Well, how is your bordello at the Peak?' I asked.

'As ever,' he said. 'Mrs. Goldfine arrived this forenoon. Old Goldfine has died since last year but she is not letting it worry her. She has a very handsome young gent with her, Italian blood, I should say and very very expensive to maintain, I should think, but she can afford him. But I don't think you have met Mrs. Goldfine.'

Goldfine. Why did the name make me think of the words 'vice under the potted palms' as if it were the title of a play like 'Desire under the Elms'? Vice under the potted palms.

'What did you say?' Sashie asked.

'Did I say something?' It was possible that I had spoken aloud, for I often spoke parts of my manuscripts aloud while typing them and now that I had shaken off my years of secrecy about my writing, I might have carried the thinking-aloud habit beyond the orbit of my bedroom and my typewriter.

'You said "vice under the potted palms",' Sashie said, and I shrugged my shoulders. 'Just a passing thought. Tell me more of Mrs. Goldfine.'

'There is little to tell. She is just one more very very rich very very dumb blonde.'

Instead of Sashie's light voice, I seemed to hear the deep voice of Twice speak the last words and I said, as I had said to Twice long ago: 'Dumb blonde nothing' as memory came flooding back. 'I know that woman,' I told Sashie next. 'The last time I saw her was years ago, at dinner at Paradise Great House.'

'Darling, you must be mistaken. Madame Dulac would never have entertained Mrs. Goldfine. Besides, they have been coming to the Peak for the last four years and old Goldfine never stopped talking but he never mentioned Paradise.'

'He wore oblong rimless glasses and was madly interested

in vice,' I said. ' "If ya wanta get ta vice," he said, "ya gotta be prepared ta get right ta the battam – ta bedrawck." '

'Bless my soul, you did meet the Goldfines, my sweet. How very extraordinary.'

'Madame was entertaining them for business reasons. Old Goldfine was a drainage-equipment-higher-levels-of-muck-shifting millionaire, wasn't he?'

'And a vice millionaire as well,' said Sashie. 'In his latter days he made a fortune out of the vice, writing books about it, you know. He wrote the books in a missionary spirit, to preach to people how wicked vice was but I am sure he inadvertently taught his readers all about vices that they hadn't previously known to exist. Anyhow, his works on vice were the most talked-of literary events in the United States since the Kinsey Report.'

'Just fancy,' I said. 'One day I must write a book entitled WRITERS I HAVE MET. And Mrs. Goldfine is a widow now?'

'Yes, but you would never notice it. Would you like to meet her again, Janet? If it would amuse you, come to the Peak with me tomorrow.'

'No, thank you, Sashie. Let the past keep its ghosts and the potted palms their vice. It is extraordinary how one's mind works. I remembered the name Goldfine in an aura of potted palms at the Great House and the old man's lecture on vice.'

'I should prefer to say that it is extraordinary how *your* mind works,' Sashie said.

'Doesn't everybody flounder about in a web of association and allusion? Don't *you*?'

'Not quite to the extent that you do, I think.'

'Twice used to say it was something to do with my memory. He said that I remembered further back and in more detail and with more continuity than most people. How clearly do you remember your childhood, Sashie?'

'I remember only little bits here and there, mostly things that I didn't like, like the time I was at prep school in Surrey.'

'How old were you then?'

'About ten. I am not sure.'

'But you *must* remember what age you were!' I protested.

'Please don't bully me, darling. I do *not* remember precisely. All I know is that they sent me there for part of a term and I did not like it and they took me away and everything was all right.'

'And you went to another school?'

'No. Not in England. A tutor came in and gave me lessons and Mama and I played the piano a lot, or *she* played it mostly and she read to me and was very beautiful. The time I remember most clearly was when we lived in Paris. I suppose I was about twelve when we went to Paris from London. My parents moved around quite a bit. My father was something to do with banking.'

'You mean that you don't *know* exactly what he did?'

'No. Why should I? He was out during the days, came home in the evenings and then he and Mama dressed and they went out.'

'And you were left all alone in the house?'

I was remembering the fuss I had made at about four years old when my father did not come home for six o'clock supper and my family was trying to send me to bed in the midst of this terrible insecurity of my father not being in the house.

'An apartment,' Sashie said, 'and there were people in the kitchen. I liked it. I used to read until I became sleepy and then go to sleep looking forward to the next afternoon. I went to school in the forenoon – but this school in Paris was all right – and came home to have lunch with Mama and then we would have the afternoon together until Papa came home. If it was fine, we went out but it was better when it rained because then Mama would tell about the night before. If she had been to a concert, she would play some of the music to me. If it had been a dinner, she would mimic all the people who had been there. She was very mischievous. And if she had been to the opera or the ballet or a play, we would do the performance all over again in my puppet theatre, only she and I acted all the love scenes and quarrels and scenes for two people ourselves. She was very small. At eleven or twelve years old, I was as tall as she was.' He shook his head suddenly, as if awaking from sleep. 'Bless my

121

soul, darling, I am talking what Twice would have called a blue streak. I am turning into a bore.'

'Quite the reverse, in a favourite phrase of your own,' I told him. 'I find it fascinating because it is so different from my own upbringing. Did you like school?'

'I liked the one in Paris. I stayed on there after my parents went back to live in London again. I liked England for holidays.'

'With me, school was the thing. I loved it. And after school, what then?'

'Nothing much. I travelled around – Europe, the States. I amused myself and other people too, I think. I found that I had a slight talent, for being amusing.'

'And then there was the war and then you came out here?'

'Yes. All very dull really, my sweet.'

'No, not dull but fascinating and different. There is something I have never thought of until now. I don't think I knew that plays or theatres existed until I was about eleven or twelve years old, while you were working a puppet theatre at that age.'

'Oh, far far earlier, darling. I cannot remember *not* having the puppet theatre. Mama loved the theatre, you see. She made all the costumes for our puppets and we made all the furniture and painted the scenery. If she had been born a little later, I think she might have been a stage designer or producer or something of the sort. But she married Papa before she was twenty and it was all very proper,' he told me smiling and then with a swoop into the present, he added: 'Janet, although you are nearly fifty, you look very young sometimes. Just now, you were like a child listening to a fairy tale.'

'Probably because, to me, it sounded like a fairy tale. It all sounds so different from Reachfar and yet there are similarities too. George and Tom used to mimic all the people we knew like your mother mimicking the people at the dinner parties.'

Sashie and I spent many evenings talking in this easy way comfortably and happily interested in one another. Sometimes, while I was drinking the tea that Trixie brought to me about six each morning, I would stand back, as it were, and examine the relationship between Sashie and myself, but I could never fit it into any of the accepted categories. It was not a love affair but it was more than a friendship in the accepted sense of that word and it was more easy and in a curious way more intimate than any relationship I had ever known. Sometimes I had the feeling that I was rediscovering Sashie, that I had known him in some former time, in the time of 'always' to use the word of my childhood, so that I had fleeting moments of belief in the reincarnation theory of Madame Zora, an old fortune-teller I had once met, which made me think that I must have known Sashie, as she would have said, 'in a former life'.

Once the day's work at Silver Beach had begun, however, ethereal theories were dispersed by the bright light and the household became very mundane and busy. While I rattled at my typewriter, Sashie would tinkle his piano in his own suite of rooms across the hall, then pause and I would know that one more island melody was being written down. Sometimes I would hear Caleb being told to come in with his guitar and Caleb's singing voice would drop its liquid notes into the sunlight. At other times, Sashie's record-player would take charge and I would stop typewriting for a little to listen to Tchaikovsky, Chopin or Debussy. I did not inquire into Sashie's activities, for he was as secretive about his doings as I was about my writing, an idiosyncrasy which I understood and in addition to this, Sashie was so knowledgeable about music, painting and many other things that I tended to stand back from him in these areas of my own ignorance with a sort of respectful shyness. During the daytime, we met only for meals or occasionally in some part of Caleb's cultivation. If Caleb came to ask my advice about some gardening matter, Sashie and Trixie would join us and look on at what we were doing but they did not take part. Trixie, although reared in the 'bush', where her family grew bananas, citrus and other fruit, had the peasant woman's attitude to the earth – the attitude that my grandmother had had – that to grow crops was to work for the menfolk, an attitude that was, I suppose, as old as Eden.

123

The other member of the household was old 'Gahta' the cook. Her name was Agatha but she herself pronounced it '*Gah*ta' and the rest of us followed suit. In her earlier days, she had worked at the Peak Hotel but Sashie had retired her along with himself to Silver Beach. She still wore the old-fashioned scarlet head-cloth of the island women and she managed us all. 'Missus Janet, you come in de house outa dat sun' she would command or: 'Mars Sashie, sah, why you go spoil you' pretty blue pants wid all dat yallah paint?' she would question with severity. She was very small and wrinkled and wizened and permanently worried by the 'great bigness' of Caleb. 'Eff you wanna joke aroun' wid Trixie,' she would say, 'take yo' great big feets outa ma kitchen' or 'I want da bottle *open* jus' – not all mashed up wid you' great big hands!'

'We look much more aesthetic,' Sashie said, 'when I pair off with Trixie and you pair off with Caleb. Yet I like you and Caleb likes Trixie. Isn't humanity awkward, darling?'

For Trixie was pretty and tiny, reaching only to a point midway between Caleb's elbow and his shoulder.

'I wonder when Caleb and Trixie intend to get married?' I said. 'He must have quite a bit in the bank by now, with all his guitar-playing at the Peak, probably enough to buy his lickle piece o' lan'.'

Caleb's ambition, the ambition of every Negro in the island, was to own a 'little piece of land', an ambition which I, a Highland crofter, could understand with the deep understanding of the blood.

'You are going to miss him when he goes, Sashie, but at least he has licked this place into shape and it is only a question of keeping it in order now.'

It was evening again and talking time, after a day spent in our diverse ways and Sashie looked out at a flower border in the fading light before he said: 'I have been turning that over in my tiny mind.'

'And Caleb is going to miss this place too,' I said. 'No matter where in the island he goes, he is never going to find a piece of land as good as this. As this property now stands, Sashie, you could get three times what you have invested in it.'

'To be precise, darling, five times,' Sashie said coolly and continued: 'The question is whether one wants five times and I don't. I merely want to be able to live here when I want to, when I am not in London or New York or wherever.'

'It is a long time since you have been to London or New York.'

Sashie loved to travel by air and had been in the habit of making several trips abroad each year. 'That is because of me. It has been on my conscience.'

'Then get it off your conscience. One always can find excuses for doing the thing that one most wants to do and if I preferred to stay here because of you to taking a trip abroad, I have the right to indulge myself. Coming back to Caleb and this place, I have been thinking of some sort of arrangement whereby Caleb would pay me a deposit and so much rent each month as long as we both live and then when I shuffle off, Silver Beach would be his.'

'But Caleb could *never* rent this place!' I said.

'When I say rent, I mean a peppercorn sort of thing. We live in a money society as you and I have agreed before and people live by money values and values are the light by which they see. If Caleb does not pay some money for this place – money that costs him some effort – he will cease to see its value but if he had to grow vegetables on it to pay the rent that will make it his own one day, he will grow vegetables like crazy, darling.'

'You mean that you are thinking of practically giving this place *away* to Caleb?'

'Only after I am dead and it is mine to give away if I want to. But I think it is better to give it away over a longish term – I hope to live for a bit yet, you know – and give Caleb the feeling that, if he works for it, Silver Beach will be his one day. I think the lawyer fellahs, as Sir Ian calls them, could draw up the kind of agreement I have in mind.'

I looked beyond the veranda screens to where the sudden tropic dark had blotted out the flower bed, the grass, the sea and I thought of the acres of sweet earth, the rising spring behind the house, the gully that flowed rich in water when rain fell in the hills inland and the well-established coconut

125

walk. Silver Beach was, to a St. Jagoan like Caleb, a veritable Eden.

'You are terribly generous, Sashie,' I said, 'and I want to say thank you, not for Caleb but for myself. I love that boy and I feel responsible for him. I don't think he will ever let you down, Sashie.'

'There is only one thing he may do and for that I forgive him in advance,' Sashie said, smiling at me. 'He may alter the name of Silver Beach to Reachfar. But do not tell me in that soulful way that I am generous. One's motives for doing anything are never pure.'

I disregarded this last. 'So many wonderful things have happened since that night of the bottle,' I said, using the phrase that always made Sashie laugh uproariously.

'I have begun to think of myself as your Knight of the Bottle,' he told me now. '*So* whimsical.'

'You look more like a genie than a knight,' I commented. 'It is not that so *many* things have happened since that night but that everything is different, as if I had been born all over again. Thursday, the fourth of September, 1958, it was. That's odd. I was born originally on a Thursday.'

'How very satisfactory, my sweet. So was I.'

'Were you really? Remember the rhyme: Monday's child is fair of face—?'

'No. I have never heard that. Go on.'

'Monday's child is fair of face, Tuesday's child is full of grace,
Wednesday's child is full of woe, Thursday's child has far to go.
Friday's child is loving and giving, Saturday's child works hard for his living –
Sunday's child dee-dah, dee-dah—

'I can't remember but Sunday's child was very good and angelic, though.'

'I am acutely aware of not having gone very far as yet,' Sashie said, 'but you give me new hope with your rhyme. Maybe there is yet time.'

'I wonder how much effect that rhyme has had on my

character and my life?' I said. 'I am sure it has done something Freudian and awful to me. When I got into bother at Reachfar, my grandmother used to say: Now then, my leddy, you have gone quite far enough! And I used to think that it was because of being born on a Thursday that I went so far that I got into bother.'

'You have known the rhyme since you were a child?'

'I was brought up on it. My birth was a big event at Reachfar, not because of me but because Reachfar's first pedigreed Clydesdale foal got herself born during the same night – Betsy, who taught me to stand on my toes – so that Thursday was marked on the family mind. How did you come to know that you were born on a Thursday, Sashie?'

'Because Mama wished me a happy birthday every Thursday.'

'She must have been enchanting!'

'She was exactly that – not really beautiful, although I thought her the loveliest creature in the world but she had the power to enchant.'

Much of the time and by intent, Sashie gave the impression that he was not made of flesh and blood but there was no doubt of his human composition when he spoke of his mother and, liking him in this mood, I longed to ask more about her but I did not dare. I felt that I was privileged in that he had spoken of her to me at all for, as a rule, he behaved as if he had no antecendents, no connection with the human race, as if he were a depersonalized commentator whose function it was to make the race aware of its foibles and failings. This attitude made people, including myself, a little afraid of him, as people of a primitive tribe might be afraid of the voice of a cricket commentator issuing from a wireless set, so I did not ask personal questions of Sashie but contented myself with gleaning every scrap that fell.

One evening, after I had spent a long day at the typewriter, he came back from the hotel at dusk as usual, hopped gaily on to the veranda and said: 'A new guest arrived at the Peak today and he asked about *you*, darling.'

'Me? Who is he?'

'A figure from your past. Darling, *don't* look so haunted!

127

He isn't a blackmailer I should say, but quite the reverse. He had a *look* in his eye.'

'Stop being so silly. Who is he? What sort of look?'

'The look of a man who has come to journey's end and sees the longed-for haven in sight at last.'

'Sashie de Marnay—'

'His name is Sir Hugh Reid, darling.'

Suddenly the warm dusk that was falling over the blue sea was transformed into the cold, dank grey mist of evening over the High Street of Cairnton, a little town in south Scotland and Hugh and I, children, were standing side by side while our two dogs, Paddy and Fly, chased a group of louts and hoydens, squealing with terror, along the pavement.

'What a *mercy*,' Sashie was saying, 'that I was in the reception office when he came in and asked about you. If Don had been there, he would have said: Oh, Janet? She's out at Silver Beach living with Sashie de Marnay and that would have ruined everything.'

'Ruined what?' I asked but Sashie swept on. 'But *I*, being a little monster of tact, not to say double-dealing, said I thought you were staying with friends somewhere and that I had heard you had not been very well but that if he really wanted to see you, I would find out what I could. And he *does* really want to see you. He is most *anxious* to see you and he had that *look*, darling, so I thought you ought to be warned.'

'Oh, shut up! You and your looks! Hugh Reid isn't here because of me at all. He is here because of – of Mrs. Goldfine.'

'Mrs. *Gold*fine?' Standing in front of me, Sashie bent on me a dark baffled stare which filled me with glee because bafflement was so rare in him. 'What *can* Sir Hugh Reid, that pillar of respectability, have in common with, not to put too fine a point on it, that demi-mondaine?'

'Why should you think she is a demi-mondaine? Lots of wealthy women these days travel with a male companion. I do it myself here at Silver Beach except that I am not travelling and I am not wealthy.'

'I do wish you wouldn't be so quibbling and muddling. I am an old man of over forty, darling, and I can recognize a tart when I see one although old Goldfine, blinded by vice, could not. Now, give with the tale of Sir Hugh and Annette.'

'She was christened Annie Black,' I said. 'She and Hugh were fathered by the same man, Annie in wedlock, Hugh out of it. All three of us went to the same school. You are right, of course. Annie has been a tart from the age of sixteen but Hugh has always taken an interest in her. I don't know whether the interest is because she is his half-sister or whether it is because he has always been a dedicated helper of lame dogs.'

'I should never have called Annette a lame dog.'

'Hugh sees her that way but then Hugh Reid could not be more different from *you*,' I said.

'That is true,' Sashie agreed solemnly. 'Hugh Reid and I are very very different. He is very respectable, Janet. I have to tell you—' He became heavily sententious '—as a candid *friend*, darling, that I don't think he is in the *least* suited to you.'

'Oh, stop that, Sashie.'

His manner changed again, became sincere. 'Janet, you can be very stupid in certain situations with regard to yourself. You know that. In my capacity as your cicisbeo – don't you think that delicious word describes me *exactly* in every possible way? – as your cicisbeo, I repeat, I have to warn you that that man Reid is carrying a torch for you, as they used to say in my youth.'

'Rubbish.'

As if I had not spoken, Sashie continued: 'I do not want you to be taken by surprise by it, so that in your obliging way, because you want everybody to have what *they* want, you say: Oh, all right, Hugh. I don't mind if I do.' He paused, cocked his head and went on: 'Are you listening to what I say? He is a very eligible parti for a middle-aged woman and I want you to *think*, Janet.'

'I am thinking and what I am thinking is that you have built a fabrication on nothing but an imagined look in a man's eye. How very romantic you are, Sashie!'

The last words were chosen to annoy him and they achieved their end.

'Let me know if you wish to see this man and I shall

arrange it,' he said shortly and went away to his rooms.

He did not re-appear until dinnertime which was two hours later and I spent the two hours thinking about Hugh Reid and also about what Sashie had said. Although I had treated the 'look in the eye' with scorn, I had an uneasy feeling that scorn was not in order and that the perceptive Sashie could be right. Hugh and I had always been fond of one another, although in recent years our only contact had been by letter once a year at Christmas or even more seldom. However, the more I thought of the matter, the more certain I became that I did not want an involvement of this kind. Now that I had accepted the death of Twice, I could look back on our time together with happiness from a new standpoint of peace and freedom and I was not going to give this up in exchange for a middle-aged relationship with Hugh Reid.

At dinner, Sashie was silent and distant and I waited until we were drinking coffee on the veranda before I said: 'If you are right about Hugh Reid, Sashie, I *do* mind if I do and I ought to thank you for warning me.'

'You would make a very dignified Lady Reid,' he said.

'And how do you think I would be on the cosy chats with people like Helen Hallinzeil? God, what a bore that woman was!'

Lady Hallinzeil was a member of Hugh's circle who had visited the island some years before.

'They could not all be like Lady Hallinzeil.'

'Look here, will you make up your mind?' I asked. 'Do you *want* me to marry Hugh Reid? If *he* wants it, that is?'

'My mind doesn't come into it. Yours is the mind to be made up.'

'Well, it is made up and stop telling me how desirable an end Hugh is for me. I am not nearly at an end yet.'

Sashie smiled for the first time since he had become angry in the early evening. 'Thursday's child with far to go,' he said. 'I wonder if poor Reid was born on a Wednesday?'

'Let's drop it, Sashie.'

'That side of it, yes. But I do think you ought to see him.'

'Lord, yes. The best thing will be for you to take me along to the Peak next time you are going.'

'No, my sweet. I shall give him our telephone number here and if he wants to invite you to the Peak, he may. Then Caleb can drive you along. In this context, I wish to remain in my character of eccentric hotelier.'

'Aren't you being a little complex, not to say silly, about this, Sashie?'

'If I am, that is how I am,' he said with finality.

'When I think of meeting Mrs. Goldfine,' I said next, 'I almost wish I had taken all those rings that Madame Dulac wanted me to have. The last time I saw Annie she was encrusted in diamonds.'

'She still is. What rings did Madame want you to have?'

'Three of those half-hoops she used to wear and the black enamel creepy-crawly with the hair inside it. Actually, she did not so much want me to have them as Anna *not* to have them.'

'But you didn't have them?'

'No. Silly, really. I could have flogged them for quite a bit, I suppose. But the very thought of them still makes me shudder. And that old woman scrabbling about among a few diamonds even when she was dying. It was all so – so ignoble.'

'How romantic of you,' said Sashie, getting his own back, 'to be disappointed that people are ignoble'.

But I was thinking of those dark days and darker nights at the Great House. 'But for you, Sashie, I would be in a loony bin by now.'

'What I fear is that, if you are not discreet, your so respectable admirer will think that you are already in one or that, if you are not, you ought to be.'

'I don't know what is the matter with you, Sashie de Marnay,' I said. 'What in the world does it matter what Hugh Reid thinks?'

'It just occurs to me that it matters in the world because he is of the world. When I brought you here from Paradise, darling, it was because I could think of no other thing to do with you. You were literally not fit to be at large. The island tittle-tattle does not matter but—'

'—you would prefer the tittle-tattle not to reach Helen Hallinzeil and the like?' I broke in. 'Listen, Sashie, that lot

131

are no part of my future as I see it. I think Hugh and his respectability have distorted your vision. I am a novelist now, remember? The Hallinzeils of this world are suspicious of even the lowest flights of the arts as you yourself have pointed out more than once.'

'How *do* you see your future, darling?'

'Among my family and a little of the publishing people and a bit of *you* of course, when you feel like it.'

'Of course?' he asked.

'Yes, of course.' I took thought for a moment, looking at his claret-coloured trousers and pale pink silk shirt. 'You would be a riot at Jemima Cottage, Achcraggan,' I added.

'We shall deal with that riot when we come to it,' he said with dignity. 'For me, the important thing is that I should be part of your future as a matter of course.'

'You haven't been thinking that one day I would leave this island and forget all about you?'

'Not exactly but certain people belong in certain parts of one's life and not in others. Somehow, the coming of your Hugh Reid made me aware that you had to be free to cast off what no longer belongs.'

'I think that you will always belong, Sashie, but the time has come to cast off Hugh Reid.'

'So I shall give him the telephone number?'

'Yes and I shall be ever so discreet and respectable but cast-offish. It sounds ruthless, but there it is.'

Hugh Reid telephoned me the following day and I went to dinner with him that evening at the Peak Hotel. I had long been familiar with this place, had once stayed here and had spent many hours in it down the ensuing years but, now, it seemed unfamiliar and strangely alien. Hugh and I dined alone while, at the other side of the room, Mrs. Goldfine, who had been known to Twice and me ironically as my friend Annie, glittered with diamonds, her beautiful eyes wide and blank, seemingly unaware of the conversation of her handsome sombre-eyed young escort. She did not recognize me and I did not make myself known to her. There was no point. Annie, as always, seemed to be entirely inside herself, self-contained in her beauty, like a flower.

From the moment of my meeting with Hugh, it was

obvious to me that Sashie, as usual, had been correct in his interpretation of 'the look in the eye' of Hugh and while he talked to me I was aware, almost as of a physical presence, of black satirical eyes and a mocking laugh in the corner behind our table. Hugh spoke of Twice, offered some conventional words of sympathy, explained that he had heard of his death from Sir Ian whom he had met at dinner along with Edward and Anna '—at Lady Hallinzeil's,' he said. 'You remember her, Janet?'

'I shall never forget her,' I told him.

There was a little more chat of Lady Hallinzeil, of Cairnton and then of Reachfar, which Hugh had visited once, long ago.

'It was sold some years ago,' I said, 'when my father, George and Tom got too old to cope with it.'

'And your father is dead too, Janet? You are very much on your own now, aren't you? That odd chap de Marnay who runs this place said that you had been ill, too.'

'Yes, I was for a bit. I got a bit run-down I suppose, but I am all right now.'

'You look too thin to me. You want looking after.'

It was all so banal, so boring that it made my mind yawn but at the same time I was ashamed of myself for this disloyal reaction to my old friend Hugh who had always been so kind. Yet, there, just behind his black-coated shoulder, was that satirical mocking presence.

'I can look after myself, Hugh,' I said. 'If I can't have Twice any more, I like being on my own. I have no definite plans as yet but life will shape itself for me. It always does.'

'You will probably marry again,' he said. 'Have you thought of that?'

'No and I don't think it probable.' I looked hard into his face and laughed. I felt a little cruel, for I was annoyed that he could see no future for a woman like me except marriage. 'I have never been the marrying sort, really, if you remember.'

He looked discomfited at this reminder of my free liaison with Twice but pushed the discomfiture aside and began: 'Ever since we were at school, Janet—'

He had an air of determination to make an honest woman

of me even against my will if need be and I was looking over his shoulder now at that mocking presence. To end its mockery, I said firmly: 'We have all come a long way from school and Cairnton, Hugh and you and Annie and I belong to different worlds.' I looked across the room towards Annie and her young man. 'She is as much like a flower as ever,' I added. 'Apart, beautiful and silent. How is she?'

'I have hardly spoken to her. After she married Goldfine, I lost touch with her. I knew she was all right. I knew vaguely that they used to spend part of the winter in St. Jago but it was a surprise to find her here. I only stopped in on my way to New York.'

Presumably he had come from London and if so, he had chosen a roundabout route to New York but I did not comment on this for the mocking presiding genius was no longer mocking but seemed to be exuding a sort of rueful pity for Hugh.

'Annie is all right,' Hugh repeated, almost huffily, as if everyone except himself was 'all right'.

'She will always be all right,' I assured him. 'And now I must go, Hugh.'

'Shall I see you again, Janet?'

'Quite probably,' I told him. 'Sooner or later I shall be in London, I suppose. In London, one meets everyone one ever knew.'

I was glad to get into the car beside Caleb and be driven back to Silver Beach where Sashie was waiting on the veranda.

'Well, darling, I die to know how it went.'

'Tediously enough, I think you were right about the look in his eye.'

'Of course I was right but how did it go?'

'For me, it was like an old song and rather a boring tuneless one at that.'

'Bon soir, tristesse, was it, my sweet?'

'Not really. More boring than sad. Hugh has come a long way, as they say and yet in my way of looking at things, he has just stood still. Very boring.'

'He is very distinguished *looking* though – you have to admit that – with all that white hair.'

134

'Is it white? I didn't notice.'

'Oh, God,' said Sashie, 'this is a requiem indeed.'

Hugh telephoned again the following day but I did not agree to meet him and Sashie read his name in the *Island Sun*, in the list of departures by air for New York the morning afterwards. 'Welladay and ah me, he is gone,' he said.

'Yes and bon jour, relief,' I said, holding up my glass of orange juice. 'Here's to the ghosts of the past and may they rest in peace. Are you going into town today?'

'Yes. Why?'

'If I parcel up that typescript, will you post it for me?'

'With éclat, darling, and by air at my expense. I can't wait for them to write back saying—'

'Shut up,' I interrupted him. 'Don't you go forecasting what they will say. You may have been right about the look in Hugh Reid's eyes but you haven't seen these publishers' eyes.'

'I feel things in my bones too, my sweet.'

'You and your bones,' I said and went to my room.

After he had gone away with the parcel, however, and I had put the copied manuscript back into the trunk, the table in my room looked bare, the typewriter lonely, sitting there with no heaps of paper around it, so I took a new parcel from the trunk, opened it and began to read through another two hundred pages of manuscript.

It was exhilarating to be able to sit down at will like this and begin to read with no qualms of conscience about the things I might have left undone. At Silver Beach, Sashie had turned my system of living inside out by making no demands on me except the implicit one that I should go on with my writing. His attitude was the opposite of every attitude that I ever encountered, just as the young life he described was as different as possible from my own young life at Reachfar. It was true that, like him, I had had a loving mother and, indeed, a loving family of seven members all told but none of these people would have spent an afternoon playing with me, as Sashie's mother had played with him. My play with the grown-up members of my family was always combined with some useful form of activity so that, while my mother amused me by teaching me to knit, there was the end-product in the form of a woollen scarf for my grandfather.

At Reachfar, reading and the writing of letters were restricted to Sundays and any other times when there was no other work to be done but these other times were theory only. My grandmother could always find some socks to be darned or some shirts to be patched so that, if I felt like writing a rhyme, as I frequently did, I had to do it in secret in one of my many hiding-places.

Along with the restriction to 'useful' activity went the training in duty. I was brought up to understand that, when my education had been completed, I would have to work for my living and my attitude to this work was carefully conditioned by commandments such as: 'If you undertake to do a thing, do it as best you can' and 'Never take pay from anyone without giving full value for it and a little bit more.'

The result of this was that, when I was old enough to begin to work for my living, which I did in the main in the homes of my employers as children's nurse, governess, secretary, if I retired to my bedroom and tried to write, I was haunted by a sense of guilt that there was some chore connected with my post that I had left undone, by the feeling that I was doing something that my employer would disapprove of in a nurse, governess or secretary. And, later, when Twice had voiced categorically his disapproval of my writing, it had become still more of a guilty secret.

This new feeling of being able to do what I wanted to do against a background of approval and encouragement was, as I have said, an exhilarating thing which made me work at tremendous speed and with immense enjoyment. The days began with a sense of adventure, ended in a slight sense of achievement and I went to sleep already looking forward to a new effort on a new day.

Having read the second manuscript and having made a few amendments, I embarked on a new orgy at the typewriter while the smooth-flowing life of Silver Beach went on around me and when my fingers grew tired I would go out-of-doors to find Caleb and see the latest developments in his cultivation.

It was late one afternoon, while Sashie was at the hotel,

when Caleb and I were kneeling by the pool, looking at the water lilies and the little black mollies that the boy said: 'Please, ma'am, Mars Sashie told you about Silver Beach and me?'

'Yes, Caleb. At least he told me a little of what he was planning.'

'We went to the lawyer when I took Mars Sashie to town today,' he said. 'It is all fixed, ma'am – not the papers, I mean. The law man is going to write the papers and then Mars Sashie and me will sign them but between Mars Sashie and me it is all fixed. Mars Sashie is good to me because of you, ma'am and I thank you.'

'No, Caleb. Mars Sashie is doing this because of yourself and because he is just good anyway, I think. And now that you have got a little piece of land, when are you and Trixie going to get married?'

'A lickle piece o' lan'!' said Caleb scornfully. 'This is the sweetest property in all St. Jago an' I'll keep it sweet, you'll see. Trixie and me been figurin'. We thought before Christmas-time because come Christmas I am at the Peak all the time playin' me guitar.'

'Will you invite me to the wedding, Caleb?'

'Sure, ma'am. You and Mars Sashie is invited for sure.'

It was at dusk a few days later that the solicitor arrived with the deed of agreement between Sashie and Caleb for the transfer of Silver Beach and Sashie came to my room, just as I was covering my typewriter for the day.

'Champagne on the veranda, darling,' he said, 'to celebrate Caleb getting a lickle piece o' lan' and my becoming his pensioner-cum-feudal-overlord. We are having the ceremony here because Caleb insists on having you as a witness to his signature.'

It did not take long to seal the transfer of the valuable little property. Sashie signed his name, S. P. G. de Marnay, in his rapid but clear script and the solicitor's secretary signed as first witness before old Gahta, with much labour and solemnity, signed Agatha Dunn as the second. Then Caleb, his big hand shaking a little, took the pen and signed 'Caleb Daley' slowly in a large clear copperplate, before I and then the secretary signed our names under his.

'That's it, Caleb,' I said, as the girl put down the pen. Caleb's huge eyes looked from me to Sashie. 'I thank you, ma'am. I thank you, sah,' he said with great dignity. 'I will always cultivate Silver Beach good,' and Sashie popped the cork of the champagne bottle.

When the solicitor had driven away and Caleb, Trixie and Gahta had gone to the kitchen, Sashie picked up the deed and said: 'I'll just put this in the safe in my room and then you and I will have a little more wine. Remarkable handwriting,' he added, as he folded the stiff paper. 'Caleb's, I mean.'

I looked over his shoulder at the signature. 'That is exactly my father's handwriting,' I said. 'He used to write to me every week and I discovered that Caleb was rescuing the envelopes from the waste-basket and copying the address on to the kitchen slate. He could write already but there came a time when, in what he called his 'good writing', he could write only the letters in my name and address at Paradise. I told my father about this and Dad wrote a letter to Caleb and enclosed with it a sheet of paper with the alphabet written in capital and ordinary letters and the figures from one to nine. After that, Caleb really got busy and that signature is the result.'

'What a remarkable man your father must have been, Janet. Twice told me a lot about him that summer you were in Scotland.'

'Yes. I think he was really a very good man and for a man of his station and education, he had remarkable vision. "Where there is no vision, the people perish" was one of his favourite quotations. I remember the first time he put me on the train at Cairnton to travel to Inverness all by myself – I was eleven – he gave me firm instructions that Tom, George and I were to telegraph him from Inverness when I arrived there. The three of us had our usual argument that we had about everything about how to word the telegram and we finished up with: "Where there is no vision the people perish Reachfar".'

Sashie listened as avidly to tales of my childhood as I did when he spoke of his own but I have since realized that I learned less of his former life than he did of mine.

'He was a handsome man, wasn't he?' Sashie asked now.

'Yes, I think so. Tall, dark, well-proportioned, you know – the right distance from shoulder to elbow and knee to ankle.'

'Like you. Did you use him as a yardstick for the boy-friends later on?'

'I don't think so. If I had, I wouldn't have had so many ghastly awful boy-friends. Were you *never* a fool when you were young, Sashie? Were there no impossible girls in your life?'

'I wasn't young for as long as you were before the war started, as I have told you before. I didn't get much time to be a fool in that way. And I liked Mama better than any of the girls I met. I don't mean anything peculiar and Oedipus but Mama was more appealing and more amusing than any other woman I came across at that time.'

'The other evening when you told me about Hugh Reid and warned me about the look in his eye and how I might say: Oh, all right, Hugh, I don't mind if I do, I was a bit annoyed with you, Sashie. But you were perfectly right. That is exactly how I was with the boy-friends. I don't mean that I jumped into bed with them. One didn't in those days. But if some bloke asked me to go to the movies with him, I didn't mind if I did and I can't remember the names of half of them or what they looked like. In fact, I can remember the movies I saw much more clearly, because the people in *them* were more interesting and one can't say duller than that. I even quarrelled with one of them finally and bitterly over a movie.'

'I shouldn't have thought that possible,' Sashie said. 'Do tell, darling.'

'His name was Hubert something and he took me to this movie called Bulldog Drummond. Hubert was terrible when I think of it. He was madly true-blue and British and old school tie and had sweaty hands when he held yours in the cinema and—'

'Stop. I wish to absorb these facts. His name was Hubert and he took you to a film called Bulldog Drummond. Was that the book that some of my colleagues at that dire prep school used to read?'

139

'That very one, I should think.'

'And this Hubert could hold his lady love's hand while watching a film like that?'

'Certainly. Hubert could hold your hand anywhere, any time, provided it was dark.'

'It had to be dark?'

'Yes.'

'And he was true-blue and British and old school tie?'

'Yes.'

'Very well. I have the facts although I don't pretend to understand them. Pray go on.'

'In this Bulldog Drummond film there was a scene in a pub in Ireland. If you check the books about Bulldog Drummond, you might find nothing about Ireland in any of them for all I know but films didn't go much by the book in those days. And it was fairly early in the sound film era, this film, so they had to have a song in it here or there. Standing at the end of the bar in this pub, there was a little insignificant-looking man in a beaten-up felt hat who suddenly burst into a song that went: There's a light in your eyes angel darlin' that makes all the world fair and bright. When we came out of the cinema, I was fed-up with Hubert. I suppose his hands had been even sweatier than usual and when he started to rave about the English actor who had played Bulldog Drummond being so much better than all these awful Americans, I said that the whole film had been a lot of tripe and that the only worthwhile thing in it had been the little man at the bar who sang the song. At least the singing had been good of its kind, I said, and one thing led to another for Hubert thought that girls should be seen and have their hands held but not heard and that was farewell to another romance.'

'How very sad.'

'But now I will tell you a thing which I think is interesting and in which I take enormous pride.'

'Hubert shot himself?'

'No. The little man who sang in the pub was Bing Crosby.'

'Darling, that *is* interesting, indeed, fascinating.'

'I never became a Crosby fan but later on I used to go to

all his films for auld lang syne or something. A lot of girls I knew used to be in love with film stars but I never was.'

'You stuck to the Huberts, darling?'

'Not entirely. In my London days I went to the theatre a lot and became interested in certain actors – not in love with them but trying to spot what you might call star quality, the thing I had spotted in Crosby.'

'With any success?'

'I shall never know. The war came, you see and everything disintegrated. I joined the Air Force and left London. Probably a lot of the young actresses and actors I had been interested in had their careers broken off short. Where were you when the war started, Sashie?'

'Mama and I were in London. My father had died the year before of pneumonia. The only places Mama really liked were London and Paris but after Papa died we settled permanently in London. We were British citizens, by the way. Papa had become British at some stage in his early life. He had some Jewish blood and a lot of Jewish friends and there was a lot of anti-Semitism in Paris at the time of the Dreyfus case. It persisted for a long time and Papa seems to have become disgusted with his own countrymen. I should like to regard his change of nationality as a manifestation of extreme long-sightedness on his part but I don't think it was. It was simply a burst of rebellion in a young man but Mama and I were glad of it in 1939.'

'That awful war,' I said. 'You know, Sashie, the worst thing about it, for me, was the number of refugees, the people exiled from their homes. I remember my father's words when he came face to face with the Nazi persecution of the Jews, when a Jewish family found refuge for a time in Achcraggan. "Anyone that would put a man out of his native country," Dad said, "for something that is no fault of his own, is not a man but a devil." My father belonged so deeply to Reachfar and the Highlands, you see, that he regarded the sending of people into exile as a deadly sin. The same feeling was in me. It is still. People should not be torn up by the roots and sent to wander the face of the earth.'

'Not having your feeling for places,' Sashie said, 'the refugees were, for me, just one more brutality. The thing that appalled me was the descent into barbarism, a barbarism that stopped people like you having fun spotting theatrical stars, that stopped the stars from developing, that put you into a uniform and made you into a cog in a killing machine. Didn't you hate the uniform, darling?'

'Not as much as many young women did but then I was always the sort that wore tailored clothes as opposed to pretty ones. The smaller prettier girls hated it though – girls like Monica. Monica at war was a riot, but then our whole unit was a riot. Talking about the war stopping stars from developing, though, I can comfort you a little by telling you that Alvah Evans, the tenor, was a member of our unit for a time. He used to sing to us in the mess.'

'You do comfort me,' Sashie said. 'I am glad to hear of even one who found his way through.'

I became conscious that we were on unhappy ground, that Sashie had suffered as much from the war as anybody and more than had many and I tried to get away from the subject by saying: 'Were you a theatre-goer when you grew up like your Mama, Sashie?'

'Yes, but even more of a concert-goer, I think. Did you go to concerts, darling?'

'I went to everything I could afford to buy a seat for, with a preference for Shakespeare and ballet.'

'I could have foreseen the Shakespeare but I did not think of you as a balletomane, as Anna so cutely had it.'

'I wasn't like Anna about it.'

'You do amaze me, my sweet.'

'All those words she threw about – fouetté, plié and all that – I regarded them as the dancer's business and not mine.'

'And rightly so.'

'And ballet in London in the 1930s was not the thing it is today but I thought I could see a resurgence in it, could see star quality emerging, as it were. I said before that I did not fall in love with film stars and people like that but that was not quite true, now that I think about it. I was dotty for a time – just before the war, it was – about a young dancer. I have always been a martyr to good looks, as you know and he was the most beautiful creature I had ever seen. As the

142

prince in the second act of *Giselle*, he took my heart and threw it away up into the roof of the theatre somewhere. The odd thing was that he was only a second string, not the star dancer I had hoped to see when I went to the theatre. But a lot of critics thought, as I did, that he was better than the star and I went on going to this theatre, hoping that the leading dancer had broken his neck and I would see my young man dancing again but I only saw him twice more during that whole ballet season.'

'Darling, what a sad story!'

'But that isn't all. I was just getting over him when there was a production of *The Tempest* so, naturally, I went to that. I didn't fall in love with Shakespearian actors because I was already too deeply in love with Shakespeare himself. I have always felt that he must have been what my grandmother would have called "a good, honest, hard-working fellow". Where was I? Oh, yes. I went to *The Tempest* and there was my young man in phosphorescent tights and all the rest of him painted green and silver being the most beautiful Ariel I have ever seen. I was a little disappointed in him though.'

'How sad. Why?'

'He spoke perfect English. I thought he was really Russian like his name. Most dancers in those days took Russian names because most people believed that only Russians could dance ballet and a Russian name was a help, I suppose. Still, I thought my young man should have had the courage and the faith in himself to dance under his own name. However, I forgave him because of his star quality.'

'He became a star?'

'I don't think so. I didn't hear of him any more but, of course, the war came, spoiling everything. Or maybe I was mistaken about his quality but I remember him with love. He will always be a star to me.'

'And what of Hubert?'

'I don't know what happened to him. I don't remember Hubert for himself at all. I have to think of Bing Crosby in order to remember Hubert and even then I don't like the memory.'

143

'And did you quarrel with any Huberts over your dancing young man?' Sashie asked.

'No. This was much later than Hubert and by this time I had learned not to go to Shakespeare or anything I was really interested in with young men, even if they were willing to take me which they mostly weren't.'

'But why ever not?'

'Sashie, this is where between your early background and mine there is a great gulf fixed. You must try to understand that all the people I knew in those days were very much like the Macleans or the Dulacs or any of the sugar people in this island. They were what *you* often call bourgeois philistines and they really thought, as Madame did, that writers were peculiar, musicians and painters what they called bohemian, actors immoral and ballet dancers, if they were female, not of the human race at all and if male they were cissy homosexuals and foreigners to boot. In fact, they preferred everybody connected with the arts to be foreigners. It explained something of their lack of respectability. Then, the sort of young men I met who took me to the cinema expected to hold hands in the dark in return for paying for my seat. A mild form of prostitution was expected of young women like me, if you like and I went to the cinema with them because I had spent all my own money and could not buy a seat for anything.'

'But I still don't understand why you let the Huberts take you to Bulldog Drummond. I am sure they could have been persuaded to take you to Shakespeare if you put your mind to it.'

'But if I went to Shakespeare with them, I would have quarrelled with them afterwards, don't you see, like quarrelling with Hubert over Bing Crosby.'

'No, I don't see,' said Sashie.

'If I went to anything *real* with a Hubert,' I explained impatiently, 'it always made me see that the Hubert-and-I thing wasn't real and I just naturally picked a quarrel on the way home. I would tell him in the end that he was a silly ass and that I couldn't be bothered with him and then I would get all lah-di-dah and highbrow and spend a few weeks going to Shakespeare and things on my own. Then all my money would get spent so that I had none left to go any-where and another Hubert would come along and there it was all over again.'

'You know, Janet,' Sashie said with mock gravity, 'I think you have a duty to give your love life to the world. Have you ever thought of autobiography?'

'No. It takes a genius to write true autobiography – some-one like Rousseau – and I am no genius. Only a genius can perceive what he is a person like, as Delgado would say and put it down in words on paper. Mark you, if you keep me talking like this, you will soon know about all my Huberts and you will be able to write my biography.'

'You over-estimate my powers, darling,' he said.

Sashie and I spent all our evenings talking like this, in rambling conversations that could begin, like the one I have quoted, with Caleb's handwriting and end, after many devious turns with my giving my views on autobiography. The letters from my family were often a starting-point for I shared those of George, Tom and my niece Liz with Sashie. George and Tom wrote very briefly, using one airmail form between them but Liz wrote at great length, on pages torn from a school exercise book as a rule and her letters came by surface mail because their weight, if sent by air, would, as she put it in the words of Tom and George 'land me in the poorhouse'.

Sashie, I had discovered, had no relations except a few distant cousins in France with whom he had lost contact long ago and 'Just as well,' he said. 'They were all very dull and disapproving of Mama for being Russian.'

We had no visitors. I had some acquaintance with the white people who constituted about three per centum of the island population but it was acquaintance only and my time at the Great House had isolated me even from this. Sashie, although he knew all the whites by name, had always stood off from them with an air of critical but reserved judgment that nobody had ever challenged him to bring into the open. Silver Beach, then, was a little pocket isolated from the rest of the world, a serpentless Eden, as Sashie said, although he added the rider: 'Of course, I don't know what Caleb and Trixie may be up to in the little house at nights but it does not matter as long as they eat their apples in private.'

Sometimes, I would give a little practical thought to my future, tell myself that I could not live at Silver Beach for ever but the thought of leaving its security was a little frightening. I was not rich but I had enough to afford a little house somewhere or a little flat in London, provided I took some sort of post that would bring in a small income, but these thoughts were all vague and would fade at the sight of a new flower in bloom in the garden or at the sound of a melody from Caleb's guitar. Sometimes, I had a sense of waiting for direction from outside of myself, for I have never been a planner. I have always lived life as it came along and no drive to leave Silver Beach made itself manifest, so I stayed, rattling my typewriter, working beside Caleb among his vegetables and flowers and talking to Sashie in the evenings and I knew a deep contentment such as I had never known since my childhood.

Among the things that Caleb and Trixie did in the little house at nights was to plan their wedding for the last Saturday in November and Sashie and I planned a trip to St. Jago Bay to buy presents and a new dress for me.

'I have to honour the occasion with new clothes,' I said. 'What in the world shall I get?'

I had not given any thought to clothes for well over a year. Several years ago, I had decided that I was too old to wear shirts and shorts. I had worn them when I first came to the island but, since coming to the privacy of Silver Beach, I had reverted to this form of dress which was cool, comfortable and required the minimum of laundry.

'It is a pity shorts and sandals won't do,' Sashie said. 'They suit you, but I suppose you have to look like a respectable matron as the rest of the world sees you.'

'Meaning that you don't see me as a respectable matron?'

'No, darling, I don't. To be truly respectable, people have to be over thirty, to give the impression of being over thirty and you have not as yet given me that impression. People who look at *faces*,' he said with candour, 'might take you for sixty but I never would.'

146

'I am deeply grateful.'

He followed his line of thought. 'I do not mean that you are mentally retarded but you look at people and things as a child looks, with intense concentration and no preconceived ideas. White, I should say,' he ended.

'White what?'

'Clothes for the wedding. White and plain with a large hat and long gloves. There are a lot of old people at Trixie's home and if they are having white people at the wedding at all, they would prefer a real old-fashioned white missis and you can look the part.'

'But I don't want to look a part as you put it!' I protested.

'It is not a question of what *you* want, as I see it, my sweet. As I see it, the polite thing is to be what *they* want.'

'But why should they want an old-fashioned white missis?'

'You and Caleb have overcome the colour bar but these old people at Pear Tree Bottom have not and they never will now. I have been buying fruit and vegetables from that settlement ever since Don and I started at the Peak but although we are all good friends on the surface, there is no rapport such as you and Caleb have established. They regard me as all right but white – madly queer and eccentric, of course – but white. And there is the fundamental truth that I *am* white. And so are you and you ought to go there dressed like what you are, the type of white they can respect and not looking like some Peak tourist of the type that they don't respect at all. And how right they are too!'

'All right, Sashie. You are far wiser than I am and white it shall be,' I agreed and cast an eye at his own peacock blue outfit. 'And you?' I asked. 'Salmon-pink or a more delicate shade of peach?'

'I can look like what Trixie's great-grandmother calls "a propah ovah-de-watah genkleman" when I choose,' he said huffily.

On our shopping day, we left Silver Beach shortly after eight in the morning, to arrive in St. Jago Bay as the shops opened, that we might avoid the crowds and the heat of later in the day. A short time sufficed to buy all we wanted, whereupon we drove up out of the sea-level hollow where

147

the town lay to the cooler cliff where the Peak Hotel stood.

The 'high' tourist season of the Platinum Coast had now begun and the lawns and beach of the Peak were littered with near-naked bodies, oiled, frying in the sun while the bars were already full of the babble of people and the chink of ice against glass. The beach, the grass and the sea of Silver Beach, that beautiful landscape without figures, seemed to be far far away.

'This is a revolting place that I have created,' said Sashie, pausing to look about him. 'May the Lord forgive me. Let's go into the office.'

Before he retired to Silver Beach, Sashie had had a small suite of rooms on the ground floor of the old plantation house which was the nucleus of the hotel but he had now given this up, retaining only his office. When we went in, Don Candlesham, was there.

'Everything all right?' Sashie asked.

'More or less,' Don said. 'Hello, Janet.' He turned back to Sashie. 'We got No. 7 Bungalow double-booked somehow but fortunately that widow from the Argentine who was in No. 9 decided to leave in a hurry last night instead of next Saturday so we are all right.'

'Why did she leave?' Sashie pounced. 'What displeased her?'

'She was not displeased. Quite the reverse, in fact. She left full of praise for us but she took Hugo Beaumont with her, hence the hurry.'

'Well, well-a-day,' said Sashie, 'so Hugo has escaped from Miranda at last!'

'Only just,' Don said. 'He and the widow had just left for the airport when Miranda came in here and found the letter he had left for her and had hysterics in the middle of the dining-room. It created quite a diversion.'

'I bet it did,' I said. 'One would like to be sorry for Miranda but—'

'One can't,' Sashie interrupted. 'Don, send in some grape-fruit juice for us and then we'll be off. We have been down town shopping.'

Don went to the door, halted, turned round. 'Janet, a chap who arrived last night was asking about you.'

'Another?' Sashie began to sparkle. 'Oh, this time, I *do* hope it is Hubert.'

'Be quiet, Sashie,' I said and to Don: 'What is his name?'

'Can't remember. I'll find out from reception,' Don said and went away.

Sadly, Sashie watched him go. 'That fellow will never make a hotelier,' he said. 'Oh, well. Darling, hadn't I better see the Hubert first? So that I may estimate the look in his eye, you know?'

'Oh, stop it, Sashie. Listen, I am terribly bored with all these people from long ago.'

'All? This one is only the second, although these two may be only the harbingers of all the Huberts to come.'

'Please stop being silly. All these old songs. Why can't the past bury its dead?'

'They may be dead old songs for you, darling, but obviously you are not a dead old song for them.'

'Well, I ought to be,' I told him impatiently. 'I am not the person they once knew at all.'

'The name is Firmantle,' said Don arriving with our drinks. 'Commander and Mrs. Firmantle from Winnipeg.'

'Crikey! Freddie Firmantle!' I said to Sashie.

'*And* Mrs.,' he reminded me.

'You have a dirty mind. Mrs. is Georgina and she is all right. Are they in the hotel at the moment, Don?'

Sashie and I had lunch with the Firmantles. Freddie said that he would have known me anywhere, that I had not changed at all except for the bits of grey in my hair but, as I told Sashie in the car on the way back to Silver Beach, with all the politeness in the world, I could not say the same of Freddie and Georgina.

'Who would have thought that the slim, clean-cut young naval officer of yesteryear would turn into all that stomach and bald head?' I asked. 'As for Georgina, she looks like an avocado pear standing on the wrong end with all that bust balanced above those tiny little feet. And there's another thing.'

'How very sinister you sound, darling. *What* other thing?'

'When I knew Freddie Firmantle, he was practically illiterate. How does he come to be an aluminium tycoon, visiting Jamaica to make bauxite contracts and coming on here to holiday at colossal expense at that brothel of yours?'

'But, darling, *all* tycoons are illiterate. Illiteracy is the basic sine qua non for tycoonery.'

'All the same,' I insisted, 'that company that Freddie is a director of had better watch itself. *His* illiteracy is not just a fact, it is a force.'

Naturally, on the veranda that evening, Sashie returned to the subject of Freddie, with the subsequent laying bare of another period of my past.

'The more I think of it,' I said, having told the story of Freddie, 'the more I become convinced that I was equipped with an invisible guardian angel. Looking back, knowing what I was, I could just as easily have married Freddie as not. I didn't mind if I did, you know.'

'I wonder just why you didn't?' Sashie asked.

I stared hard at the moon-tipped waves of the sea rolling quietly on to the beach. 'I honestly believe we would have ended up together if he hadn't written that letter,' I said.

'What letter?'

'Well, this old Madame X that I was secretary to did not allow her employees to use her telephone, especially if young men were involved. Freddie and I used to arrange our next meeting before we parted but when he had this rush of blood to the head that made him think he was in love with me, he wrote to arrange a special meeting. He said in his letter that if I could meet him, he would be fearfully bucked.'

'Darling, he didn't!'

'Yes, he did and I think that that letter put me off although I did not know it at the time.'

'And of *course* you had a guardian angel,' Sashie said. 'It was your love of the written word. The angel insisted that the word be well written.'

'You could be right at that. How complex everything is.'

'Not for Freddie. Oh, Janet, how I adore your past!'

'I hope no more of it turns up,' I said. 'It is all too embarrassing – not the Freddies but the looking back to myself when young.'

Every time, now, that Sashie went into town, I would greet him with some apprehension when he came home, in case he was bringing with him news of yet another spectral visitant and when, one day, he brought me a letter bearing British stamps and addressed in type to 'Miss Janet Sandison', I sat looking at it with deep suspicion.

'Janet,' said Sashie, his voice snapping with impatience, 'the only people who know you as Miss Janet Sandison, care of me at this address are those publishing people. Open that at once!'

'I am scared. You do it.'

Sashie slit the envelope, unfolded the sheet of paper and began to read aloud: 'Dear Miss Sandison, After reading your second manuscript which Messrs. Bush forwarded to us, I am taking the liberty of writing to you direct to express our appreciation—' Sashie's glance moved to the bottom of the sheet '—and it is signed by a gentleman called *Arden*!' he said. 'Now, for pity's sake, will you read your own mail?'

I read the remainder of the letter which told me that the publishers were accepting the second script and would arrange a contract with the agents and then said: 'He sounds nice, doesn't he, Sashie? I wonder what he looks like?'

'I don't *care* what he looks like! The import of the letter is that you have succeeded for the second time.'

'Oldish, I should think, bald, rather wizened up with those spectacles that are only crescents that you look through when you are reading and look over the top of when you're not.'

'Never mind his spectacles! Don't you understand at *all* what has happened?'

'Not quite,' I told him. 'It is easier to wonder about Mr. Arden's spectacles.'

The remote world of London and publishing did not seem real and the Janet Sandison to whom the people of that world wrote letters was not myself, not anybody I had ever been but some new person that I did not yet know. I felt that if I could clothe this signature: 'Aubrey Arden' with an appearance, the outer aspects of a personality, I might come to some knowledge of this man and through him to some knowledge of the new Janet Sandison.

151

This feeling of loss of identity was not new to me. I had felt before, at different times in my life, that if my contacts with my fellow creatures – those people to whom we refer to loosely as our 'friends' – were suddenly broken, my own personality would disintegrate. I had always felt that my identity was reflected back to me by the people about me and it seemed to be logical that the identity of the new Janet Sandison must be a reflection given back by people like Mr. Arden, without whom she could not, in a practical sense, exist at all.

'Drat Mr. Arden's spectacles!' said Sashie. 'The important person who merits a bottle of champagne is Janet Sandison.'

'No. The important person is Mr. Arden, without whom Janet Sandison the writer person would not exist.'

'And where would Mr. Arden be without writer persons, may I ask?'

'True. My professor of philosophy long ago would have said there is a functional relation between us. Very satisfactory.'

'How maddeningly calm you are!' he complained. 'Have you no spark of temperament at all?'

'I never count my sparks until they catch fire,' I said, 'and these novels, so far, are only so much dead matter.'

'Oh well, how far advanced is the latest heap of dead matter?'

'Another two days should see the typescript finished.'

'Then don't *sit* there talking about this man's spectacles! Get you to your machine, get it finished and let us mail it.'

'But, Sashie—'

He struck an attitude, one arm held high, the other hand on his hip. 'Am I not your presiding spirit? Have I not served you well so far?'

'You have, Sashie and I thank you,' I capitulated. 'I shall finish it and you shall mail it.'

Two days later, Sashie left for town with the parcel of typescript and, so much of day-to-day life being habit, I now had a habit of spending much of my days at the typewriter, so I unearthed another parcel of scribbled pages from the steel trunk and began to read them through prior to a fresh bout of typewriting. When I look back, I think the hours I spent at the typewriter were an escape from thought of the future. I still did not regard the activity as work; I still did not think of myself as a writer but the typewriting kept my mind engaged, kept thought of the future at bay. I was marking time, clinging to the security of Silver Beach, ignoring the world that went on its way beyond the boundaries of the property.

The days passed quickly and our main – almost our only – contact with the outside world was the mail which Sashie or Caleb fetched each day from the local post office and one day about mid-November, Caleb arrived back at the house wearing the broad smile that informed me that he carried letters from my family. He had known how important my father's letters had been to me and any letter that bore a Scottish postmark was identified for him with pleasure for me.

'One from Mars George and Mars Tom, ma'am,' he said, putting the blue airmail form beside my typewriter, 'and one from your brother and one from little Missy Liz.'

'Thank you very much, Caleb.'

I began with George and Tom and the first part was written by George:

'My dear Janet, This is to tell you that Jean took a fit of rage at Tom and me lately and when we came down the stairs the other morning we found that she had run off with all her belongings and one or two other things and the parlour carpet. She went in the car from the garage at the smiddy and young John the Smith says he put her on the train at Inverness to go to Glasgow, so now Tom and I have no housekeeper.

Tom now took over:

'It is foolish of George to say that we have no housekeeper for Jean has been too cripplé with the rheumatics for the last year to do much more than sit in a chair and George and I are not good at the housekeeping and sick, sour, scundered with it forbye. We hope you are right well

153

now. Our respects to Mr. Sashie and love to yourself. Write soon. Tom.

I laid this missive aside and opened the letter from my brother:

'My dear Janet, Those two worthies Tom and George arrived here this afternoon with no warning, bringing with them the keys of Jemima Cottage. They say they have written to you to tell you that Jean made a sudden departure and I am afraid I can add very little to what they have told you except that I suppose that she has gone to those Graham sisters who came up for their holiday every summer.

I can get little sense out of George and Tom for the obvious reason that they don't want to make any sense but I would like to know what they have been up to. It seems odd that, during the three years since Dad died, they have coped with Jean fairly smoothly and that now, in the comparatively short time since Twice died, things have reached the point where Jean has run away. I also find it significant that they have never been down here to us since Twice died when, before, they spent at least half the year here.

They have also been to see the lawyer in Dingwall – they let this slip by mistake – who has told them that since Jean occupied the house by a courtesy agreement within the family and left the property without making suitable arrangements for caretaking and upkeep, she could be held to have forfeited further claim to it.

It is obvious, of course, that they have done whatever it is they have done in order that you will come home.

You said I was not to tell them or anyone about the acceptance of your novel and I have not and they are worried about you financially. So am I, a bit, if it comes to that, for Twice's long illness must have eaten into any capital you had and the advance on a first novel can't be very much. Naturally, you know best what you want to do but I do ask you to think about coming home. You would be welcome here, as you know and more than welcome at

Castle Jemima. Of course there is a risk of Jean coming thumping back like a bad penny but if that happened, you, George and Tom could come here until you found some other place. Not that Jean has any right to the cottage but I know that you promised Dad that she could have it for as long as she wanted.

Anyhow, think carefully about it and let us know your plans. Liz is writing and you will get all the family gossip from her so I shall get this in to the post. Yours, Jock.'

Liz's letter was also an air mail form this time.

'Dear Aunt Janet, I made the boys whip in tuppence each, including Sandy-Tom to buy this air letter for I said that if I wrote the news it was fair for them to pay for it the air letter I mean. The news is that George and Tom are here because they have no socks left without holes in them and the shirts they were wearing were not ironed either but Mum has done them now. I do not suppose you know about Granny-Jean who used to stay with them but she has gone away to Glasgow now. It is fun to have Tom and George here and we wish that you were here too and Dunk says if you come to live at the cottage to be with them we could all come up for holidays. Gee does not remember being at Achcraggan ever and of course neither does Sandy-Tom because he has never been there really. He has red Wellington boots and a red barrow and he digs in the garden all the time. George says that he is just another danged crofting Sandison. This paper is getting full up but if you do not want to leave Mr. Sasha de Marnay with the beautiful name behind you could put a bed in the parlour at the cottage where the asperdester is. I send him my kindest regards. Love from Elizabeth, Duncan, George, X (Alexander Thomas his mark).

There was a postscript in very small writing.

'P.S. If he did not like to sleep with the asperdester he could come to us.'

155

I carried the three letters out to the veranda and handed them to Sashie. 'Read them in the order I did,' I said. 'Tom and George first, then Jock and then Liz.'

Sashie gave his attention to the letters and soon looked up to say: 'I must sleep, if only once, with the asperdester' then to add: 'What a wonderful family you have, Janet!'

He looked suddenly small and forlorn and sounded wistful which was unusual and disconcerting in him so that I said briskly: 'That is as may be. I am crazy about that bit from George and Tom about how they came down in the morning and – surprise, surprise! – Jean and the parlour carpet were gone. You couldn't drop a pin in the house night or day without their knowing about it but I am expected to believe that Jean, her luggage and the carpet got out of the cottage and into a car while they slept on in blissful ignorance. Those two must think I have gone soft in the head!'

'You sound positively vindictive, darling!' Sashie protested.

'I feel vindictive. You would too, if you knew them as well as I do. They have jacked Jean out of that house as sure – in their own coarse phrase – as there is dirt in a cat.'

Sashie laughed before he asked: 'But being what she was, are they to be blamed if they did? From what you have told me from time to time, they have probably had some very unpleasant years with her.'

My uprush of vindictive indignation at the cunning of George and Tom was a familiar reaction from my childhood which had risen in me now to cover my unease about those very years they had spent with Jean since my father died. During those years, I had spared hardly a thought for them although I knew how difficult life with Jean could be and now the guilt for my neglect of Tom and George began to writhe in me like a black snake.

Sashie waved Liz's letter at me and said: 'This young woman has more of the subtlety that life needs than her father, Tom and George put together.' He looked down at the blue sheet and read aloud: '—because they have no socks without holes in them and the shirts they were wearing were not ironed either.' He looked up at me. 'This young woman knows not only what she wants but how to get it.'

'She is an interfering little brat,' I said and I meant it, for Liz had shattered my peace of mind completely with her picture of George and Tom untended, their clothes unmended and unironed. 'Sashie,' I burst forth, 'I am a selfish bitch, sitting here in luxury all these weeks when George and Tom—'

'Let us be quite calm and reasonable,' Sashie broke in. 'You have been sitting here in luxury as you call it all these weeks because you were very seriously ill and needed some time to gather yourself together. And during these latter weeks, you have been working extremely hard, doing a ten-hour day at that typewriter.'

'Working! That isn't work!' The deeply ingrained law of Reachfar that writing was a leisure occupation had now come to the fore. 'I have been *enjoying* myself while George and Tom—'

'From what I have heard of George and Tom, they would want you to enjoy yourself. Now, let us make a little hard sense, Janet. I am convinced that you can establish yourself as a writer but, in the meantime, have you any money?'

'Somewhere around three thousand pounds. Long illnesses like Twice's had cost a lot of money in this island. I was paid while I was at Paradise but I spent most of it on whisky.' I was bitterly ashamed as I made this confession. 'I haven't enough to live on for any length of time but I can get some sort of job when I go home, can't I?'

'A woman of nearly fifty in a Highland village? Do you propose to be a charwoman?'

'No matter what you say, Sashie, I have to go home and I'll manage somehow.'

'Of course you must go home,' he surprised me by saying. 'I have known ever since Twice died that you must go home. It is the only place where you have ever belonged but you had to get around to it in your own tortuous and self-torturing way. The point I wish to make is that you must put your faith behind your pen. You have to stop looking upon your writing as a sinful pastime and look upon it as the job you do, as your *work*.'

'But it has brought in only a hundred pounds so far and

maybe another hundred for that second script. I could earn more—'

'Let us not argue about this, Janet. You have enough capital to live in Achcraggan for at least two years. I wish you to promise me that you will live on that capital and *write*. I believe that in two years you will be established but if not, I have more money than I shall ever need, thanks to my exploitation of the class of exploiters who come to this island.'

'Don't talk nonsense, Sashie.'

'It is far from nonsense, darling. I have no heirs and I would rather spend my money on you than leave it to a home for fallen women, if there are such places nowadays.'

The thought of being able to sit in the cottage at Achcraggan, pushing my pen or rattling my typewriter, while George and Tom pottered around the house and garden was very appealing, almost too appealing to be within possibility as a way of life.

'Tom and George have some capital,' I said, 'and they both have the old age pension.'

'And they own the house, don't they?'

'Yes or, at least, I do, actually. Old Aunt Betsy left it to me.' I remembered how little Jemima Cottage had meant to me when I had inherited it at the age of about sixteen. 'Then I refuse to think any more in financial terms. Between us all, we have more than enough.' Sashie held out his small hand. 'But, Janet, I want you to put your hand in mine and promise me that, if things are slow or if anything unforeseen happens, you will not fly into a panic, abandon your writing and take a job in an office or behind a shop counter.' I leaned back in my chair and clasped my hands firmly in my lap. 'Come along,' he said. 'Before you do anything like that, you will apply to me,' I did not move. 'Doesn't it occur to you that, when you leave here, I shall be like a tiny tragic Othello with his occupation gone?' he asked.

The web of time since Twice died until the night of the bottle spread itself out in my mind, ugly, dark and dead, redeemed only by the brilliant little figure of Sashie that seemed to float over it like the spirit of the future. I already owed him so much that a promise to apply to him for mere money was very little to give him. I leaned forward and put my large hands between his two small ones.

'I promise,' I said. 'And you would make a better Ariel than an Othello. You will come flying over to see George, Tom and me now and then?'

'*All* the time, darling.' He released my hands and stood up. 'Now that we understand one another properly, I feel like Ariel and I fly to fetch us some wine.'

Over his glass of sherry, he said: 'Far be it from me to pry, my sweet, but how many more novels are there left in that trunk?'

'Three. No, four. I had seven altogether.'

'That will keep those people in London publishing for a year or two,' he said.

'Oh, Sashie—' I pleaded, suspicious, uncertain of the future. 'Just because two have been accepted don't—'

'Oh, pish and tush! I am sure that nice old gentleman with the funny spectacles is going to love every one of them.'

'I must start making arrangements about going,' I said, clinging to the practical level.

'I shouldn't hurry too much. Although the stepmother person has gone with the carpet at the moment, she may come back.'

'I don't give a damn if she does,' I told him. 'I have always sworn that I would never live under the same roof as Jean but I see it differently now. If it comes to it, I can look after George and Tom and handle Jean as well.'

'Darling, in that tone, I should *hate* to be handled by you. But you can't go until after Caleb's wedding, don't you feel?'

'That is true.'

'But I shall book a flight for you any time after that. Your passport is in order?'

'Yes but not a flight, Sashie. I shall go by sea. I don't like to fly and ten or twelve days at sea will give me time to sort of re-orient myself.'

'*I* know! We shall book you so that you will be at sea all anonymous among strangers over Christmas and the New Year. Would that be comfortable, darling?'

'Yes. That would be perfect. And George and Tom

always spend Christmas and the New Year at Jock's place anyhow.'

'Then that is arranged. And may I have one tiny bit more of my own way?'

'I suppose so. You always get your own way anyhow.'

'I shall put you on the passenger list as Janet Sandison for that is who you are now – Janet Sandison, the writer person.'

'But Sashie—'

'You must begin to think in terms of publicity, my sweet.' He cocked his head, his eyes glittering with mischief. 'You are quite extraordinarily contrary. You used to be so good at getting publicity of the wrong sort among the veranda gossips when you didn't need it and now that you need it, you don't want it.'

'Oh, please yourself,' I said. 'Let's have lunch and let me get back to my typewriter.'

Within the few hours since Caleb had brought the letters, the entire face of life had changed. Mechanically, I copy-typed from the manuscript that lay beside the machine while I tried to envisage the future. I had written a brief reply to Mr. Arden's letter and I now tried to visualize him and his London office but the only London office I had ever known at first hand was in the City, where I had worked as a sec-retary for a short time long ago and Mr. Arden had written from a west central address. Besides, the offices I had known had been those of a shipping firm and the offices of pub-lishers must be very different. I then tried to remember the details of Jemima Cottage at Achcraggan but the only things there that came to mind with any clarity were the little stair-case with its wrought-iron balusters and what Liz called the 'asperdester', which sat on the window sill of the parlour in a pink china pot. I had hardly been inside the cottage since my father and stepmother went to live there and old Aunt Betsy, who had occupied it when I was a child, had been such a domineering overpowering character that, when I was sent to call on her, I had been aware of little other than her rather frightening self.

When I looked back like this, the river of my time seemed to be very long and very broad, smooth-flowing here and with stony rapids there and with many back-waters and deep still pools under its banks, along which all the people I had ever known seemed to stand, as trees and woods stand on the banks of the Thames, their reflections colouring the water, their shapes, in turn, being reshaped by the water. The death of Twice stood up like a rocky cliff, a black eminence round which the river had to flow, changing its direction, forming first a sullen pool before finding its way forward again and now the course before it seemed to lead into new country of a kind that it had never traversed before.

The typewriter, meantime, rattled on and two days before Caleb's wedding, the third typescript was completed.

'Cardboard, brown paper, string,' said Sashie, dancing round the table. 'A little letter to the agent, darling, do up the parcel and your Ariel will fly to the post office.'

'Sashie, all that money for airmail!' I protested. 'I can take the thing with me when I go and post it on the other side.'

'I shall spend my own money as I choose. Do up that package at once.'

I did up the package, Caleb came round with the car and they set off for the post office, leaving me to look out over the grass to the long calm waves that washed on to the beach. I found myself thinking of the singing at Twice's funeral, the metrical version of the twenty-third psalm.

> Mid pastures green he leadeth me
> The quiet waters by.

The time among the green pastures of Silver Beach by the quiet waters of the Caribbean was coming to an end and the future looked very frightening until I thought of George and Tom, those members of the 'always' of my childhood, who had always protected me from all the uncertainties and had helped me over all the rough places.

I went to my bedroom, put the manuscript I had copied into the trunk and took out another, but not to put it into type. I had finished, for the moment, with the copying of manuscripts but I felt the need to have some of these papers where I could see them, to remind me of this strange new

161

turn in my life. But automatically, escaping from thought of the future, perhaps, I began to read the manuscript which had been written over a year before and discovered that I had quoted in it the rhyme that began: 'Monday's child is fair of face' and that it stopped short at the final couplet that applied to the child born on Sunday.

'Try as I may,' I said to Sashie on his return from the post office, 'I can *not* remember those last two lines. I bet it is because of Tom and George.'

'You sound positively sinister towards Tom and George. What can you mean?'

'They always put me off things they didn't like. Sunday's child in that rhyme was what Liz would call holy-oly although I can't remember the exact words. Tom and George don't like the holy-oly. Oh, well, the words will come back to me, I hope but in the meantime it is irritating. Or could I be losing my memory in my old age?'

'I doubt that very much,' Sashie comforted me.

A day or two later, Sashie booked my passage in *Mnemosyne*, a banana boat that carried twelve passengers, which was scheduled to sail from St. Jago Bay on the twenty-second of December and I now telephoned Mackie, the Chief Engineer at Paradise. When his voice answered me, it sounded like an echo from the cave of the past.

'How are you Missis Janet?'

'Very well, thank you, Mackie. Look, I know how busy you are but I am sailing for home in the *Mnemosyne* on the twenty-second of December. When will it be convenient for me to send for that stuff of mine that is in the Great House cellars?'

'Leave it to me, Missis Janet. *Mnemosyne*, 22nd. I've got that. The stuff is all labelled, isn't it? I'll send it down on the 20th or 21st. That will be the passenger wharf?'

'I suppose so.'

'Don't worry about it. I'll see to the shipping papers and all that.'

'You are very kind, Mackie. Thank you.'

'Give my regards to Scotland. Good luck, Missis Janet.'

I put the telephone down. All that remained of the years at Paradise was packed into five wooden crates that could be disposed of in a few words. Yet, not all. There were more memories than could ever be put into words.

'Mail,' said Sashie. 'Just one for you.'

He handed me an envelope addressed in the handwriting of my friend Monica, re-addressed at Paradise. The letter was written from London, was short and to the point.

'My dear Janet, Our lives continue to follow their oddly parallel courses. Torquil died at Beechwood two weeks ago, following a coronary thrombosis. I have taken a flat here for the present and have left the twins at Beechwood for a bit. The others are at school. I have put Poyntdale up for sale and there is already a prospect who wants to turn it into a hotel. I have nothing to keep me up there now that Torquil is gone and I want to be near Beechwood and the children's schools. Forgive this scrawl. I have so many to write. Love, Monica.'

'They all seem so far away and long ago – Monica, Torquil, all the people I ever knew. They are only names now. I don't feel them as people any more,' I said to Sashie. 'In one way, my world has come down to just you and my family and in another way, when I think of Canterbury, Arden, it has grown monstrously big and strange.'

We talked of Monica for a little before Sashie said: 'But I had a letter today too and as a very special favour, you may read it.'

He handed me an airmail form addressed to himself in the firm hand of my niece Liz.

'Dear Mr. Sasha de Marnay, Tom and George gave me the money to buy this letter so that I could write to you to thank you for looking after our Aunt Janet. We are very glad she is coming home and we hope that you will not be very lonely without her. We were very lonely when she went back to St. Jago from here. She is a very useful person to have staying with you.

George and Tom are out playing football with my brothers. They play football all the time even when it is snowing and they are very well, George and Tom I mean and send you their best respects. We are all looking forward to our New Year dinner and the turkey. I always get the wishbone and can choose who I pull it with and I wish you could be here for me to pull it with you. I would want you to get the top and get your wish. Mum says that you come to London sometimes and that you may come to see us one day. The train comes to Aberdeen and we would meet you there or it would be better still to come in the aeroplane to Dyce. I have never been to meet anyone at the aeroplane at Dyce.

We all send you our very best wishes. Yours sincerely, Elizabeth Sandison. P.S. Aunt Janet said you were very interested in the aspidistra. This is how A. J. spelled it so I suppose it is right. George and Tom said that they often hoped the ugly booger would die but since you like it they will take care of it. E. S.'

'You said once that people's motives are never pure,' I said, returning the letter to Sashie. 'If that child's mother knew about that ugly booger bit in that letter, she would go through the ceiling. The sole motive for writing it was to mark her secret defiance of her mother.'

'I don't care what the motives were. It is a splendid letter and it was charming of Liz to write it.'

'Charm my foot,' I said. 'She is absolutely fascinated by your name. She probably talks about nothing but you and she talks all the time. Tom and George probably suggested that she write to you to shut her up for a little.'

'I will *not* have my new friend deglamourized!'

I relented a little. 'Your name is something quite new under her sun and I know exactly how she feels. I was a little younger than she is when I met an American woman called Madeleine-Louise de Cambre and I went around singing her name for weeks.'

Sashie sat looking down at the blue paper between his hands. 'I feel I have been adopted,' he said with a shy upward glance that was foreign to his normally mischievous or satirical eyes, 'as if I were part of a family again'.

'The Sandisons do seem to be putting their clutches around you,' I agreed.

'And I am quite inordinately pleased to be clutched, I find.'

'By the way, I rang Mackie at Paradise. He is going to get that heavy stuff sent down to the ship and put on board for me.'

'Good, so we have no more to worry about before you sail except to *will* those publishing people to write to us accepting your latest parcel before you go. They have almost four weeks.'

'Sashie—'

'No protest, if you please. No more Highland caution. Let us live in faith and hope and go dancing at Caleb's wedding.'

On the evening before the wedding, Trixie and Caleb left for their homes, Gahta going with Trixie and Sashie and I were to be driven to Pear Tree Bottom the next day by one of the chauffeurs from the Peak Hotel.

'Have you been to what they call a bush wedding before?' Sashie asked me that evening and I shook my head. 'Then we shall simply have to play it by our wits,' he said and then: 'You are quite extraordinarily calm at the prospect of leaving this island and taking up a new way of life, darling. You are truly calm and not suppressing things in your absurd way?'

'I am not suppressing anything, Sashie. If you are thinking of my ringing up Paradise to ask Mackie to ship the remains of Guinea Corner, that was a mere matter of a business arrangement that had to be made. As Twice used to say, I have *had* this island but I am grateful to have had it. The only thing I am sorry about is that I have to leave you and Silver Beach. I don't regard this place as part of the island. It is part of *you*.'

'But you are not leaving me. I will not be left for I have Liz now should you not want me any more. I shall come to sleep with the asperdester very soon and should these publishing people prove in any way difficult, I shall come speeding to your aid.'

'I admit to being nervous about them. Sashie, have you ever known any publishers?'

'One or two. They were quite human. They don't belong to a race apart as you seem to think.'

'I do feel they belong to another world, like all the people connected with the arts.'

'But *you* belong to that world, Janet.'

'Not really. I am just a sort of accident.'

'Aren't we all accidents, little microcosmic explosions? But I think you are a pleasant little accident – not a nasty little disaster like some.'

'You do work hard to bolster me up,' I told him.

At noon the following day, we set off to the wedding, Sashie very conventional in a pale grey suit, a white shirt and with one of Caleb's crimson 'coronations' in his buttonhole. When the car turned out of the Silver Beach gates on to the Coastal Highway, it went to the right and westwards, towards St. Jago Bay which surprised me for, for no good reason, I had thought that Pear Tree Bottom would be somewhere in the hills to the east.

'Where exactly is Pear Tree Bottom?' I asked.

'Up in the gorge of the Rio d'Oro,' Sashie told me.

I looked down at my white silk skirt. Once before I had paid a visit to a Negro home in a river valley where, as dusk fell, the mosquitoes came out in battalions until my arms, legs and face were spotted with blood. To be the favourite food of the mosquitoes was a thing that embarrassed and shamed me, for it put distance between me and the Negroes who seemed to be impervious to the black humming insects.

As if he knew what was in my mind, Sashie said casually: 'I had speech with Caleb on today's programme. The wedding ceremony is at two o'clock, then there is the feast and then the dancing begins. We are not expected to dance so we shall make a dignified departure before the darkness and the mosquitoes come down on us.'

'That is a relief,' I said. 'I don't mind the itching so much as the revolting bloody mess they make of me.'

'I know. They are still over-fond of me too. I once stayed a little late at Pear Tree Bottom and Don suspected me of coming down with measles.'

'Have you ever got malaria, Sashie?'

'No. I would never let any mosquito take quite *that* much of a liberty with me, darling.'

When we had passed through St. Jago Bay, where the

166

sunlight shimmered off the chromium of the cars and the shop fronts, we began to climb again, turned off the Highway on to the road that followed the gorge course of the Rio d'Oro and then on to a rough track that went down through dense vegetation for a long way until it ended in an oblong patch of brown earth by the riverside. Around this small clearing, there were patches of thickly-planted bananas, less thick citrus trees, a patch of coffee, a patch of cocoa. Every inch of the fertile alluvial soil bore fruit of some kind and here and there, through the dense dark green, there showed the wall of a wooden house.

We left the car and followed a track between two patches of bananas which brought us to the fenced enclosure with the house at its centre which was Trixie's home and here the entire population of the settlement was gathered, including a number of goats, pigs and chickens which had taken advantage of the open gate. Older people sat on forms at long trestle tables covered with white cloths, younger men and women stood about in groups and there were children everywhere, running in circles and crawling under the tables which were arranged round three sides of a square. When Sashie and I arrived at the gate, an old lady rose from one of the forms and came to greet us.

'Good afternoon, Mama Martha,' Sashie said. 'I brought Mrs. Alexander.'

The old lady bobbed the old-fashioned curtsey of the island.

'I very happy to see you here, ma'am,' she said.

The dignity of people like Mama Martha always made me feel inadequate and unworthy of the respect they paid me but there was little time to feel anything as a number of old men gathered round Sashie as if he were a favourite friend. I had never imagined Sashie in a situation like this and I noticed that he did not make the mistake, as I considered it, that many white men made, of trying to speak the dialect of these old islanders. He spoke to them in his own clear standard English and there was a curious atmosphere of respect on both sides.

Mama Martha, I discovered, was Trixie's great-grandmother and had been given the role of lady for the day. She

167

sat with some ten female guests of her own age and me, while the other women of the family attended to the drinks and the cooking of the feast. These women were marshalled and managed by Caleb's ancestress, the wizened but redoubtable Missy Rosie, who had come here, with the generations of her large household, from her own equally fecund place in another lush valley.

Sashie and his group of older men were joined by the minister who was to conduct the service and then by a brash young Negro in a dark 'city' suit, a gaudy tie and yellow shoes.

'Him de parish councillor, ma'am,' Mama Martha explained to me in an apologetic tone, as if she hoped that I would understand that such men in public office expected to be invited to any celebration in their area as a matter of course.

The young man had obviously modelled himself on Kevin Lindsay, the island's leading political agitator, who was very anti-white in his views but this youth had neither the personality, the education nor the political subtlety of Lindsay and succeeded in being merely loud-mouthed and offensive, with an offensiveness aimed at Sashie and me but which had the effect of making old Mama Martha and the old men very uncomfortable. The strident voice cut through the air, echoed off the walls of the house and dominated everything and even during the marriage ceremony, I felt that the voice was only gathering strength for a fresh attack, for the youth did not sit in his appointed place, but prowled around behind the guests seated at the tables.

The minister performed the ceremony at the middle table where Sashie and I were given places of honour, facing the bride and groom who were supported on either side by the more intimate members of their families. Trixie, dressed all in white, flanked by two rose-pink bridesmaids, looked shy and pretty and Caleb, in his white drill suit, looked very large and very solemn but the short ceremony was soon over and Missy Rosie and her minions began to serve the feast. The thick soup was ladled from buckets, the huge pig which had been roasted in an oil drum was hacked into portions of immense size by Trixie's brother and then the two pink bridesmaids came down the steps from the house, carrying between them a small table on which stood the wedding cake.

I had never seen such a masterpiece of ingenuity as this. Like the cakes made by professional confectioners, this one was in five circles of decreasing size, but the white-iced circles were not separated by chromium pillars like those used on a confectioner's cake. Instead, the branch of a tree had been carefully selected and carefully cut and then every minor branch bound with white ribbon. The main branch seemed to grow out of the big circle of cake at the bottom, above which three branches spread round the central stem, each of these supporting a circle of cake, while the main stem rose above these, pierced the smallest circle of cake and emerged through its top to hold a bunch of wild lilies tied with a bow of white ribbon.

'I have never seen anything so beautiful,' I said across the table to Mama Martha.

'Me dahtah Clara do it, ma'am. A good cook is Clara,' she said.

The beautiful confection was taken apart by Clara and cut by Trixie while Caleb handed paper plates and Caleb's brothers or cousins or nephews or uncles walked round behind us all, pouring more rum into our glasses, but now the parish councillor had found his second wind and standing on the steps that led up to the house, he began to make another speech. Missy Rosie, in the doorway of the house, was now directing her minions in the clearing of used cutlery and crockery from the tables and in the serving of coffee and at her feet she had a large bucket into which the women tipped bones and scraps as they went past. The heat in the crowded space among the lush vegetation was intense; the heavy smells of roast pork and strong rum were trapped in the thick air of this green tent and the insolent voice of the parish councillor was like the persistent thud of a heavy hammer. I could not hear what Mama Martha was trying to say to me from across the table and the old men sat sullen and silent under the political barrage. Suddenly, there came cutting through the thuds of the hammer the eldritch voice of Missy Rosie on the top step of the flight. 'Shut yo' big mouf, you wid yo' black folks an' white folks an' pol*it*ickin! Dis hyah is a *weddin*'!' whereupon she picked up the bucket of slops and scraps and bones and tipped it over the parish councillor's head, the grease making shiny rivulets down the smart 'city' suit.

Under the white tablecloth, Sashie's hand took a hard grip on mine while we stared at the shoulders of the padded coat that supported the bucket. Then a child laughed into the silence, followed by another and another until the entire green place was filled with laughter which grew even louder as Missy Rosie reclaimed her bucket, lifting it from the grease-dripping shoulders to reveal the councillor's face and the black hair which was crested, as if wearing a coxcomb, with a rib bone from the roast pig. The young man now descended from the steps and slunk away through the gate and out of sight among the dense vegetation, whereupon Mama Martha, the perfect hostess who could not be ruffled by any contretemps, leaned towards me across the table and said: 'Caleb is telling me that you are leaving us, ma'am, to go home ovah de watah?'

'Yes, Mama Martha. I sail just before Christmas.'

'We are sorry you go, ma'am.'

I believed her, but I knew that I had not merely imagined the hatred in the eyes of the parish councillor as he looked at Sashie and me while he removed the rib bone from his hair and held us responsible for his humiliation. Mama Martha and her generation might be sorry to see me and my kind leave the island but there was a rising generation that would be glad to see us go.

But the rest of the party did not suffer from the white guilt that made Sashie and me so conscious of the further implications of Missy Rosie's spurt of anger with the councillor. They were simply relieved that he had gone, leaving them free to celebrate the wedding in traditional style and in a trice the tables were dismantled, the forms carried to the perimeter of the yard and the dancing began with Caleb the bridegroom leading the music with his guitar.

At four o'clock, Missy Rosie appeared at my side bearing a tray that held a pot of tea, sugar, milk, two cups and a plate of biscuits, the strange eccentric meal that white people took at four in the afternoon.

'You will be so good to help yourself, ma'am an' Mars Sashie, please,' said Mama Martha. 'Missy Rosie an' me, we will drink coffee.'

Again I felt unworthy of this thoughtful attention but I could only thank her and pour out the tea which, I felt, had been specially bought for the occasion as, possibly, the china on the tray had been bought as well.

When, between us, Sashie and I had drunk all the tea, which was very strong, he began to make our excuses and I rose to my feet.

'Thank you, Mama Martha, Missy Rosie,' I said. 'It was a beautiful wedding and I shall always remember coming here.'

'Me sorry me tip de bucket on dat fellah,' said Missy Rosie and then: 'No, me not sorry neither. Him wid his pol*itic*kin' an' nuisance! T'ank you for all you do for Caleb, ma'am. Good-bye, ma'am.' She bobbed her little curtsy.

'T'ank you an' Mars Sashie for bein' wid us folks today, ma'am. Good-bye, ma'am,' said Mama Martha and again there was the little curtsy before Sashie and I went away between the green bananas to the car. We could hear the music, coming as if from the hidden heart of the island, until we turned the corner and came out of the vegetation on to the road that followed the river gorge.

We arrived home at Silver Beach just as darkness fell. As Sashie switched on the lights, I threw my hat, which I had taken off in the car, on to a chair and said: 'Going free, one expensive hat that Trixie or Gahta wouldn't be seen dead in. I always have to pay too much for hats. My head is too big and cheap hats are always small.' I realized that Sashie was looking at me with intense concentration.

'What is it?' I asked.

His face seemed to come alight. 'I didn't know it until this very moment, Janet, but in a tremendous number of ways you remind me of Mama. *She* always took her hat off the moment she came into the house although, in those days, most women wore hats even at lunch in their own homes if they had guests. And there are other things—' he wrinkled his forehead and smiled '—the pinned-up hair is part of it, of course. Mama did not follow fashion into the bob or the shingle. At first sight, you and she could not be more different and yet there are curious resemblances.'

I sat down, hoping to hear more of this woman who had taken such a hold on my imagination but Sashie dismissed the subject and said: 'I think there is some champagne on the ice. Let's drink to this wedding in a civilized way.'

As he poured the wine, I said: 'That wedding nearly became very uncivilized when Missy Rosie tipped that bucket over that councillor bloke.'

'Yes indeed, a horrid moment, although comic in retrospect and it made me come to a decision. I had thought of ending my days here at Silver Beach but I don't want them ended for me too soon. Caleb, my Negro partner in the property, will be some protection of course but I find that I want some place where people are not actively *hostile*, don't you know. I am going to take a small flat in London, darling, so that if people here, like that councillor bloke as you called him, get really out of hand, I can run like a tiny stag, for I have not Missy Rosie's expertise with a bucket of pig swill.'

'I think you are wise, Sashie,' I said.

Sashie was always wise, shrewd, far-sighted. I remembered the evening when he first told me about the agreement he intended to make with Caleb regarding Silver Beach.

'One's motives are never pure,' he had said and I saw now that Caleb, as a partner in the property, might act as a safeguard if serious civil disturbance between white and Negro broke out.

'But let us not be weather, as Mama used to say,' Sashie said now. 'Mama was very conscious of being British and tried very hard to speak English but she spoke it in what I can only call an atmospheric way. She found the London weather dreary but she found it drearier still that the weather was so often a topic of conversation and she would describe a dull dinner party as "weather".' His face changed to become, I was sure, very like the face of his fascinating mother as he mimicked: "Very weather, mon petit autre" she would say.'

172

'She called you her little – other one?'

'Yes. That is rather embarrassing and schmaltzy, as private language always is, like that dire passage in Proust where Swann and Odette speak of doing a cattleya. But it is less embarrassing if one knows the origin, I think, for it arose out of Mama's attitude to language. One of the people who came to visit her shortly after I was born was an Englishwoman, and she bent over my no-doubt snivelling self in the cot and said: "What a sweet little thing!" Mama was furious. I was not a *thing*, she said. I was a *boy*, a new *person*, another *being* – un autre être. So Papa used to inquire after autre être each evening when he came home.' Sashie smiled. 'There are more resemblances between you and Mama here when I think of it. She did not like to speak Russian any more and tried to manage in French and English and this made her very word-conscious, like you. And again like you, she had a very keen sense of the individuality of people, of their diversity, their otherness. She brought the "autre" into play in all sorts of ways. If I misbehaved, she would say disgustedly: "Ce n'est pas autre", accusing me of being not what she expected but a mere ordinary ill-behaved little monster like all the rest and it at once made me behave as she wanted me to. And if I drew a picture for her that really pleased her, she would say: "Oui. C'est de Sashie de Marnay. Bien. 'C'est autre." It was her highest praise.'

'I could listen about her, as Tom used to say, for ever,' I told him.

'Our relationship paralleled what you have told me about your own relationship with George and Tom in a curious way. In the words of Percy Soames, it was not a huggery-kissery affair. Indeed, I don't remember ever being kissed by Mama. In a physical way, she stood off from one rather and mentally she was interested in one as a separate individual more than as her child, an individual who could develop. It was Mama who educated me really, in so far as I am educated at all, not my schools.'

'She certainly educated you and developed you as an individual,' I said. 'You are the most individual individual I have ever encountered.'

'She was not in the least what they call maternal, or what

173

she in her atmospheric way called wombsome. When she went to dress for the evening, I had to go to my own room. In the earlier days, I had a nursemaid called Mariette who undressed me and so on but very soon I began to look after myself because Mama contrived to imply that it was undignified to require a Mariette. So I would go to my room and read or paint something for the puppet theatre and when Mama had dressed, she would come in to see me before she went out or downstairs if she were having people to dinner. It was a formal call. She knocked at my door and waited to be asked to come in. I would open the door to her and approve of her toilette. I always genuinely approved, for to me she always seemed beautiful and I am aware now that she did dress very well. She always wore flowers in the evening. Papa had them sent every day from the florist. After we had talked for a little, about what I was reading, perhaps, she would nip a little bud or a violet out of her corsage and hand it to me with a deep curtsy. "A demain, mon petit autre", she would say and I would bow and wish her good night.'

As Sashie spoke the last words, he mimed the action, both hands holding the flower raised to his lips, then the right arm extended, with the palm of the hand upward, the fingers curved, in the gesture of an actor acknowledging applause. 'What I am trying to convey,' he added, 'is that she contrived to make me feel loved and secure and yet at the same time independent, with a place of my own that even she did not enter uninvited and the little ceremony of the flower seemed to symbolize the tie between us and at the same time our separateness – Janet, you should not let me mumble into my beard in this maudlin way.'

'You are not being maudlin. You are telling about a very happy time long ago. All the happy times are long ago. We never notice the happiness while it is happening.' I wanted to hear more of Sashie's childhood. 'Did your father ever take part along with you and your mother when you acted? In my family, George and Tom were the actors.'

'No. Papa was much older than Mama, a little more than twice her age. When they married, he was thirty-seven and she eighteen. At that time, I gathered, he was quite a gay young blade. It seems that my arrival aged him. Responsibility does age people. I don't mean that he was appalled by what he had done in producing me exactly—' Sashie grinned '—but people react to events in different ways. My arrival seems to have turned Paul de Marnay from something of a man-about-town into a respectable papa overnight while it seemed to make Mama grow even younger. When Papa came home from his office early, he would sit and watch our antics in an affectionate indulgent way as if we were both children. Of course, when he and Mama were alone, he would be different and she would be different too. He died in 1938, of pneumonia, as I think I told you. He was only in his early fifties. Mama was thirty-eight and looked about twenty-five but his death changed her. I suppose the change had been going on for some time but I had not noticed it until then. I had long outgrown the petit-autre stage and was a very selfish self-centred youth, fluttering around, amusing myself and other people. After Papa died, Mama took against Paris and settled in London, in spite of the weather. I think now that she moved partly to get away from an admirer who had designs on her and partly because she was more politically intelligent than I was. I think she foresaw the trend of events in Germany fairly clearly. I was enjoying myself too much to foresee anything.'

There was a note of self-accusation in Sashie's voice now and a heavy frown darkened and stilled his gay mobile face.

'Most of us were like that in the thirties,' I said, 'except for the few who took part in that muddle and shambles in Spain. They didn't do much good but at least they tried. I didn't even try.'

'Neither did I. I don't mind not having tried about the big general mess but I minded afterwards not having tried about Mama. In the summer of 1939, I had arranged to go to the United States for about two years. There were all the rumours of war, of course, and I tried to persuade her to come with me. She wouldn't. She told me that I was grown-up now and that, as she put it, I must tell my own story. I said that I would cancel my trip to the States and she became angry. The States was part of the story I had to tell, she said. And then, she had acquired an admirer in London and I thought he might be the reason for her staying there. Also, I didn't like him. Everything we do is coloured and shaped by so many factors that there are never clear reasons or motives. Anyhow, I went to the States, the war came and there was that period when armies sat on either side of the Maginot Line and looked at one another. Seen from New York, it did not look like war at all but then there was the débâcle at Dunkirk and I came to my senses. I tried to get back to England but it was not possible. I had left it too late. Then the bombing of Britain began and Mama was killed in one of the first raids on London. I had left it too late,' he repeated.

I knew the numb sense of guilt and failure that he must have experienced for I remembered my own state of mind after my father died, a time when Sashie had helped me as no other person could have done.

'I know how you felt,' I said. 'I had the same feeling of too-late and never-again when my father died. It was because of your mother that you were able to help me then, Sashie.'

'But I could not help myself when Mama was killed,' he said. 'Like you with your father, I could not accept the fact that I would never see her again. Instead of standing still and facing it, I escaped into a black desire for vengeance – very melodramatic and stupid. You indulged in a bonfire in the garden at Guinea Corner. My bonfire was an internal affair, a flaming desire to be avenged on the people who had killed Mama. Melodramatic rubbish. It still shames me to think of it.'

'But, Sashie, that was natural. You were so young. Twenty-two or three?'

He shook his head. 'Young or not, if I had thought of Mama instead of thinking of nothing but myself and the people who had killed her, I would never have gone to Canada and joined the Air Force. Mama would never have approved of my turning into a killer and I *was* a killer after I was trained. Although it sounds immodest, I was a very deadly fighter pilot.'

'We were all killers in one way or another at that time,' I

said. 'Even I was one in a small way but I do everything in a small way.'

He smiled a little but grimly.

'Why did you choose the Air Force?' I asked on a more practical level for it was uncomfortably strange to see Sashie puzzled and uncertain as he had looked when he spoke of the death of his mother.

He smiled now in his mischievous self-mocking way and when he answered my question his voice was light, all the gravity gone. 'Darling, I should never have done for the army. I should have had to carry a *rifle* and they did not have them in my size. And I should not have liked the navy – those great ships where you slept in a hammock below the water line. But I was perfect for a fighter aircraft where I could be all alone with nobody to order me about. I have never been good at co-operating with other people in the way of turning left or right when a sergeant or somebody says so. If a sergeant says "right", I invariably feel morally obliged to turn left. And then, being small was an advantage, if anything, in the cockpit of a fighter and I was an agile sort of person in those young days. I could always run very fast and jump very high and dodge around very quickly so all I had to learn was to do these things up in the air in my little flying machine and that was not difficult.' He looked thoughtful for a moment and then: 'After I was trained and went into action, I stopped seeing myself as seeking revenge. It all became rather fun. It was only after I was repatriated and in hospital in England, learning to walk on my tin legs that I discovered what a terrible creature I had been. I did not regret the killing so much as the descent into sub-humanity that had made me find it fun. Why is one talking in this boring self-analysing way do you suppose? I think it must be all that roast pig and rum this afternoon. It would be different if all the self-analysing made one understand oneself and things in general any better but it doesn't.'

'But it does,' I argued. 'Your self-analysing has made you understand things like me very well so that you have been very helpful and I am grateful.'

'There is no need for gratitude, darling. I ought to thank *you* for making me talk about Mama. I have never talked about her to anyone before and hardly even to myself. She is more present with me now than she has ever been since she died.'

I observed that he said 'she died' and not 'was killed', implying that no blame for her death attached to himself or to anyone. Down the months I had discovered that this is the only attitude that makes death acceptable to the mind. We have to look upon it not as an outside force that overtakes a life but as the final act committed by the life itself.

The next day, the only evidence of the wedding was the ring on Trixie's finger for, having danced the night through, she and Caleb, along with Gahta, came back to Silver Beach and resumed their duties. With the coming of December, however, the tenor of our life changed and there was in the air the sense of an ending. Each day was marked by some little reference to my departure and a little of each day was given to some detail connected with it.

'I am hoping these blood-root seed show through before you go, ma'am,' Caleb would say, 'for I ain't exactly sure about separating them.'

'What about clothes, darling?' Sashie would inquire. 'You land on the fourth of January and there will probably be a blizzard in Liverpool. The white silk will hardly be suitable.'

'I have a few sweaters and skirts left over from my trip to Jock's place,' I told him. 'They will have to do until I get myself organized.'

And one evening he said: 'This parting is indeed going to be a little death, my sweet. I have grown accustomed to talking about myself and my ego is going to miss its audience.'

'I apologize for being inquisitive, Sashie, and I have really tried not to ask questions.'

'I don't remember that you asked any,' he said. 'If you had, I would probably have told you nothing. You know how contrary I am,' but then he made a gesture that dismissed the words he had spoken. 'It is not contrariness. It is simply that I am afraid of people knowing about this disability of mine – afraid that they will pity me or find me grotesque. But you don't pity me?'

'Indeed I don't,' I told him. 'I never have. You made it fairly obvious when I first found out about your legs that pity would not be in order.'

'I pitied myself terribly at first, when I discovered that I had no legs any more. I pitied myself nearly to death. It was so offensive to be mutilated and Mama would have hated it so much. But I came to understand that it was part of what she would have called my story, an integral part of how I had told my life, as it were. I brought the thing on myself. When I joined the Air Force, if I thought of anything at all as the end, I thought of being shot down in flames, looking dramatic and rather magnificent and leaving no trace. I did not think in terms of gross mutilation.'

'The acceptance must have been very difficult, Sashie.'

'There were things that helped. One of my colleagues was blinded. I don't think I could have coped with being blind.' Mischief suddenly lit the black eyes. 'I use my sight a great deal and I do so enjoy what I see.' He changed direction. 'Talking of seeing, when you depart from this cultural desert, darling and get to civilization, you will be able to start star-spotting again.'

'In Achcraggan?'

'But you will be *bound* to go to London to see those publishing people. You must.'

'Oh, I don't know,' I said hesitantly, feeling scared. 'After all, we don't have to *see* one another. It would be so sort of embarrassing.'

'Embarrassing? Why, for pity's sake?'

'My writing is a sort of personal peculiarity like your legs,' I tried to explain. 'That is how I see it. I would be embarrassed to see it—' I hesitated, '—mirrored in the eyes of people. I can talk to *you* about it because you have never read any of it. But these people have *read* it!' I ended on a loud note of protest.

'But if you write things, the only result that makes any sense is that they should be read!'

'When I wrote them, even when I write them now, I don't

think about results any more than you did when you joined the Air Force,' I told him and myself as well for this was a new discovery that I had just made. 'The writing is part of my story, something I had to do, that's all.'

'And now that you have done it, you have to cope with it, like me with my tin legs,' Sashie told me, 'and you might as well get used to the idea that what you have written is going to be read, that you will have to meet those publishing people, mirrors in their eyes and all. The moment is bound to come and when it does, think of me the day I left hospital. I went to Green's Hotel in London and walked, if you could call it that, into the lounge where Don was waiting for me. There were acres of carpet between him and me as he came towards me and a mass of people sitting round having drinks and tea and things. And you know how Don draws the eye, especially the female eye. It was obvious to my morbid imagination that all these people thought that Don had been waiting for a young woman and that my arrival changed their whole attitude to his Adonis appearance and that was the moment when I lost control of my new legs, so that I toppled towards Don and had to be caught in his arms like a ballerina being held in a swooning lift by a danseur. I was sure that it looked like the most impassioned meeting between two long-separated lovers and I longed to yell at the spellbound audience that I was neither a eunuch nor a queer but merely slightly lame, that I hated Don and that if they didn't stop staring, I would take off one of my legs and brain them all with it.'

It was in Sashie's gift for mime to make the episode take pictorial form so that I seemed to see the people staring at the handsome Don and the wilting Sashie and I began to laugh, not at the picture of Don and Sashie but at the startled staring audience that had been conjured up.

'Actually,' I said after a moment, 'it isn't funny at all. It must have been absolutely soul-searing.'

'In point of fact, it proved to be of the greatest possible help. It was that débâcle that led to my fairy act which has been such a comfort down the years. I don't know why it is that I don't care what people may think of me as long as they don't know that I am physically deformed.' He made

180

that gesture that dismissed the words he had spoken. 'Actually, I do know. It is—' He broke off short. 'How did we arrive at this extraordinary subject anyway?'

'With your saying that when I met the publishing people I was to think of you at Green's Hotel.'

'Ah yes. I am being lightsome and silly about your encounter with the publishers, Janet, but I do realize that you are going to find it difficult, you know, after all these years of secrecy about your writing. What I don't understand is what made you send that first manuscript to London last year. After the years of secrecy, why did you?'

I sighed. 'Another complicated why. It was partly your fault that I sent it. You had been going on about people who fiddled about with things that they were afraid to put to the test but that was only a small part of the reason. A larger part was that nothing seemed to be *happening* in my life. Twice and everybody at Paradise were fooling about with the cricket tournament, which seemed to mean something to them but it meant nothing to me. And you were flying about to London, getting books of folk music published and having things happening to you. I can't really explain at all, Sashie. A day came that seemed to be my day for sending a manuscript to London and I sent it. That's all.'

'An unconscious recognition of the flood-tide that leads on to fortune?'

'Nothing so grand and fortune didn't come into it. I have never thought of my writing as in any way connected with fortune or fame or anything like that. It is simply something I have always done, that's all. I shan't mind meeting the publishers at all as long as they don't *talk* about my writing.'

'But, darling,' Sashie protested, 'this is the sole reason for your meeting them. Of course they are going to talk about your novels in every conceivable aspect, advertising, contracts, the colour of the boards that bind them—'

'I don't mind that as long as they don't talk about *them*,' I told him.

'Them?'

'Yes, them.'

'This conversation has me floundering. Why mustn't they talk about *them*?'

181

'Because I would have nothing to say about them. They are just *there* and that is all that is to them.'

'You mean that they are there and that we all simply have to take them or leave them?'

'That's about it. There they are and there is nothing you can do about them and there is no point in talking about them.' Sashie sighed. 'I suppose that someone who took dance lessons from a horse is capable of almost anything,' he said.

As part of the preparations for my departure, I had written to Mr. Arden, telling him of my intention to return to Scotland and giving him my Achcraggan address and a day or two after this conversation with Sashie, there came a letter suggesting that I come to London direct from Liverpool.

'We would suggest that you spend at least three days in London before travelling to Scotland,' the letter said, 'and if you will let us know where you would like to stay here, we shall be glad to book accommodation for you.'

'Oh dear,' I said, handing the letter to Sashie, 'life is looming very large.'

'Take it firmly by the loom, darling,' he said. 'Write at once to the nice gentleman and tell him that the *only* place in London where you like to stay is at Green's Hotel.'

'Nonsense! It is far too expensive.'

'A pox upon your scurvy faithless cheese-paring! If you don't do as I say, I shall cable Green's from here.'

'All right, Sashie. I'll do it. I have to, don't I, when you have been so right about everything else? I think you must have Second Sight.'

'Not exactly, my sweet, but, like yourself, I have a tiny talent for talent-spotting.'

'I didn't help any of my spotted stars as you have helped me.'

'With respect,' he said gravely, 'that is something that you cannot know. You may have created a tiny matrix in the ether that affected Bing Crosby's stars and led him on to a White Christmas and countless millions.'

Time seemed to flow faster and faster, like the sand in the narrowing chamber of an hour-glass and I felt more and more that my body was hollow except for a tight knot of nervousness located somewhere in my stomach. When the support of Sashie, to which I had grown so accustomed, was withdrawn, I felt that I would cease to exist, for I was no longer Janet Alexander, the wife of Twice and not as yet Janet Sandison, the writer person. I tried to conceal my feelings from Sashie, although he was probably aware of them and I tried to scorn myself into courage by apostrophizing in myself what my Aunt Kate would have called 'herring guts' but still the blue sea that stretched away from Silver Beach to the shore of Britain made me hollow with fear.

Two days before I was due to sail, Caleb and I were busy separating the beetroot seedlings – the plants that Caleb called 'blood roots' – when Sashie came out of the house and asked Caleb to drive him to the post office.

'Can't the mail wait a bit?' I asked. 'Caleb and I want to finish this job before the sun gets too high.'

'No, it can't wait,' he said shortly. 'I wish to go to the post office *now*.'

'All right,' I told him, 'and I hope there is nothing in the mail except a letter from your French cousins saying that they are all coming to stay with you for six months.'

I went on separating the little seedlings and had just finished when the car came back. 'Come on, Caleb,' I said. 'Get the shade over them as fast as you can.'

Caleb began to fix a framework of wooden slats over the bed while I laid over them the palm fronds that would protect the little plants from the scorching sun.

'Come and open this at once,' Sashie said. 'It is from the publishing people.'

'Open it yourself and stop bothering me,' I told him, dragging palm fronds over the grass. 'It will only be about that room at Green's.'

Sashie created the disapproving silence that was at his command, a silence that was palpable, almost audible, before retiring into the house and when, a little later, I went to the veranda, he was sitting there with a glass of champagne in his hand, the bottle in a bucket beside him.

'You'll get as high as a kite,' I said. 'It isn't ten o'clock yet,' and went through to my bathroom to wash my muddy

183

hands. I was scrubbing my nails when he arrived at my side. 'You clod!' he said. 'You lump of clay, you – you *vegetable*!'

'What is the matter with you?' I asked.

'They have accepted that third manuscript!' he shouted at me.

'Oh,' I said, looking down at the muddy water in the wash-basin. It was all too strange. Sashie and I had not been together in this little room since the night of the bottle when I had been so disgustingly sick and so much seemed to have happened since then.

'Is that all you have to say?' he was asking.

'Yes,' I told him. 'At the moment, that is all I have to say.'

'I take it back. You are not a vegetable, darling. Come out and have some wine.'

When I joined him on the veranda, I felt apologetic. 'Sashie, it isn't that I am not pleased about the manuscript and that I am not grateful to the publishers and you and everybody but everything is so peculiar. I seem to have lived through a whole lifetime since you brought me to Silver Beach. I *am* a bit like a vegetable. I want things to happen in an orderly predestined way, like Caleb's blood roots taking so long to germinate and so long to grow big enough to separate. All this suddenness and unexpectedness bewilders me. I feel as that councillor bloke must have felt at the wedding, when Missy Rosie tipped the bucket of swill over him.'

Sashie laughed. 'Don't worry about how you are, my sweet. The way you are seems to do very well for you.' He moved away from the subject and I felt relieved. 'I have been thinking quite a lot about that wedding,' he said. 'The whole affair had extraordinary drama and atmosphere, all that hot purple-green shade and the red fire under the drum where the pig was roasting and the violent colours of the clothes, with Caleb and Trixie in the middle all in white and the councillor bloke, as you call him, prowling about in his dark city suit like an evil genius. I can see it all on stage, as a ballet.'

I was remembering the hot fecund hollow at Pear Tree Bottom. Seen from this clear light that sparkled off the sea, it did have the other-worldly atmosphere of a stage beyond footlights where brightly-clad knots of people grouped, moved and re-grouped amid the murmur of guitar music. I looked at Sashie. Probably he knew something of ballet and stage design, after all his play with his puppet theatre as a child.

'Sashie,' I asked, 'how does a choreographer record a ballet? I mean is there a way of writing down the movements in the way you can write down sounds in musical notation?'

'There are systems of ballet notation, I believe but they are rather cumbersome. I suppose every choreographer has a system of his own but the early classics were handed down by memory mostly, like folk song. Nowadays, I suppose they would use film.'

'Of course. I hadn't thought of that.'

'Janet—'

'Yes.'

'Nothing after all.' He smiled at me and changed direction.

'I had a letter today too,' he said and handed me an airmail form addressed to him in the hand of Liz. 'Dear Sashie,' I read. 'Thank you very much for your letter. It is the first letter I have ever had from the Unseen and Unknown and I like it very much. George and Tom say that you are to have the pink china pot as well as the aspidistra and the pink silk cushions out of the parlour too if you would like them but they have hard tassels that dig into you when you sit down so maybe better not. George and Tom say that some people rub the leaves of their aspidistras with castor oil to make them shine but they think this is not natural because even in countries where aspidistras belong it does not rain castor oil and besides there is the smell. We are looking forward to seeing Aunt Janet and wish that you could come too but we understand about you and Caleb being busy with the coconut crop. Gee thought you dug coconuts out of the ground like potatoes but he is only rising seven. I hope you will write again when you have time and feel that way inclined. Love from (my friends call me) Liz.'

'Feel that way inclined,' I commented. 'That is straight

out of George and Tom. They never do anything unless they feel that way inclined. "I'll incline them!" my grandmother used to say, "if they don't mend that gate before tomorrow". I used to think that if they didn't do what she wanted, so that she inclined them, they would walk for ever afterwards at an angle of forty-five degrees to the earth.'

Sashie never tired of my tales of Reachfar and in these last days in the island, before I had to face the new unknown way of life that was looming before me, talk of the secure days of long ago provided an escape for me. When I was alone, I would try to face the reality of the future, try to convince myself that everything would be 'all right'. Yet, in spite of myself, I wished that time would stop for a little while, give me a little longer to collect myself but time is relentless. It sweeps us along as a river carries flotsam, unheeding of our rights and wrongs, our joys and fears and the dusk of my last evening at Silver Beach came down over the sea.

Mechanically, I packed the last few items, locked my typewriter into its case, locked the steel trunk that held the manuscripts. Then, looking down at it, I changed my mind, re-opened it and took out the manuscript on which I had been working, putting it into Twice's briefcase, along with the books I had bought to read during the voyage. Perhaps, I thought, the sight of the manuscript while I was on board the ship would help to convince me that I did exist as a writer person.

When I came down to the veranda, Sashie handed me the Peasant Girl portrait. 'Darling, I am sorry. I should have given this back sooner. Have you locked everything?'

'I don't want that damn' thing,' I said. 'Burn it.'

'May I keep it?'

'If you want it, yes.'

'Thank you. I do want it very much.'

He went away to his room and I sat staring out at the sea, black now and mysterious, with the moonlight glittering as it moved from wave-crest to wave-crest. I wished that Sashie would come back to anchor me to the earth before, like a hollow bubble, I floated away to be lost in the nothingness between the dark sea and the silver sky. When he did come back, I burst into speech at once but on a strictly practical, even trivial note.

'I still can't remember the last two lines of that silly verse,' I said, referring to the rhyme that began: 'Monday's child is fair of face.'

'It must be in some book,' he said, 'although I can't find it in any of mine.'

'You have been looking for it?'

'Of course, darling. You know how helpful I try to be always.'

'It is not the sort of thing that would be in your books, surely?'

'*My* books?' His black eyebrows rose, as if he were about to fire one of his barbed shafts but it did not come. I suddenly became aware that he was sad at my going and would show any sort of mood rather than the sadness. 'I still have all the nursery books I had as a child,' he explained, his voice apologetic now.

Still, I felt that I had been rebuked for making assumptions about the books he might own. 'I hope that George and Tom have still got some of mine,' I said, 'but that rhyme isn't in any of them.'

'George and Tom will remember it, I am sure.'

'My father used to use the phrase "a willing forget",' I told him now, keeping our talk impersonal. 'He maintained that if one forgot something, one did it deliberately although perhaps one was not aware of doing it.'

'Freud would have agreed with him and so do I.'

'Then I have a reason for forgetting those two lines. I have either been put off them by Tom and George or there is a word in them that I don't like.'

'Then let us think of all the words that you don't like,' said Sashie.

As if the wide expanse of the ocean beyond the beach lay between us, we talked of trivialities from shore to distant shore as the last evening ticked its minutes away. With Sashie sitting only a yard away from me, I felt sad and alone and earlier than usual after dinner, he rose to his feet.

'Bed, I think,' he said. 'We should leave for the docks at seven-thirty in the morning.'

'Yes.'

His face changed. 'I am sorry to be so dull, not to say ill-natured, darling, but' – wry little wrinkles of self-disgust formed at the sides of his nose '—I find it impossible, this evening, to be—' he hesitated, '—blithe. Good night.'

He went from the veranda into the house, across the hall and the door to his rooms closed with a click of finality. I darted a glance over my shoulder at the sea. Surely it was nearer than usual, flowing up over the beach in a threat to overwhelm me? I hurried to my own room, shut the door and leaned my back against it. Blithe. Ugly word.

> But the child that is born on the Sabbath day
> Is blithe and bonny and good and gay

the final lines of the verse spoke themselves inside my head.

'Got you!' I said to them and opened the brief case to enter them in my manuscript before they could elude me again. Inside the buff folder that held the manuscript, there was a large manila envelope that I had never seen before. Slowly, I took out of it three photographs and a single sheet of paper. The photographs were large, of the kind that are displayed in glass cases in the foyers of theatres. The first was of the Ariel I had seen in London long ago, the Ariel with the silver wig and the tights streaked with silver, the second was of a male dancer in the tights and short tunic of classical ballet, caught by the camera at the peak of a high leap and the third was of the head of a young man, with high cheekbones and dark eyes under brows slanted and thin as antennae. The head was turned slightly to show the strong line that ran from behind the ear down to the collar-bone. Printed under the first photograph were the words: 'Paul Gregoriev – *The Tempest*', under the second 'Paul Gregoriev – *Giselle*' and under the third were the words 'Paul Gregoriev' but the face was indubitably the face of Sashie, Sashie as a young man.

On impulse, I wrenched open the door, took a first quick step on the way to Sashie's room but stopped short. I had not been intended to discover this package until I was on board the ship or later. I closed my door quietly, sat down on my bed and spread the photographs around me. I found myself bending over the leaping figure of the Prince in *Giselle*, studying the muscles of the legs and feet that had lifted the body high into the air and suddenly my mind was invaded by the thought of Sashie's body as it was now. The thought was sickening, grotesque and unbearable. I turned the photograph face downwards and stared through the window at the sea, rippling and whispering in self-communion under the white moon. I had always wanted to 'know all about Sashie' and now I knew. Knowing can bring deep sadness.

I unfolded the single sheet of the letter. 'My dear Janet, Ever since the time when you told me of your "dancing young man" I have been trying to tell you what became of him. I feel that I have talked incessantly about music, the theatre and ballet but I found it impossible to come to the ludicrous and grotesque point. Yet I do want you to know and this is the easiest way of telling the story but I do not want you to be made unhappy by it. If Mama had not been killed, I would have decided to die in that prison camp, but Mama was dead and I went on with my story which reaches the end of another chapter tomorrow morning. Thank you for staying with me and making it possible to speak of Mama, her *petit autre* and even Ariel. I hope to come soon to sleep with the asperdester. Love, Sashie (Paul Gregoriev de Marnay).'

Before I went to bed, I put the photographs and the letter back into the envelope and the envelope back into the manuscript folder exactly as I had found it and in the morning I was at pains to walk far along the beach before breakfast so that Sashie, if he changed his mind, might remove the package from its hiding-place but when I gave the briefcase to Caleb to be put into the car with the rest of my luggage, the large envelope was still there.

We spoke hardly at all during breakfast or in the course of the drive to the docks. I was hardly aware that the dreaded moment of embarkation on a new life was upon me, for I could think of nothing but Paul Gregoriev and do nothing but try to conceal my thoughts from Sashie's over-keen perception.

189

He had timed our arrival at the passenger wharf very precisely, so that the ship would sail only about fifteen minutes after I went on board. Her cargo of bananas had been loaded during the night and I seemed to be the only passenger from St. Jago.

When Caleb stopped the car at the foot of the gangway, two seamen hustled my luggage on board while Caleb, with pride, produced from the boot of the car and presented to me a bunch of pink rosebuds, still wearing the dew of Silver Beach, like tears, upon their petals. I was afraid to speak in case I should begin to cry.

'I am *not* going to climb that gangway,' Sashie said in a pettish voice. 'Those steep things give one away utterly to the staring crowds.'

The wharf was deserted except for two wharf-hands who were waiting to remove the gangway. The ship's deck was deserted except for two young officers in white uniforms who stood by the rail. *Mnemosyne* blew a blast on her siren. Sashie took my hand, raised it to his lips and said: 'Au revoir, darling, and bon voyage,' and one of the young officers ran swiftly down the sparred wooden slope, took my arm and led me on board.

From the rail, I looked down at Sashie's upturned face and the brilliant, early tropical sunlight made me think of the lights upon the stage of a theatre long ago, a stage where a young dancer was receiving applause. I nipped a rosebud from Caleb's bouquet and dropped it into the still air.

Deftly, Sashie caught it and there came the beautiful gesture of the dancer as both hands carried the rose to his lips before the right arm was extended, palm upwards, the delicate fingers curved against the black backdrop of the wharf buildings. Time and place became confused. I did not know whether the figure far below was a distant unknown called Paul Gregoriev or whether it was my friend Sashie.

THE END

NOR THE MOON BY NIGHT BY JOY PACKER

For two years they had written letters to each other – Alice Lang, the English nurse, and Andrew Miller, the Game Warden of Velaba. And now Alice stood in a Pretoria garden listening to Andrew's sister . . .

'You'll hate me for this,' said Meg. 'But Alice, don't marry my brother! You don't know Andrew . . . what can you possibly know about a man with the wilderness in his blood. I know the men of my family, and what they expect of their women . . . they've broken the hearts and the health of their wives for generations . . .'

It was sound advice – but Alice was a young woman keen for life, longing to love and be loved, wanting desperately to meet and marry the man whose letters had sustained her for so long . . .

0 552 09305 X   40p

THE MAN IN THE MEWS BY JOY PACKER

Ravenswood was the country estate of the Fleet family. It had its own quiet magic, that old Queen Anne manor house set in the soft Sussex countryside. Ann Olivier knew that this graceful and dignified home would belong to her daughter, Rachel one day . . . if nothing occurred to upset the plans for Rachel's wedding to Jim Fleet. Ann was intelligent enough to know that there were serious gaps in her own past, unaccounted for by a sojourn of twenty years in South Africa, Jim's father, Sir Jasper, was disconcertingly shrewd . . . he watched every move she made on her first visit to Ravenswood. He's dangerous, she thought, I must go carefully . . .

0 552 10173 7   65p

A SELECTED LIST OF
FINE FICTION FOR
YOUR PLEASURE

*All these books are available at your bookshop or newsagent: or can be ordered direct
from the publisher. Just tick the titles you want and fill in the form below.*

CORGI BOOKS, Cash Sales Department, P.O. Box 11, Falmouth, Cornwall

Please send cheque or postal order, no currency.
U.K. send 19p for first book plus 9p per copy for each additional book ordered to a
maximum charge of 73p to cover the cost of postage and packing.
B.F.P.O. and Eire allow 19p for first book plus 9p per copy for the next 6 books thereafter 3p per book.
Overseas Customers: Please allow 20p for the first book and 10p per copy for each
additional book.

NAME (Block letters) ....

ADDRESS ....

(SEPT 76) ....

While every effort is made to keep prices low, it is sometimes necessary to increase
prices at short notice. Corgi Books reserve the right to show new retail prices on covers
which may differ from those previously advertised in the text or elsewhere.